Outst:

"Scott feeds the reader bits and pieces of the plot, keeping interest high. Not as technical and certainly shorter than Tom Clancy's books but can be read in lieu of them."
—*Library Journal* on *Burst of Sound*

"*Burst of Sound* is another mystery/thriller that is highly entertaining and ends all too soon for the reader's taste. Caruso and Panzer are a great investigative team!"—*Midwest Book Review*

"Fast action and good characterizations make this launch title of a new imprint a good summer read."—*Library Journal* on *Boom Town*

"Trevor Scott manages another winner with this exciting tale set in the middle of the Cascade mountain range on the Northwest. Scott's background and knowledge of all things relating to bombs puts him in the driver's seat, and the reader is the fortunate recipient of an excellent plot, well-crafted characters, and constant action. He never fails to please."—*Midwest Book Review* on Boom Town

"A damned good writer."—**David Hagberg**, bestselling author of more than 70 mysteries and thrillers.

"*Global Shot* is a deftly written, highly recommended action/adventure suspense novel that will have the reader gripped in total fascination from first page to last with its plot twists and unpredictable developments leading to a memorably vivid conclusion."—*Midwest Book Review*

The
COLD EDGE

The

COLD EDGE

Trevor Scott

Salvo Press
Portland, Oregon

THE COLD EDGE

Copyright © 2009 by Trevor Scott

Salvo Press
Portland, Oregon

www.salvopress.com

Cover istockphoto by Chris Schmidt, London
istockphoto of woman by Leva Geneviciene

Visit the author online at www.trevorscott.com

Library of Congress Control Number: 2009920399

ISBN: 1-930486-91-X
9781930486911

Printed in U.S.A.

For Andrew and Trevor

Acknowledgments
Thank you to the people of Norway and Sweden for your hospitality. Although I didn't make it as far north as Svalbard, I hope I captured the essence of the area after growing up in the frozen tundra of Northern Minnesota. A special thanks to one pretty, young waitress at Blomonn Restaurant & Bar in Lillehammer, Norway, for convincing me to try the whale. After doing so, I finally understood Melville's Ahab.

PROLOGUE

Spitsbergen Island, Svalbard Archipelago, Norway
October 9, 1986

S wirling lights of blue and orange and green and red marked the Northern sky above the thick glacier, as if aliens or some unearthly force was about to invade this remote island halfway between the northern tip of Norway and the North Pole.

One man sat on a snowmobile in Arctic clothes, the wind biting into any exposed skin around the edges of his goggles, while a second man adjusted a small satellite dish hitched up by wire to a cumbersome SAT phone the size of a small briefcase.

"Any time now," Korkala said from the snowmobile, as he adjusted the volume on the phone. John Korkala was the CIA's assistant station chief in Oslo, and his colleague, Steve Olson, the military attaché, an Air Force captain and communications officer.

"Just about there." He made a final adjustment and the phone went hot with a squawk.

"Got it."

Captain Olson stood and gazed at the strange swirling of the Aurora Borealis. He had seen them in his youth in the Upper Peninsula of Michigan, but nothing like this. They appeared to be encased in a lava lamp. "Check out this crazy sky."

Korkala didn't even raise his eyes away from the phone. "Seen them a hundred times. Let's focus here."

It was early evening, but the sun had not come out all day. And at this time of year, it was so low on the horizon the entire island would be lucky to see an hour or two of fog-obscured glowing. Two days ago they had flown five hours from Oslo on a commercial flight to Longyearbyen, the capital and largest city of some twenty-five hundred people, mostly Norwegians, stayed one night in a hotel, and then flown by a charter helicopter to the even more remote Pyramiden, a Soviet mining settlement. From there they had rented the snowmobile from a rather skeptical Russian, who wondered why two Americans would want to venture out onto a barren ice field as winter approached. Their cover story? They were preparing for an expedition to the North Pole next summer. The story was as good as any, since many explorers had used the remote islands as a staging point before heading to the Pole.

"Damn it!" Korkala said, shaking the SAT phone.

Olson stepped closer, the snow squeaking beneath his Sorrel pack boots. "What's up?"

Korkala tried to adjust the phone to grab a signal again. Nothing. "We lost it." He jumped from the snowmobile, pulled the binoculars from his chest and crawled to the top of the snow drift that hid them from activity nearly a mile down a glacial valley. There were two snowmobiles and four men, as far as they could tell, working around the wreckage of a plane that was scattered for a hundred yards, much of the parts already covered by the treacherous blowing snow. A few days, Korkala knew, and the entire wreckage could be lost in the glacier, swallowed up by the ever-changing environment.

Olson crawled up next to the CIA man. "What you suppose is so important?"

That was the problem. They had no way of knowing. The Oslo station had gotten word from the Helsinki office that a Soviet plane had gone down on Spitsbergen. Details were sketchy, but when known KGB officers had passed through Oslo days ago, Washington had insisted on an escort. Something wasn't right. They could have been simply recovering codes and destroying communications equipment on the aircraft, but Korkala and Olson would have to get closer to even determine the aircraft type. The Why would have to follow the What.

Korkala ignored the Air Force captain. "Let's find out. Make a direct approach." He backed away from the edge and scurried toward the snowmobile. He unhooked the trailer skid and took a seat on the snowmobile.

"What about the SAT dish?" Olson asked.

"Get on. We'll come back for it." He turned the key and then pulled the starter cord. Nothing. It had been giving them problems since they rented it from the Russian earlier in the day. He pulled again. Still nothing. Finally it cranked over on the third try, the lights coming on immediately.

"Should we turn the lights off?" Olson yelled above the whining engine.

"No," Korkala yelled back. "That would be more suspicious. Get on. We'll say we're lost."

The Air Force captain straddled the seat behind Korkala and held onto the side handles. He barely sat down when the assistant station chief thumbed the throttle and the snowmobile surged off.

It took them only a few minutes to round the outcropping drifts, angle down the hill toward the glacial plain, and then slow down as they approached the men working at the debris field. All were wearing pure white suits, just like them.

Korkala stopped near the other two snowmobiles and shut down the engine.

One of the men approached, his flashlight shining into both of their eyes.

Glancing through goggles at the debris, Captain Olson saw the tail of the aircraft, which had settled against a snowy outcropping. He whispered into Korkala's ear, "MiG twenty-five. What the hell is that doing here?"

"Be ready," Korkala said, swinging his legs off the seat and moving toward the Soviet KGB officer. "Thank God we saw you," he said in Russian to the man, who stopped a few feet away, hands in bulky mittens at his side.

Confusion on the Russian's face, his eyes shifted behind large goggles.

The other three men started to approach and the captain saw the hunting rifle for the first time at the side of one man's leg.

"What are you doing here?" the Russian asked Korkala.

"We're lost and running low on fuel."

The three other Soviet officers stopped ten feet away, hands in pockets, except for the man with the rifle, whose naked finger was pressed against the trigger guard.

Something was wrong. The Soviet officer wasn't buying the story.

Everything seemed to move in slow motion. First, the rifle started to rise. Then hands started coming out of pockets.

But Korkala was the first to pull his 9mm handgun, his first shot entering the closest Soviet in the neck, bringing instant blood spurting outward. The next few shots struck the man with the rifle, first in the chest and then in the forehead.

By now the captain had rolled off the snowmobile and retrieved his gun from inside his coat, also a 9mm handgun.

The next few seconds lingered. Bullets flew in each direction. The cold air filled with clouds of gunpowder.

When silence finally came, Olson looked down at his gun—it was out of rounds, the slide back and steam rising from the exposed barrel. He dropped an empty magazine and fumbled in his jacket, found another full magazine, and slammed it into the handle. Then he released the slide, sending a round into the chamber, the hammer cocked, and rose up from behind the snowmobile.

Slowly he stepped through the squeaky snow, his gun pointed toward the Soviets. But they were all down, their bodies merely white lumps in the snowy glacier, spots of red seeping through the white. His eyes reluctantly went down and saw Korkala lying face down.

Olson knelt down and touched the side of Korkala's neck. No pulse. He rolled him over and saw that most of his face was gone, having taken a bullet in the mouth. Damn it!

The captain went slowly to the Soviets, checking each man. They were all dead. He felt light-headed. Then the pain came. As he returned his gun to the holster under his left arm, he felt the moisture. He had been hit in the left shoulder. But he was breathing all right. It had not struck his lungs.

He put pressure on his wound and then turned on his headlamp and shuffled toward the MiG debris. The first thing he noticed was that the pilot had gone down with the plane. He was still strapped into the cockpit, which had rammed into a snowbank and was nearly covered already with new snow.

The Soviets had been gathered near the main fuselage, the captain remembered. Had this aircraft been carrying a nuke? Maybe they had been about to destroy it.

No. Captain Olson had worked on nukes and he didn't see any sign of a large weapon. In fact, the wings had sheared off and blown quite extensively. Probably external fuel tanks. This MiG was on a long mission. But what kind of mission?

Moving to the main fuselage, Olson found where the Soviets had been working. They had removed a panel and exposed a compartment. Inside was a silver container of some sort, encased in foam rubber, which had been partially cut open by the Soviets.

The captain tried to grasp the container with his free hand, but it was starting to go numb. He'd need both hands. With a great deal of pain, he was able to pull the container from the spray-foam padding. It was a one-foot cube, perfectly intact. He swirled it around and found no way to open it. What the hell was it?

As he turned to go, his mind seemed to swirl as his eyes

centered on the Aurora Borealis, which nearly filled the sky now. With great determination, he shuffled back toward the snowmobile. He thought about his friend, John Korkala, and realized he was in no condition to drag him anywhere. They would have to come back for him.

Looking up for stars in the sky, all he saw was the morphing, shifting clouds, a distorted distraction of his current reality. He had to move. He was getting weaker and had more than twenty miles to travel across the rough, desolate terrain to reach the nearest village. And he wasn't sure he should even go there, since it was the Soviet mining settlement. How could he explain a bullet wound? Or the absence of his partner?

Somehow he got onto the snowmobile, the square box on the seat at his crotch, turned the key and pulled the cord. Nothing. Damn it! He pulled and pulled until it finally turned over and sputtered to life.

He rode slowly back toward the location where they had left the SAT phone equipment and the trailer sled. By the time he had hooked up the trailer and strapped the small satellite dish onto the back, he was feeling weak and cold. He was sure the actual temperature had dropped, but also knew he had lost a lot of blood. It had soaked down his shirt and gotten into his pants. He could feel it down to his knees.

He would never make it twenty miles on this snowmobile. Sure he had grown up driving snowmobiles in Michigan, and could drive as fast as the machine would go in these conditions. But the wind had picked up now, blowing snow obscuring his view beyond a dozen feet. He could be swallowed up in a glacial crevasse without him knowing what had happened. No, he had to go somewhere to get out of this weather. At least until morning. Needed to get the bleeding to stop.

Then it came to him. Just before they had found the crash site, they had seen a rock overhang that could have been the entrance to a cave or at least a protected area from the blowing snow.

It took the captain fifteen minutes to find the rock over-hang. He had gone right past it a few times, since the snow had drifted against the front. Eventually he was able to pull the snowmobile and the trailer entirely under the rock. With some clarity of thought, he decided to bury the cube in the back of the crevasse. He had no idea what it was, but if the Soviets had sent four officers to pick it up, it must have been important.

Satisfied that he would be safe there until morning, he pulled out his sleeping bag and crawled inside boots and all. Wrapped up and curled into a ball, he was chilled for a moment but eventually started to warm. His thoughts drifted like the snow to his wife and two small children. He would have to endure. Have to make it through the night. Have to. For them.

Then he went to sleep for the last time.

CHAPTER 1

Oslo, Norway
Present Day

The hotel door slammed with a resounding thud, startling Jake Adams from his nap. He looked around and found himself on the floor in the center of the room, an empty bottle of Schnapps a foot from his head. His mind drifted back, remembering vaguely how he had checked into the posh Grand Hotel on Oslo's most favorite Karl Johans Gate, the pedestrian enclave between the country's Parliament and The Royal Palace, across from the national theatre.

The room was mostly dark, with only a sliver of light at the edges of the curtains. His eyes tried to adjust to the movement—legs and feet. He knew those nice black leather pumps. Had purchased them for his girlfriend Anna at a shop in Vienna, his current place of residence.

The shoes stopped a yard away and the right foot started tapping on the low-pile gray carpet.

Jake rolled to his side and finally caught the expression on Anna's face. Disturbed? Concerned? No, definitely pissed off.

"What?" Jake said, scratching the hair on his bare chest. Coming to a sitting position, head spinning, he realized he had no clothes on at all. "What?" he repeated.

Her foot stopped tapping, but she crossed her arms over her chest. Okay, now she was mad as hell.

"I thought we were on vacation," Jake protested. He knew he should have just kept his mouth shut at this point. Take the ass chewing like a man. Usually he knew precisely when he screwed up, but now he was baffled beyond the norm.

"Vacation assumes you have worked," Anna finally said in German.

Damn! She spoke English during normal conversation, mostly to learn the idioms and idiosyncrasies of the language, muttered perfect, sensual French during sex, and her native Austrian German when she was either working or royally torqued at him for some reason or other. Her German could travel anywhere from kinder-kind to Hitleresque. Now he thought he saw a small mustache forming above tight lips.

"That's cold," he said, sticking with English. "Listen, I made a hundred thousand Euro on that last case."

"Three months ago," she said, still in German.

Okay, so it wasn't about the money. He should have known that much anyway. As an officer in the Interpol stationed in Vienna, Anna made less per year than he had hauled in for one-month of work. Maybe that did piss her off. Maybe it was the fact that he had done nothing in the last three months but drink beer, wine and schnapps, when he wasn't out at the range shooting his guns, walking to stay in shape, and lifting weights. All right, most of the walking was from the apartment the two of them had shared over the past two years to the bar six blocks away, the trip always faster on the way there than the way back.

"You look like hell, Jake," she said. "Take a shower and get dressed." A tear streaked her alabaster face, rolling off the high cheek bone until she caught it with her fingers and briskly wiped it away.

Jake got to his feet, unsure what to do, and even more unsure if he could stay standing. He had not neglected her. Had not taken her for granted in any way. If anything, the reverse was true. She had traveled so much in the past year, they had spent more time away from each other than together. Yet he knew when it was time to fold the cards and shut up. He shook his head and made his way to the bathroom. Hadn't he just taken a shower that morning? What time was it now? He caught a look at the clock radio on the nightstand just as he entered the bathroom. Crap! No wonder she was pissed. He was supposed to meet her at 1800 at the restaurant downstairs. It was 1830 now.

He took a quick shower, toweled off and came back in the room. Anna had picked up after him and placed his fresh clothes on the bed.

As she glanced at his clean, naked body, Jake thought he saw a new attitude in Anna. Maybe she had calmed down.

She sat onto the end of the bed and threw his underwear at him, which he caught and slipped on.

"I'm sorry," he said. "I must have overslept."

"Passed out." English. That was better.

"Tomato potato."

"That's not the way it goes," she said.

Putting his pants on, he said, "That's my way. Why'd you want to meet me downstairs at the bar anyway?"

"I didn't. The restaurant."

She had a point. Although they were technically connected. "Right. Why don't I take you someplace nicer. I'm sure Oslo has a decent JapaChinese place. Tai? Indian?" He strapped his watch to his left wrist. "Where have you been for the past three hours?"

"Shopping."

"You have no bags."

"Shopping is not buying."

"It is when you go," he reminder her as he stretched a polo shirt over his head and then combed out his longer than normal hair with his fingers. Jesus, he had let his hair get long again.

"Must you always be a smart ass, Jake?"

"That's rhetorical, right? That's like asking me to piss sitting down."

A slight smile crept up the right side of her mouth. Okay, he had her now. She was cooling down.

Reaching his hands to her, he said, "Come on. I'll buy you some Sushi."

"Sushi with a hangover?"

She put her hands out and Jake pulled her up from the bed and into his arms. They kissed and she pulled away from him.

"Hangover assumes I still don't have a shine on," he said, knowing she had pulled away because of the alcohol on his breath.

"You've got to slow down, Jake. It's not good for you."

No shit! Maybe that was the point. He was bored out of

his skull. "I know. I need to get back into the game."

A knock on the door surprised Jake, but Anna didn't seem to flinch. Maybe she had ordered room service.

After hesitating another moment, Anna went to the door, looked through the peep and opened the door.

Jake expected to see some room service dude. Instead, there stood a man in his late 50s, gray hair in a military flat top, and dressed in nice tan Dockers and tight black polo shirt that showed the guy was still full of muscle and vitality. Even though it had been ten years since Jake had seen the man, that time passed would not hide his ex-commander, Colonel Russ Reed.

"Jesus," Jake said, his head shaking. "What the hell you doing here, colonel?"

The two of them embraced like brothers, for that's what they had been, first in Air Force intelligence stationed in Germany, and later, when the colonel retired and Jake moved on from the military early, where their paths crossed many times in the old CIA. Jake had spent much of his CIA time in Western Europe, and Colonel Reed had been assigned at various embassies in Eastern Europe. Although they hadn't seen each other in years, they had talked on the phone and corresponded by e-mail.

Anna closed the door and stared at Jake.

"I'm sorry, Russ," Jake said. "This is Anna, my—"

"We've met," the colonel said.

Jake was rightfully confused. But then he remembered that Anna had opened the door without hesitation. She had recognized him. His head swirled and he had a feeling the alcohol was only part of the problem.

"Have a seat, Jake," Colonel Reed said. It was more of a order than a request.

He would have protested, but Jake felt like shit and maybe close to throwing up. Reluctantly, he sat on the end of the bed. "What is this some kind of intervention? I admit I've been drinking too much. But come on. . . ."

Anna pulled a chair from a small table, took a seat, and cast her gaze on the colonel. "You want me to talk?" she asked the colonel.

"Let me start," Colonel Reed said.

He remained standing, his fully-expressioned, ruddy face his only tell. Something was seriously disturbing him, Jake could see.

"I contacted Anna in Vienna," the colonel continued. "You had mentioned she worked for Interpol, and more specifically The Public Safety and Terrorism Sub-Directorate."

Jake looked at Anna and said, "That wasn't exactly a secret. After all, your mother and father in Zell am See know that much."

She didn't say a word.

"Anyway," the colonel said, "you had also told her about my background. So Anna knew, to a certain extent, where I was coming from. As you might know, there's been a huge shake-up in the U.S. intelligence community."

Jake knew. Nearly a decade ago the old CIA, FBI, NSA, ATF, and nearly every other alphabet soup agency had been swallowed up in one major intelligence agency, the American Intelligence Network. The Network also included members of the military intelligence community. Unfortunately, the expected streamlining had also developed at times into an even more cumbersome bureaucracy. Jake had been called back to the Network, which he had never really been a part of, on a number of occasions over the years. And it was always the same old mantra— your country needs you. Each time had almost cost him his life.

"What's the Network need this time?" Jake asked callously. "Who do you need killed."

Colonel Reed laughed. "You're still a funny guy, Jake. But it's nothing like that." His eyes shifted toward Anna and then settled back on Jake.

"Wait a minute," Jake said. "You could have just dropped by our flat in Vienna. Oslo is kind of out of the way. A connection too far. You convinced Anna that she and I needed a vacation in Norway in August. But why?"

Anna leaned back in her chair, her expression defiant yet defeated.

"Well," Colonel Reed said. "Glad to see your training hasn't entirely been washed away by schnapps."

"Did you come here to insult me, or tell me I just won the Megabucks Lotto?"

The colonel hesitated, selecting his words. "You remember a guy named Captain Steve Olson?"

"Of course. You only had seven officers at any one time under your command in our tactical intel squadron. Steve and I hung out a lot. But you know that. What about him? He was reassigned as a military attaché here in Oslo until he died in a plane crash."

"There was no plane crash," the colonel muttered.

Jake's mind tried to recall the circumstances of his old friend's death, but it had been nearly two decades ago, and too much had happened between then and now. "A cover story," he finally surmised.

"Right."

"Okay. . .so how did Steve die?"

"We don't know for sure," the colonel said somewhat reticently. "But we might know now."

Glancing at Anna, Jake said, "And how does this impact Anna and Interpol?"

"It doesn't," Reed said. Perhaps too forcefully.

"It doesn't but it does," Jake said. "Otherwise you wouldn't have asked her to be here. You would have just called me in Vienna and told me what you're going to tell me right now. Come on, Russ, before my buzz wears off."

"Right to the point. I always liked that about you, Jake. All right. Steve and the assistant Oslo station chief, John Korkala, went missing together back in October of 1986. They had heard of a plane crash on Spitsbergen Island in Svalbard and went to investigate. Last the CIA heard they were following four KGB officers. Something went wrong up there, because not one of the six ever left that island."

Thinking of the scenario, Jake tried to remember the Svalbard Archipelago. He had flown over the islands once during a mission. To call them remote would be like calling the sky blue.

"Svalbard made news recently," Jake said. "The Norwegian Seed Bank."

"Exactly."

The Norwegian government had recently completed a cave-like structure under the permafrost where they would store as many species of seeds as possible, just in case the world decided to blow itself up. Then the Norwegians could come to the rescue and help the world re-plant and survive. Of course, they might not have taken into consideration that whole Nuclear Winter, and the fact that they would need someone to till the soil, fresh water, etc.

"So, what happened to Steve?" Jake asked. "You sure the Ruskies didn't just kidnap him?"

"We weren't entirely sure, but his failsafe intel had never been put to the test."

All intel officers were given a piece of information that could be exploited after a little intimidation or torture. None of the officers knew what their own failsafe response entailed. That was the only way the other side knew the officer was not lying, especially under drug-induced lie detectors.

"Interesting. But now you know. Who turned?"

"A retired Soviet intel officer with GRU. He told me about a MiG going down in Svalbard in October of 1986."

"You believe him?"

"Yes. His brother was the MiG pilot."

"So officially that makes seven," Jake said.

"Seven?"

"Seven dead in Svalbard."

"Right."

"So, this Soviet GRU officer told you more." It wasn't a question.

"Yes. This officer has been going to Spitsbergen every August for the past five years to search for his brother. This has been an unusually warm summer up there."

"Global warming," Anna finally said.

"That or fairies and dwarves," Jake said. "He found something?"

The colonel smiled. "Last week. The tail section from his brother's plane."

Jake couldn't hold back a flash of incertitude. "Why do

you need me?" he asked.

Colonel Reed cleared his throat. "Our governments can't get involved with this."

"Why not?"

"That's one thing I can't tell you, Jake. All I need you to do is go up there and find whatever remains of your old friend, Captain Steve Olson. Anna has agreed to go with you. She thought. . ."

"That I needed something to do."

A slight smile tried to escape from Anna's mouth, but she was doing a fine job holding back.

"Well, she said it's been a while."

"Can I think about it?"

Colonel Reed pulled his wallet from his back pocket, retrieved a plastic card, and handed it to Jake.

He looked at the Visa symbol and then read his name on the card. "A platinum debit card with my name on it. Pretty sure of yourself. How much is on it?"

"Just under ten grand. Pin number is the last four of your Social. Kept it simple. You'll need to buy some gear. You have e-tickets waiting for you at Oslo Gardermoen international airport. Flight to Longyearbyen, Svalbard leaves tomorrow at thirteen ten. I've already given Anna a programmed GPS, maps, a satellite phone, and instructions on who you'll meet up there."

"You've thought of everything," Jake said. "What if I just want to hang out here in Oslo and party?"

"Your sense of duty," the colonel said. "And Steve was a good friend. Plus, you could never turn down a good adventure."

He had Jake right on that one. Duty was more than something you stepped on in a cow pasture. Adventure was a reason to live. And, other than for Anna, Jake had not found many reasons in the last few months.

"Fine," Jake said. "But I hope to hell you plan on providing some polar bear prevention."

"You'll get some guns when you reach Spitsbergen," Colonel Reed assured him. With that he went to the door and turned back to Jake, who had followed him from the bed.

The two of them shook hands and turned that into a hug.

"You two take care up there," Reed said. Then he whispered, "That's a beautiful lady you have. Don't let her get away."

Jake smiled and nodded and let him out the door. Then he turned to Anna, who was looking at the floor.

"Shopping?" Jake asked her.

She shrugged. "The GPS and SAT phone. It's like shopping."

Something wasn't settling properly in his stomach, and he guessed it had nothing to do with the schnapps. Regardless, he rushed to the bathroom and puked his guts out.

◆

Colonel Reed got downstairs, strolled through the lavish hotel lobby, and out onto the street. Gazing left and right, he eventually went to the left and then down a narrow side street. Darkness from an overcast sky had nearly enveloped Oslo, but the city lights of the downtown shone brightly as he got behind the wheel of his rental BMW. He glanced up to the fourth floor and tried to guess which room held his old friend, Jake Adams, and that pretty little Interpol agent. He hated this. Hated to lie to Jake like this. But what choice did he have? Some things were bigger than mere individuals.

He checked the rearview mirrors and thought about starting the engine.

Suddenly the passenger door swung open and a man slid onto the leather seat, closing the door behind him.

"How'd it go?" the man asked with an indeterminate accent. A voice that resonated with each syllable. His gruff intonation was probably the result of the skinny cigars he always smoked. He had one now hanging out the right side of his mouth, smoke rising up and making him close his right eye.

"Jake looked like shit," Colonel Reed said. "I don't know if he's up to the task. Looks like he's trying to drink himself to death."

"What's his problem? I've seen his girlfriend. They don't get any warmer than that." He moved the cigar to the front of his mouth and puffed the end red.

"You mean hot," Reed corrected. "Don't get any hotter than that."

"You know what I mean," the man said, exhaling smoke in a straight stream at the windshield. "Try to say that in Russian. Has Jake Adams ever failed to complete a mission?"

He had good points. The colonel smiled thinking about sending Jake to Kurdistan back in the 80s, and how he had come back with first-hand evidence that Saddam Hussein had used nerve agents on his own Kurdish population. No. Jake had never failed him. But he had also never led Jake this far astray. And that bothered him.

"Keep an eye on him," the colonel said. "We'll feed him

more information as needed."

The Russian nodded and got out, disappearing in the darkness like a ghost in a cloud of cigar smoke and car exhaust.

How the hell had it come to this? He thought he had left the game long ago. Now he was pulled right back in. He started the engine and pulled away from the curb, blending in with light traffic.

CHAPTER 2

Jake and Anna checked out of the hotel early the next morning and then went shopping for warmer clothes. After his stomach settled the night before, Jake had checked out the weather forecast for Spitsbergen on the internet. Even though it was summer there now, there was perpetual permafrost and glaciers and they would have to be ready for any weather. Layers would be the best way to go. Jake had also researched the Svalbard Archipelago on the net. Interesting place.

Then the two of them headed to the Oslo airport and waited for their flight. Colonel Reed had not only arranged for tickets, he made them first class. When they got onto the plane, the flight attendant asked if they'd like Champagne. Jake considered it but declined. His right hand shook and he grasped his leg to calm himself. He needed to clean up. Not just for him, but for Anna. She didn't deserve a drunk. Had put up with him like a saint the past few months as he had descended deeper into a funk that even he didn't understand. He hadn't been sober long enough to decipher why he was drinking so hard in the first place.

The flight took three hours, and most of that over the North Pacific. When they finally set down in Longyearbyen, the Svalbard capital of some 1,800 Norwegians, clouds shrouded the little town in near darkness. It was amazing the pilot had even been able to land in that soup.

They took a cab to one of the only real hotels in the town and plopped down onto a feather bed. Jake closed his eyes and his body felt like he was spinning. He needed a damn drink. Couldn't come down this hard.

Anna ran her hand across his forehead. "You're sweating like a pig, Jake."

"I need a drink."

Her hand moved to his chest and she grasped him by the shirt, catching a handful of hair. "No. You need to tell me why you're drinking so much. Don't you love me?"

Opening his eyes, he said, "Of course I love you, Anna. It has nothing to do with you."

"But it does, Jake. It affects me. What happens to you happens to me."

He rolled to his side and gazed at her. She was so beautiful. Colonel Reed was right, though. He couldn't let this woman get away. They had had a good two years. Not perfect, with both of them gone on business so often, but pretty damn good when they were together. And even while they were separated by distance, they maintained contact by cell phone and e-mail. It wasn't perfect. But what relationship was perfect? Maybe they needed to get away more often. . .together. This would be good for them. He only wondered if she knew how much pain he was in at this moment. God he needed a drink.

"Are you okay, Jake?"

He hesitated. "I will be. A part of my mind is telling me I need a drink, and the other part is telling me I can't have one. My body is agreeing I can't. Two against one."

"Why don't you take a shower and we'll go get something to eat."

"Reindeer steaks?"

She laughed. "Or salmon."

His stomach became unsettled with the thought of fish. He thought he might lose his lunch, which had consisted of a large pretzel at the airport before the flight. He rolled off the bed and went to the shower.

Once the shower started, Anna pulled the satellite phone from her backpack, turned it on, and punched in the long number from memory.

"Yeah, we're in place in Spitsbergen," she said in French. She listened carefully as the shower droned on in the bathroom. "I understand. We go to the site tomorrow." She listened again, hoping Jake would take a long shower. "All right. When I know, you'll know." She clicked off the phone and quickly plugged it into the wall to make sure the charge was full.

Then she pulled out her cell phone, found a full signal, which amazed her, and hit in another number.

"I know it's short notice," she said in German, "but I need to extend my vacation beyond the weekend." Listening, she heard the shower stop. Hurry. "It's personal. And I haven't taken vacation in almost a year." Pause. "Thank you." She flipped her phone shut just as Jake came out of the bathroom, naked, wiping his long hair with the towel.

"That feels much better," Jake said. "You should give it a try."

She moved close to him and placed her hand onto his penis, which almost immediately responded to her touch. "I plan on it. But first. . ."

Once they had tested out the bed, Anna went in for a shower. Jake picked up the SAT phone and checked the last number dialed. Interesting. Then he did the same with Anna's cell phone. Not as interesting.

Knowing Anna would be a while with the shower, the blow drying and the make up, he took out his own phone and made a call across the pond to an old friend in Washington.

"Sidewinder Three Eight Four," Jake said. A pause of silence on the other end. He had only used this call sign a few times in the past few years. Only when he really need- ed information he could not get anywhere else. And why not? Since he had left the old CIA, the Network had called on him many times for help. Now it was his turn to get help from them.

"Lindberg one three three."

Jake smiled as the shower continued. He still had time. "Your favorite ex-officer. I take it this is a secure line on your end."

"Of course, Jake. What about your end?"

"Where do you have me located?"

Hesitation. "What the hell you doing in Brazil?"

"I'm far from it," Jake said, smiling. "Tell me every- thing you know about any Op in Norway."

His contact hesitated too long before saying, "You know

I can't talk to you about anything ongoing."

"I understand." More than he was letting on. "Tell me if Colonel Reed is involved."

"Jake, you know the rules. What have you gotten yourself involved in this time?"

How the hell should he play this? He could need their help down the road. Better to come clean. Jake explained what the colonel had hired him to do, and then waited.

Heavy sigh on the other end, just as the shower stopped. "You're on Spitsbergen Island right now." It was a statement. "Colonel Reed was correct. Captain Olson, we believe, either died up there or was taken by the KGB or GRU. Either way, he's long dead. It happened around the time of the Reagan Gorbachav Summit in Iceland."

Jake remembered that now. He thought his old friend had died on a flight to Iceland, where he was supposed to provide intel support.

"What really happened?" Jake asked. He heard the hair dryer turn on.

"Jake," Anna yelled. "I hope you plan on taking me out to the best restaurant in town."

Jake turned the phone away from him and yelled back, "Of course."

"What was that?" Jake's contact asked.

"I have a lady friend."

"The Interpol?"

Shaking his head, Jake guessed the Network had done a complete background check on Anna. "Yeah."

"I've seen photos. Very pretty."

"Thanks. Now can you tell me what kind of shit I'm stepping into?"

"I'll need to do some research and get back with you."

He guessed as much. "I leave for some glacier in the morning." He checked his watch. "I'll call you in twelve hours." He flipped his phone shut just as the hair dryer turned off.

Anna opened the door to the bathroom and looked at Jake in the mirror as she put on mascara, dressed only in a thong and a bra. "Who were you talking to, Jake?"

Jake shook his head. She had to have the best ears in the business. "Asking for a little help." He came up behind her and placed his hand on her bare cheek. "I hope you have something to keep these cute buns warm."

She wiggled away from him. "Hey you just got that. And you saw me buy the silk long underwear."

He leaned against the door frame. "Well, I think I was still a little wasted."

She set down the mascara. She rarely used much make up and needed to use none at all. She was a natural beauty. "What did the Network tell you?"

"Not much. I have to get back with them in the morning. Ready to eat?"

"Famished."

They headed out. Their hotel, the Radisson, was situated on the edge of Longyearbyen, which wasn't saying much. The town was a cluster of colorful wooden structures in yellow, red and green. Walking the streets for a few blocks and finding only a pizza joint and a couple of cafes, they decided to return to the restaurant attached to their hotel.

They had barely sat for a short moment, when Jake had a strong urge for a drink. He needed a drink. No.

Anna ordered them both a strong cup of coffee, which came in a few minutes. Then they both ordered the salmon.

"You could have ordered a glass of wine," Jake told her.

"That's not fair. We need to have clear thoughts. Besides, I think I might be getting a beer gut."

He laughed. "You have the nicest tummy I've ever seen." And if she wasn't so hot it would have pissed him off. She could eat damn near anything and not put on a pound. "Did you make a pact with the devil to keep that beautiful figure?"

"Ha, ha."

Jake casually glanced at a picture on the wall, as if admiring the photo of mountains and glaciers, but in reality was looking at the reflection. He pointed at the photo. "Isn't that a beautiful place," Jake said to Anna.

"Yes, I hope we see that tomorrow."

Their food came and Jake kept his eyes on the food, Anna, and through the corner of his eye, the man across the room.

"You all right eating fish?" Anna asked him.

"You know I love fish." He smiled, put a piece of salmon in his mouth and mumbled. "We have a friend."

She smiled and said, "Are you sure?"

He held back a laugh. "What do you think?"

"I think you should know." She finished her fish and continued, "Let me take a trip to the lady's room and get a good look. Which one?"

"Big guy. Dark hair. Your five o'clock."

She dabbed her mouth with her napkin, put it down and left. The guy tried his best not to watch her, which was hard for any man, and confirmed to Jake that the guy was watching them. Otherwise he would have checked her out more thoroughly.

A few minutes later Anna returned. Same result from the man.

"Well?" she asked.

"The guy barely looked at you," Jake said. "And, if I'm not mistaken, you added a little sway to your normal gate."

She took a sip of water and said, "Perhaps. But maybe the guy is more interested in you."

"I don't think so. Let's head upstairs."

They paid and left. When they got to their room, Jake quieted Anna with his finger as he moved about the room. "Salmon wasn't too bad," he said, searching under the lamp shade. He moved along the curtains, checking inside the edges. "I was really tempted to try the whale or the seal. But I hear they're both out of season. And I'd hate like hell to have my first whale of the frozen variety."

Jake stopped and glanced about the room. Anna looked confused. Settling his gaze on the nightstand, he picked up the small clock radio and smiled. He went to his bag and found a Swiss Army knife; then he opened the radio with a screw driver. Inside, stuck to the small speaker, was what he was looking for. A bug.

"Let's see what the weather report says," Jake said, switching on the radio and cranking up the sound. With the local radio blaring at its highest level, Jake pried the bug loose and brought it to the bathroom, where he flushed it down the toilet. He swept the room for anything else, including going through their bags, until he was satisfied that was the only device. Only then did he turn down the radio.

"All right," he said.

Anna sat on the edge of the bed. "I thought you were

being paranoid. Why would someone bug our room? And how did you know it was bugged?"

"I wasn't sure until I saw the clock radio had been moved slightly. It had been parallel to the back and side of the table."

"Someone placed it while we went to dinner?"

"Yes. They had to move it from the other room, which was supposed to be ours."

"That's why you had us move rooms at the last minute?"

He nodded.

"Wow. What's going on?"

"I didn't want to be, but I'm back in the game."

She put her hand over her face. "I did this."

"In the future, when a former friend of mine, a former spook, comes calling, make damn sure you tell me about it immediately. It's usually not good news."

"But you'd always spoken so highly of Colonel Reed," she pled. "In fact, he's one of the only people you freely talked about. Why is that?"

Jake sat on the bed next to her, his eyes glancing to the table at the SAT phone, which was still charging. He had already opened the battery compartment to check for bugs, but there was something else.

"Anna, there's a reason for that. Half the people I've worked with are either retired or dead. The other half are divided into the covert realm or at the headquarters. I can't mention those."

"I understand. But what I don't understand is why the colonel would put you in danger like this. I thought he was your friend."

"He is. He knows that I know that any time he would

ask me for a favor, it could involve something nefarious and dangerous." Jake got up and picked up the SAT phone from the table, checking the call record again. Even though he had cleared it, she didn't know that. "Why did you call Interpol headquarters?"

Her eyes gave away her embarrassment. "I work for them," she said. "I needed to extend my vacation for a week."

Jake was going to hate himself for this, but he plowed forward. "That's why you'd call your Vienna office."

She rose to her feet. "You bastard! You've been checking up on me." Her fists were clenched at her side.

He set the SAT phone down and came to her, grasping each of her wrists and moving his face along the side of hers. "I'm sorry. I checked the phone while you were taking a shower, seeing if Colonel Reed had left any numbers in there. I saw the number to your headquarters had been made while I was taking my shower, and deleted the record. Good thing, because whoever planted that bug would have checked the call record and known you work for Interpol."

Her arms went limp and she leaned into Jake. "I'm such an idiot. But I still don't understand why this is happening. Isn't it a simple search for an old friend?"

"It's never that easy, Anna. The colonel knew I was good friends with Captain Olson. I couldn't refuse. At least not from Oslo. From the comfort of Vienna, maybe. He must have known I had been down and out lately, and figured I would jump at an opportunity. Especially if it involved you."

He let her hands go and she wrapped them around his back, pulling him tighter to her. "He used me."

"Yeah. And he did a damn good job. Just like he was trained. Now you need to tell me anything else the colonel might have told you, and what your bosses at Interpol know about this whole thing."

She sat back onto the bed and Jake followed her down.

"Vienna knows nothing," she started. "Just think I'm on an extended vacation. But I was required to contact Lyon after any contact with a foreign intelligence officer. You know that. They told me something was up, but they weren't sure what at this time. Told me to keep checking in while they looked into it."

"You trust them?"

"Of course."

Jake thought about it. Maybe this could work to their advantage. Pull info from them and the Network and see how far off each of them is to the truth.

"All right," Jake said. "But from now on let's be open with our contacts and agree on how much to feed them. We don't give them shit unless they give us something first."

She nodded and then kissed him.

"Let's hit the sack. Have a feeling tomorrow will be a long day."

CHAPTER 3

Edinburgh, Scotland

Rain came down in a steady flow, the darkness of midnight broken by the lights of the Edinburgh Castle at the top of the hill at the end of the Royal Mile. A few blocks down from the castle in the Old Town and two blocks down a side street off the Royal Mile, a lone figure walked at a slow clip. He was dressed in dark clothes from top to bottom, no umbrella. When he came upon the pub with the photo of Robert Burns hanging out from the front entrance, he hesitated before stepping inside.

Jimmy McLean, although an officer with British Secret Intelligence Service, MI6, was working undercover as an agent with the MI5 Security Service, looking into domestic terrorism.

At this hour the place was still fairly crowded, and that bothered him. He should have never agreed to meet here at this time. Knew better, that was for sure.

There he was in the corner booth. The little man from Aberdeen. His stubby legs swung with the traditional Scottish music a foot from the floor. Gary Dixon had been picked up by MI5 so many times, he damn near had his own coffee mug in the Edinburgh office. They had never stuck him with anything, though, because he was far more valuable on the street. He collected information like a pack rat and sold it to the highest bidder. All MI5 had was leverage to avoid prosecution, and the fear that they would throw the man into a cell with a large man wanting an ass buddy.

Removing his coat, he hung it from a hook at the end of the booth before taking a seat across from his contact.

"You're ten minutes late," his contact said, his voice a combination of effeminate and Lilliputian.

"Don't get short with me."

"Hey, no need to start in with the short jokes."

"Right. I guess you'd be a little concerned with that." He placed heavy emphasis on the word 'little.'

"Ha, ha." He picked up his pint of Guinness with both stubby hands and downed the last of it, placing the glass down hard onto the thick wooden table. "Why don't you get me another one of these."

McLean got the attention of the pretty, slim young bartender with multiple piercings, her tight stomach exposed, showed her two fingers and got a nod in return.

"What you got for me?" McLean asked the little guy.

"Right to the damn point," Dixon said. "Jesus, don't they teach you guys any people skills?"

The two pints of Guinness showed up on the table and McLean handed the young woman cash and a heavy tip. She smiled and left them alone.

"I take that back," Dixon said. "Hot girls still get your attention." He took a sip of beer and ended up with foam on his thick mustache, which he licked off with his enormous tongue. He caught McLean staring. "It's not the only thing big on me. And the ladies like both."

"You were saying?" This was getting old.

"All right, all right." The little guy tried to lean across the table toward McLean, but he couldn't get any leverage to do so. "I was home for a week and heard of something going down across the pond."

"America?"

He shifted his thick head and said, "Other direction."

"Scandinavia?"

"Norway. But off the coast on some island."

McLean thought for a moment, but didn't know what to think. What of importance could possibly come from a Norwegian island. They had huge oil production facilities along the coast. Maybe someone was planning on hitting those. That would be a huge environmental disaster, and could shift the oil wealth equation.

"What's going on? What have you actually heard?" McLean pressed the guy.

"All I can say is it's something big. What's that worth to you?"

"Without details, not a helluva lot," McLean said. "Who told you, and under what circumstances."

The little man's eyes shifted around the room. "Listen, if I start giving away names at this point, my life will be shorter than my legs."

McLean held back a snicker. "Right. But I need more details. Get me more and you get another get out of jail free card. Otherwise, we picked up this massive man recently. . .could have been a basketball player. I understand he's getting lonely. Needs a friend."

"Hey, hey," the little man protested. "I came to you, remember. Soon as I heard something might be going down."

"Then take me to your contact," McLean said.

"No can do. They'll see MI5 coming a mile away."

McLean considered his options, taking a long drink from his beer. He didn't have many. He shifted in his chair and reached for his jacket.

"Wait a minute," Dixon said. "What about a little help."

Moving back to the center of the booth, McLean said, "You want money for telling me you might have something to tell me? That's incredible." But he also expected the man would ask for it, so he was ready. He reached into his pants pocket and retrieved a debit card, then slid it across the table at the man, who quickly scooped it up with his stubby fingers and looked it over front and back.

"Who the hell is Amus McCloud?"

"That would be you. That's how you get paid from now on. There's fifty Quid on it now. You give me what I want and there'll be much more." He pulled a pen from his shirt pocket and handed it to the man. "Sign it."

"Fifty Quid. That isn't much. How do you sign Amus? Let me practice a couple of times." He scribbled on his coaster a couple times and then made it official on the debit card. Then he put the card into his wallet, which was so stuffed it was hard for him to find a spot for another card. "What if someone asks for additional I.D.?"

"Right." McLean was also waiting for this. "Here." He handed the man a new driver's license. "Sign this also."

"Where'd you get the photo? Wait a minute. . .that was

my last booking shot."

"Right. Well, we had to Photoshop it a little."

Then he looked more closely. "Hey, I'm not three six. I'm three seven, maybe eight on a good day."

"Close enough." McLean sucked down most of his beer, slid to the end, and got out now, putting his long jacket over his shoulders. Then he leaned closer to Dixon and said, "I want a call by noon tomorrow." He left without waiting for a protest.

Out on the sidewalk the rain had slowed to a light mist. He looked across the street at an alley no wider than three feet. Alleys like that were all over the old town area. They cut off distances, but had also been know for their underground activity across the centuries. McLean saw a dark figure slip down into the shadows, so he crossed the street and made his way to the alley.

By the time he got to the edge, he checked his watch and then slid around the corner, stepping lightly down the wet cobblestones. His only lighting came from a building around the corner ahead, giving him a distinct advantage. He could see better than anyone from that side.

A couple more steps, where the alley widened slightly, he stopped. A hand touched his arm.

"I thought you would come in," McLean said. "Watch my back from there."

"No, it works better this way," came a soft woman's voice. "What did he tell you?"

"Nothing. . .yet."

Her hand moved from his arm to his crotch. "You gave him the cards?"

McLean cleared his throat. "Listen. You work for me. What do you think? Of course he has them. And you can bet your ass he'll drain the money from it as soon as he gets a chance."

Her hand moved from his crotch to his buttocks. She squeezed down and said, "That driver's license is brilliant. Are you sure the embedded GPS will work?"

"As advertised. State of the art." What the hell was she up to this time? She was an attractive woman, but not quite his type, for she was an inch shorter than his contact Gary Dixon. She had been trying to seduce him for the past six months. Ever since she had been reassigned from Vauxhall.

Without further warning, her deft little hands unzipped his pants and one hand went inside. "Let's let the Loch Ness Monster out for some Midnight air."

He gasped but didn't stop her. She was at the perfect level, and his mind had actually gone to that thought a few times. In seconds he was to his full glory and her warm mouth took it in. Now he couldn't stop her if he wanted to. And he sure as hell didn't want her to deviate from the task at hand.

American Intelligence Network Headquarters
Camp Springs, Maryland

Deep within the command center, more than one hundred feet below the surface of what had been the old Andrews Air Force Base bowling alley, Kurt Jenkins swiveled in his wide chair like a starship captain, his eyes flicking from one LCD screen to the next, observing ongoing operations worldwide. He was the newly appointed governor of the American Intelligence Network. He had been career CIA before congress had combined the CIA, FBI, NSA, DEA, ATF, and all of the military service intelligence functions into one organization years ago. He had been the first manager of external operations, a position that controlled all covert operations away from U.S. territories, and had ascended to the top job a month ago.

Jenkins checked the bank of clocks, which ran along the top of the wall above the LCD screens, each indicating a different time in various locations around the world. Zulu plus one to Svalbard Archipelago. Twenty-three hundred here. That would mean Zulu minus six, or zero five hundred there. Jake would call at any time now.

He needed to get home to sleep, but guessed he would spend the night again on the sofa in his office. He should have just had a bed brought in and forget about the pretext of his current situation. Sure he didn't really want to go home, but he needed to help his old friend, Jake Adams. After Jake had called, Jenkins had researched the current situation in Svalbard. He glanced at a briefing paper. It was more than Jake understood, he was sure of that. Only time would tell for sure what Jake had gotten himself into this time, though. His men had tried to pick up Colonel Reed for questioning, but somehow he had disappeared from Oslo. Vanished.

Then Jenkins had wanted to contact his counterpart in Moscow to see what he knew; yet, he knew that would show his hand. No, he needed to give Jake everything he knew to date, and then keep digging. Even though relations with Norway were good, he didn't want to talk with them directly either. This would have to be handled with great discretion. Jake would be on his own. He would give Jake technical assistance when needed. Nothing more. He looked at the brief once more before slipping it into the shredder at his side.

CHAPTER 4

Jake had woken early as usual, around zero six hundred, but what was not normal for the past three months is that he did not have a huge headache hangover. At some point he had come to expect the stiff neck, the throbbing pain radiating from there to his temples and eyeballs, and the dry throat. Expected the feeling of weakness that he thought he could vanquish with the early hour and some push ups and sit-ups. Yet, deep down he knew he was fooling himself. Still, it wasn't like he had been falling down drunk for the past three months. He had simply taken things a bit to the extreme, finding whatever comfort he could with Anna's absence without cheating. The numbness had prevented any possible intimacy with another woman, not that he had tried to find it, but had also bled over into those times when Anna had been home. He could see that now, with his mind clear and not clouded with the after-affects of alcohol.

In fact, he felt pretty damn good this morning. Felt like taking a run, which he did while Anna continued to sleep.

A dark fog wrapped the town of Longyearbyen in isolated obscurity as Jake jogged along the main drag of the capital. He made his way toward the airport, his lungs sucking in the cold, damp air and feeling as if they might explode with each struggle for air. When he got to within a few blocks of the airport, he slowed his pace to a walk, his hands on his hips.

He thought about Anna and why they were there in that isolated set of islands in the Arctic. What had Colonel Reed gotten him involved in this time? Was it just a simple case of him finding an old friend in the snowy glacier? Closure?

Stopping alongside the road, Jake swung his fanny pack from back to front and pulled out the SAT phone. He punched in the number for his old friend Kurt Jenkins. If anyone owed Jake a favor, it was the current Network governor. Jenkins had ridden some of Jake's successes over the years right to the top.

Before the call went through, Jake checked the distance between himself and any possible parabolic microphone. He guessed he was beyond the range of most that would be within view. It's why he had selected the site on the ride from the airport the day before.

"Well? What ya got for me?" Jake asked.

"Right to the point," Jenkins said. "No weather report. No how's she hanging."

"I'm on a run," Jake said. "If you must know, it's dark, damp and foggy. And I've got a flight to catch in less than two hours, assuming the helo can fly in this soup. That better?"

"Much." He hesitated and Jake thought he had lost the signal.

"You there?"

"Yeah. I had to dig deep for this one, Jake. I was just a field officer like yourself in nineteen eighty-six."

"I was still an Air Force officer," Jake corrected.

"Right. Anyway, your friend Captain Steve Olson, as you know, was assigned to the Oslo embassy as a military attaché."

The wind swept across the open tundra and Jake shivered from the sweat he had worked up.

"No offense, Kurt, but could you cut to the chase. I'm standing out in the middle of nowhere, freezing my ass off."

"Absolutely. Anyway, as far as we know, a Soviet MiG Twenty-five went down on Spitsbergen Island a couple of days before the Reykjavik Summit. At the time, we had no way of knowing its flight path. So, Captain Olson and John Korkala, the Oslo assistant station chief, were sent to investigate."

"What made the CIA so interested?"

"One of our contacts in Finland said the Soviets were sending a team to recover something from Svalbard."

"How many?" Jake asked.

"At least four."

"That would have gotten our attention. Send one or two and it's a search and destroy mission. Send four and it's a sanitation mission. What was on the plane? A nuke?"

"That's what we thought at first. But there was no radiation release."

"Chemical or biological?"

"Don't know."

"Hang on."

A car came along the road toward him and slowed when

the headlights hit Jake. He waved and the car continued toward the airport. A pretty woman, a blonde who could have been Anna's twin, smiled at him and waved back.

"Everything all right?"

"Yeah, just a car with a hot blonde."

"Some things never change. Christ, you have a beautiful girlfriend."

"I know. And you don't have to deify me."

"Funny guy. Anyway, we never heard from our men and the Soviets never heard from their men. I have that on the best authority. Of course if it had happened today we would have a direct GPS position, SAT photos, you name it. But somehow the decision was made to forget about this whole affair. Reagan and Gorbachav had damn near French kissed and nobody wanted to make waves. Later, once the Soviet Union went tits up, the entire case was closed when the new Russia had admitted that one of their pilots had defected with the MiG and crashed in Norway in bad weather. That's the last note we have in the official file."

Jake let out a deep breath, the air escaping in a cloud of vapor. "There's more to this. Always is."

"I don't know that for sure."

"But you suspect I'm correct."

Pause. "I don't know."

Context. Jake always knew that what was not said was usually as import as what was said. It was all context and juxtaposition. This would be no exception.

"Thanks, Kurt. Appreciate the effort."

"Jake?"

"Yeah."

"Be careful."

Those words hung in his brain like the fog on the muskeg of Spitsbergen.

He jogged back to the hotel and caught Anna in the shower, where he joined her. They had a quick breakfast, checked out, and took a van to the airport.

They were directed to a helo out on the pad, where the pilot was already behind the controls and a ground crewman was making final preparations for the flight. Piling all their gear in, Jake strapped Anna into a seat before heading to the cockpit.

He was surprised when the pilot turned out to be the pretty blonde who had passed him while he talked on the SAT phone that morning. She handed him a headset as she powered up the engines and clicked switches to get ready for flight.

"Kjersti Nilsen," the pilot said, reaching out her gloved hand to Jake.

He shook and she squeezed down hard. It surprised him, since she had the build of a cross country skier like Anna. But then Anna's strength had also surprised Jake on more than one occasion.

"How was your run?" she asked him through the headset.

"A little cold and moist," Jake said.

"Welcome to Svalbard. It doesn't get any better where we're going."

Moments later they were airborne, and Jake wondered how in the hell they could even lift off in that thick fog. He got his answer seconds later as the helo lifted out of the low clouds and an obscured sun appeared.

Jake pulled out his GPS handheld, waited for the satellites to get picked up, and then punched in their destination. He watched as their elevation fluctuated and the distance counted down. By air they were about 120 miles from Pyramiden, a Russian coal mining settlement that had once had a population of 1,000 before being abandoned in 1998. But the Russians had re-established mining operations in 2007, and Jake had heard the population had already gone back up to 500. Which is how someone had found the wreckage of the MiG-25 a week ago.

The scenery was surprising—high glacial mountains, mostly barren, with deep fjords that cut through rocky coasts. It was breathtaking and Jake guessed not many people had actually seen the place. Other than those hardy coal miners, Norwegian fishermen, or those stopping off on their way to explore the North Pole.

They stopped in Pyramiden to drop off mail and pick up another package of the same, topped off with fuel, and then quickly lifted off again. Total ground time about ten minutes.

Anna had not said a word since they left the capital. Jake knew she hated to fly by helo. She tried to sleep through the experience.

Jake pulled up their next destination on the GPS and saw they were only about 20 miles away. He gave the pilot the location. He had read in the briefing from Colonel Reed that Captain Olson and John Korkala had taken snowmobiles from Pyramiden back in 1986. Looking at the terrain below, he guessed it had been some pretty rough sledding.

"How would you get to our destination by snowmobile?" Jake asked the pilot. "It's so rocky."

She glanced to the ground. "Couldn't do it this time of year. Well, not true. I hear last year you could have. This is an unusually warm summer. August is the warmest it gets up here, and the melt is at its peak. Global warming."

"Looks like the glaciers are doing all right up here," Jake said.

"I'm just saying the only reason anyone saw the plane was because the snow hasn't melted this far down in more than twenty years. A pilot saw the tail from the air."

Moments later Jake saw the plane for himself—what was left of it. The debris field stretched for dozens of yards. The pilot set down the helo right near the center, where the main fuselage was still partially covered in snow. In fact, there had been a couple of inches of new snow the night before.

The pilot shut down the engine, unstrapped, took off her headset, and then pulled a pistol from under her seat and strapped it to her hip.

"Forty-four magnum," Jake said. "That's a powerful gun."

She opened the door and said, "Polar bears laugh at a nine mil or a forty cal." She slapped her gun. "But this will take one down. We've got two more rifles in the back—a thirty-ought-six and a three hundred mag."

"Great," he said, slipped toward the back. "Let's hope we don't need them."

"Need what?" Anna asked. She looked a little green.

"The rifles," Jake said. "A lot of hungry polar bears up here."

"This is crazy. You know my idea of roughing it is having no hot tub in the hotel room."

The side door opened and Kjersti held out her hand to Anna, introducing herself and helping her out onto the frozen ground.

Jake got out and first went to the largest aircraft parts, the main fuselage, which had broken in two. The wings had sheared off and probably lay back fifty yards or so, but the cockpit was still attached to the main fuselage, just in front of the large engine intakes. He checked the cockpit first. The canopy was gone. No pilot. He didn't know what he had expected. Bones perhaps. Maybe more, considering the glacier. But something wasn't right.

"Jake!"

He turned to see Anna brushing snow from something. He walked to her and said, "What ya got."

"A snowmobile."

Jake looked a few feet away and saw a second one. "Make that two snowmobiles."

Kjersti pulled a digital camera from inside her flight suit and started taking photos.

Immediately Jake saw that they were Russian sleds. Which made sense, since the CIA had rented a snowmobile from them in Pyramiden. He already knew that. But wait. They had rented one snowmobile and a sled for their gear. These had to be from the GRU or KGB.

"What's going on?" Kjersti asked. "I thought this was supposed to be a plane crash."

"As you can see," Jake said, "it is. I have no idea how these snowmobiles got here." Not a total lie.

His friend at the Network, Kurt Jenkins, had said they had sent four Soviet officers. That would be at least two snowmobiles. Must be their sleds, he guessed.

"Anna, see what you can find here," Jake said. "I need to check out the aircraft."

Anna nodded and started to dig around.

"We have a metal detector in the helo, if that will help,"

Kjersti said.

"Sure thing."

Once Kjersti went back to the helo, Jake came closer to Anna and said, "These have to be the KGB or GRU snow-mobiles. You keep digging and you might find their bodies."

"That's what I'm looking for," Anna said.

"Something is wrong here," he said. "This isn't a MiG-25. It's a MiG-31. Very similar but not the same. In '86 it might have had more significance. Although both aircraft never really lived up to their hype. This one had a little more range, though. Perhaps two thousand miles at ferry distance. More importantly. This was a reconnaissance version. I doubt if it would have been carrying a weapon."

But then that didn't really explain why the Soviets had sent a crew to sanitize the place. The avionics were not that different from the MiG-25, which the U.S. had already taken apart at that time from defected aircraft. In the '70s the U.S. Air Force had gotten their hands on a MiG-25 when a Soviet pilot defected and landed in Japan. The Americans had taken it apart, studied it piece-by-piece, and then shipped it back to the Soviets in pieces. Talk about a slap in the face.

Kjersti came back with a metal detector. She and Anna combed the immediate area while Jake went back to the opened MiG-31 fuselage. The crash had not opened that panel. There were too many panel fasteners, and all of those were intact and had been opened with a screw driver.

Looking around in the compartment, Jake saw something that wasn't normal. There had been a cube about one foot by one foot surrounded by spray foam, which had been mostly chipped away. Whatever the Soviets had come for, they had found it and pulled it from the wreckage.

"Jake!"

He turned and saw Anna and Kjersti standing and looking down at something. He hurried over there and saw what they saw. What was left of a man. Animals had chewed away most of the man's face, ripped through his chest to get at his innards, and left only bones. They had not chewed through the rifle, the AK-47, at his side. Moreover, it was pretty easy to determine the cause of death for this men. He had a bullet hole in his forehead.

"What's going on here?" asked Kjersti.

"You suppose the polar bears did this?" Anna asked, glancing around toward the horizon and to closer snowy outcroppings.

"When's our drop-dead time to leave?" Jake asked Kjersti.

"I don't like the way you phrased that." She thought, calculating the time against distance. "We've got a few more hours. The weather is supposed to turn bad later this evening, with heavy winds, snow, and more fog."

"Could we stay the night?"

"Only if we're complete idiots."

Anna laughed. "You don't know Jake very well."

"Hey." Jake gave her a mock cold look.

"I'm just saying. They don't call you the crazy American for nothing."

"Who's they?"

"I promised not to tell."

"You aren't really serious about staying the night," Kjersti said.

"Only if we have to," Jake said. "You two keep looking for more bodies. I'm going to scan the area."

"You better take one of the rifles," Kjersti said. "They're fully loaded, there's extra rounds also, and the scopes are zeroed to one hundred meters."

"Great." Jake took off, picked up the 30.06 and another box of 20 rounds, and then headed off to the west, toward a slight rise. Now he was up above the crash site, about two hundred yards away, with a view in all directions.

He took out the SAT phone. Once it acquired a signal, he punched in the number and waited. Nothing. The signal was suddenly lost. That's strange. He turned off the power and gazed around. What the hell had gone on here? It looked like there had been a shoot-out. Fighting over what had been in the aircraft? Must have been. Then it was only a short time before they would find all six of the bodies. Unless someone had made it out alive. Four against two. It was more likely that if anyone had survived it would have been one of the Soviets. He tried the SAT phone again, but got the same result. Damn it!

Putting the rifle to his shoulder, he scanned the horizon in all directions through the nine power scope. Something bad had happened in this pristine place, and Jake had a feeling he'd uncover what that was soon enough.

CHAPTER 5

Stockholm, Sweden

Having flown from Oslo earlier that morning, Colonel Reed had wasted some time at two museums, waiting for his hotel in Central Stockholm to allow him to check in, and also waiting for his 1800 meeting with another contact. Now he sat somewhat subdued in the back of the taxi as the driver negotiated late rush hour traffic, bringing him from his hotel to Gamla Stan, the Old Town.

The clouds were so thick it looked like midnight, with the rain starting now to beat down on the cab's windshield. He hated Stockholm. It was like a clean, cold Venice. Yet, whereas the Venetians were welcoming and boisterous, the people of Stockholm were as cold as the outside air. And the damn women were self-absorbed flaxen giants. Italian women were nicer, that was for sure, but they were too hairy. At least the Swedish women were fairly hairless. One consolation.

Finally the taxi pulled over to the curb near the stock exchange. Reed paid the guy and got out.

The little café was a block away and he was ten minutes late. Screw it. This was his meeting. He could wait.

The rain started to pick up and Reed wondered if it was snowing right now way up north on Svalbard. Had Jake Adams actually found what he had been sent to find? Or did he find more? That was the hope.

As he got to the front of the café, he didn't hesitate—just rushed in out of the rain as if he had done it a hundred times. Now he stood, taking off his coat and giving it a slight shake to release the rain, which brought stares from one of those blonde giants, the waitress with hair to her strong shoulders.

His contact would be wearing a red cap. That's all Reed knew. Glancing around the crowded room, he saw the only red in the place, and it sat atop a huge head in the corner. A perfect spot for a view of the entire joint, but not close enough to the front windows or the door to concern him. But that's about all Reed saw was the head and the red cap. His contact was a little person. A dwarf? Midget? Crap!

Reed approached the man in the corner and stopped before sitting down. "You Oberon?"

"King of the Fairies," the guy replied, his voice a mixture of Swedish and effeminate Slavic. He gestured with his stubby fingers for Reed to sit across from him.

Reed sat and studied the little man. His skin was dark, his eyes green and narrowly set in his large skull. The crow's feet gave away his age to be around mid-fifties, but Reed already knew that, since he had read a briefing on the man earlier in the day. Oberon was really Victor

Petrova, a former KGB officer who had retired nearly five years ago, and, according to intel briefs, started his own underground syndicate. He was into nearly anything he could get his stumpy little fingers on.

"I've heard a lot about you, Victor."

The man looked annoyed. "Please. . .my name is Oberon."

"Sorry, I thought that was just your code name," Reed said.

The leggy waitress came around and Reed asked for a cup of coffee. She left without acknowledging.

"Let's get down to business," Oberon said. "What the hell does the CIA want with me?"

"As I'm sure you know, the CIA is no longer the CIA," Reed said. "Besides. I'm an independent contractor now. Just like you?"

The little man laughed, his thick chest bouncing up against the edge of the table. "Right. That's a good one, Colonel Reed. And I plan on trying out for Russian National Basketball Team."

"Believe me or not." Reed had heard that Petrova was a genius, a chess master, and had worked at the highest levels in the KGB's First Chief Directorate in the Disinformation Department. But why had his briefing not mentioned the man's physical description?

"So why did you hire Jake Adams to fly to Svalbard?"

Reed tried not to flinch, but he guessed he might have failed, he was so put off by this revelation.

"I'll take your silence as an affirmation," Oberon said. "I hope you don't play chess or poker."

"Never found the time for either," Reed said.

The waitress finally brought his coffee and set it down

on the table with a tinkling of China. The coffee had a film of foam on top and Reed hoped that wasn't spittle.

"She doesn't like you much, Colonel. Let's get down to business. You sent Jake Adams to Svalbard to find something. You think I know something about why he's there. This is a chicken and egg conundrum, Colonel. You think I know something about the MiG, so you should have asked me before you sent Jake Adams there. Does he even know what he's looking for there?"

The colonel took a sip of the coffee. It wasn't that hot, but the caffeine would help. He was having a helluva time staying awake recently.

Finally, Reed said, "I want you to buy what he finds."

The little guy shook his enormous head, a smile on his face, revealing teeth that looked as if they had been ground to points but were just crooked and oddly spaced.

"Why would I buy something that should already be mine?" Oberon asked.

"You mean the Russian government."

"Technically that was before the Russian government," Oberon reminded the colonel. "Old Soviet."

"Set a price."

"For what?"

Silence as they stared at each other. Colonel Reed finished his coffee and gently set the coffee cup on the saucer, his eyes never leaving those green orbs.

Oberon broke first. "I need to know what I'm buying."

"I understand you sent that MiG on the mission in the first place," the colonel said. "So if anyone knows what was onboard, it's you."

Silence again.

"Assuming you're correct," the little man said, "why

wouldn't I just send some of my own men to take what should be mine in the first place? Or maybe we already got what was there years ago."

Now the colonel smiled. He had him. The colonel did play chess. Had been the Air Force Academy champion for three years. "But you haven't. Your men failed to retrieve. . .the item, back in eighty-six. The location was only known by your men back then, who failed to relay it back to you." He was bluffing now. "And your superiors called off the mission, deciding to let it go."

"Superiors? I had a bunch of dolts who ran the First Chief Directorate back then. Glasnost. Perestroika. What the hell was that all about?"

Colonel Reed hunched his shoulders.

Oberon continued, "What makes you think Jake Adams will find anything in that Arctic wasteland? I understand he's a drunk now."

The colonel tightened his jaw. "He has personal reasons."

The little man laughed. "You mean Captain Olson?"

Damn it! Did this man know everything?

"Your men killed him." Another guess.

"Maybe he's alive," Oberon said. "Took what was ours."

What the hell was he talking about? Remember, he had been in charge of the disinformation department. He was playing him. If the captain had lived, he would have turned over whatever the Soviets had been up to at the time. There would have been no other reason not to do so.

"Will you buy what we find?" the colonel asked again.

The little man shifted his head to the side and said, "You find something, you give me a call. Then we'll talk. You can't sell what you don't have." His eyes shifted toward the outside window. "Get down."

As he said it, the colonel looked at the window as he dove toward the floor.

Bullets crashed through the glass and sprayed the wall where they had both been sitting. People screamed and scattered.

The colonel looked up over a table, but the shooter was gone. As fast as he had shown he was gone. On his knees now, Colonel Reed scanned the recovering patrons. But Oberon, Victor Petrova, was nowhere to be seen. He had vanished.

Glasgow, Scotland

After Jimmy McLean got a call from his little friend, Gary Dixon, around noon, telling him he was going to Aberdeen to meet with his contact in person, McLean had told the guy to call him as soon as he had more information. McLean had gotten a call shortly after from his people, saying Dixon was on the move—not to the north in the direction of Aberdeen, but to the west toward Glasgow.

Now, just after the supper hour, McLean pulled his Rover to the curb in a nasty little neighborhood a dozen blocks southeast of the city center. Litter was strewn about the street. Graffiti plastered upon brick walls. Among all the chaos of this rundown enclave, written in large red letters on a white background on a poster on a beat up bus stop shelter, was the phrase 'Love Something.' Government do-gooder, McLean guessed. Hopeful thinking in this neighborhood.

He checked the address one more time to make sure it was correct. Then called his contact to verify Dixon was still there. He was. He hadn't moved.

McLean got out and walked toward the apartment building. This dwarf was starting to piss him off. They had gotten a vague confirmation of chatter similar to what Dixon was trying to sell him. Something was going down in Norway. But nobody was sure of the details.

Inside, McLean checked the mail boxes. There were only six apartments. Three down and three on the second level. Which one? Looking at the first door down the hall, he smiled. He pulled a device from his pocket and put it up to the peep hole. The reverse peep-hole viewer allowed him to look inside the apartment, which contained an older couple watching the news. The next two were empty.

He quietly went upstairs. About to use the viewer again, he realized he didn't need to do so. The peep hole was around crotch level. What were the odds of. . .

Getting to his knees and placing the viewer over the hole, he saw his little friend scurry across from one side of the room to the next. The lock was a piece of crap. In less than thirty seconds he had it unlocked, and with a quick shove he was inside.

Dixon's eyes got big when he saw McLean enter. The little guy's legs shuffled toward the kitchen, but McLean caught him by the scruff of the neck and pulled him back into the living room.

"What the hell," Dixon yelled.

McLean threw him onto a battered and torn sofa and loomed over the man. "This doesn't look like Aberdeen."

"I had to stop by here and knock one off with the old

lady. I'm a little guy but I got big needs."

McLean glanced about the room and saw that everything there was feminine. Flower pillows, dainty doilies, a knock off tiffany lamp. "I thought you might be a little light in the loafers."

"This coming from a guy who frequently wears a dress?"

"It's my clan kilt you fugly troll."

"Jesus. Back to the short jokes."

He felt like pummeling this little dwarf. But he needed him.

"How'd you find me anyway?" Dixon asked, genuinely confused.

"We have our ways, Gary. But I'm guessing your contact, if there is a contact, is not in Aberdeen. You're gonna take me to him now. Let's go." He waved his hand toward the door.

Dixon hesitated and then shoved his short legs over the side of the couch and hit the floor. "All right. All right. You got me, big guy. I was gonna call ya."

"Sure."

They left and went down to McLean's Rover.

Settled into the passenger seat, Dixon said, "Nice ride. Leather seats for MI-5? You must be a big shot there."

"This is my private auto," McLean said, cranking it over and pulling out onto the deserted street. "Nice neighborhood."

"Hey, my people have been repressed since the beginning of time. Can't get a decent job. Can't get a nice place without that. Everyone tries their best to keep the little guy down."

"But you're not a tiny bit bitter."

"Screw you."

McLean drove nowhere slow.

"You gonna tell me where to go?" McLean asked.

Dixon smiled.

"Better yet. Give me directions to your friend's place."

"He's got a kiosk down in The Barras."

Great. The Barras was a market in Glasgow where one could get just about anything, including mugged. Kiosks and booths lined the streets, which had been closed off. Many of the items were of questionable legality. It took them a half hour to get there.

McLean got out, made sure his wallet was securely buttoned into his back pocket, and checked his gun under his left arm. A comfort. For every step he took, Dixon took four.

They found the kiosk, which sold everything from Scottish trinkets to Troll dolls. McLean noticed he even had his clan crest on key rings and coffee mugs. The man behind the counter was much older than Dixon, but around the same height. Only this guy's gut was bigger than his head. He had built a ledge that ran the length of the booth, putting him close to McLean's level.

"This is the guy," the kiosk man said. His voice came out like it traveled across broken glass.

"Yeah," Dixon said. "Tell him what you told me."

"What about a little consideration?"

"So, you want me to pay you by the inch? Or the quality of the information?"

"You were right, Gary. He's pretty funny for a big guy."

McLean glanced around and finally pulled out a combo cell phone slash PDA, caught a signal, touched in a figure, and closed the browser. "There. I just transferred some money to Dixon's bank account."

"You're shittin' me, right?" the kiosk man said.

"Dead serious."

"You can check the balance at the ATM at the end of the street," the man said to Dixon.

Dixon started off but McLean grabbed him by the collar. "You'll have to trust me. Now quit yanking me around and tell me what you know. Or I can take the both of you in and we can talk in a little room."

The kiosk man leaned onto the counter toward McLean and said, "All right. I heard there was a Soviet MiG that went down back in the eighties on some Norwegian island up in the Arctic. Some kind of spy mission. Real secret type stuff. The Americans, the CIA, were on it like a Highlander on Haggis. So were the KGB. But none of them got off the island. I heard that for some reason both side gave up on it, but I don't know why."

"What was on the plane?" McLean asked.

"My contact said it was some kind of weapon. Something the old Soviets had developed. Word was sent out to start the bidding."

"Without even knowing what it was?" McLean asked. That was almost impossible to believe.

"Well, the Russians know what it is," the kiosk man explained."

McLean had him. "So your contact is Russian."

"I didn't say that," the man said emphatically.

Not wanting to argue, knowing he already knew the answer, McLean leaned in a little closer and said, "Where is this going down?"

"I don't know. Some island in the Arctic. Spits or Swallows."

"Spitsbergen?"

"Sounds about right."

McLean considered that. He had never been to the Svalbard Archipelago, but he had seen a BBC documentary on the islands a few years back. "Why is something going down now? How do you know?"

"How much money did you put in Gary's account?"

"Enough. There'll be more once I verify the information. Now answer the question."

"He has a temper," the man said to Dixon. To McLean he said, "Some American hired a guy named Jake Adams to find the MiG. He's there right now."

Jake Adams? McLean had never met the man, but another friend of his at MI6, Sinclair Tucker, had mentioned the man often. Adams was former Air Force Intel and former CIA. He was now a security consultant of some kind. Private. But he had been called back by the Network a few times in the recent past. If Adams had been hired, something big was about to go down. Trouble seemed to follow him around like a mist on the glen.

CHAPTER 6

American Intelligence Network Headquarters
Camp Springs, Maryland

Kurt Jenkins slammed down the SAT phone for the tenth time in the past hour. He had tried to call Jake Adams for hours from his private office, but had not been able to get through. A communications specialist now stood at his side, a former Navy nuclear submariner who had retired from that service directly into the Network a year ago.

"Tell me I'm not going crazy, Johnson," Jenkins said.

Johnson pushed his thick black glasses higher on his nose. "Sir, you're not going crazy. There is SAT coverage on Spitsbergen, but for some reason the signals are being disrupted."

Jenkins thought for a second. "Is someone trying to jam our signal?"

"Not a chance, Sir. There's a ton of Boreal activity, though."

"English, Johnson."

"Boreal, Sir. Referring to the Aurora Borealis."

The Network governor's face distorted. "You're telling me the Northern Lights are fucking up my SAT Comm?"

"Yes, Sir. A qualified maybe. The Sun flares and sends ionic. . ." He stopped short. "The Sun causes the Northern Lights and screws up our satellites."

"You're a quick learner. Thank you, Johnson. Now how long will it last?"

Johnson's eyes rolled up in thought. "On Svalbard? On and off until the Sun goes Supernova."

"So SAT images are also a no go."

"Sir, we have no assets in that region at this time. We could re-direct, but that would take a while. And then we'd still have the Sun problem."

"Great. Thank you. That'll be all."

The communications specialist left Jenkins in his office alone. Great. Great. Great. The charter helicopter was hours overdue. No communications. Now Jake Adams was stuck out in the middle of nowhere, probably freezing his ass off. At least he was there with a beautiful woman.

Spitsbergen Island, Norway

The Arctic sky streaked with swirling greens and orange of the Aurora Borealis. With the darkness came the cold of the northern wind whipping off the glaciers.

The three of them had spent hours digging up the remains of five men; four Soviets and finally the body of the Oslo assistant CIA station chief, John Korkala. All of the bodies showed signs of animal predation—probably polar bears and Arctic foxes. Only one man remained missing. Jake's old friend, Steve Olson. Also missing was the snowmobile the Americans had rented in Pyramiden.

Jake stood now outside the helicopter, mesmerized by the Northern Lights, the hunting rifle over his right shoulder. He heard the side door open behind him and seconds later arms reached around him, followed by a kiss on the side of his neck.

"Kjersti, my girlfriend is right in the helo."

Anna slapped him on the butt and came to the front of Jake. "You'd like that."

"She's a very attractive woman."

She smiled and said, "I agree. You think she might be up for a three-way?"

Jake knew that was a no-win question, but he played along. "Maybe. But it might go over better if you approach her. See what she thinks."

"I'll bet you're getting hard just thinking about that." She looked around Jake toward the helo and then placed her hand on his groin.

"It's so cold out here I'd be lucky to find it to piss."

She took her hand away. "You're no fun."

"That's what I hear. Did Kjersti get through to anyone on the radio?"

"No."

"We need to stay the night," Jake said. "I've got to find Steve."

"I know. The two of us agreed."

"Might get a little cold and cozy in the helo tonight."

Anna smiled. "That's what I'm talking about."

"In the meantime, I'm heading up to that ridge to see if I can get through on the SAT phone. I'm sure coverage is not great for this region under normal circumstances, but with this Boreal activity there's probably not much chance of getting through."

"You want some company?" Anna asked him.

"No. Stay down here with Kjersti. Let her know what I'm up to. Stay warm."

She kissed him on the lips and said, "You stay safe. Don't let the polar bears get you."

Jake patted the butt of the rifle. "Got this."

He took off toward a ridge a couple of hundred yards away. With the Northern Lights swirling above the stark white glacier, he could see fine without turning on his head lamp.

Half way there his lungs started to give out on him, the cold, damp air making him labor with each step. How had it come to this? A simple walk on a glacier and he was feeling it. His body started to shake and he stopped for a moment to catch his breath and steady himself. It wasn't the cold, he knew, but his worst fear. He had been drinking too much over the past three months, and now had been without for days. His body was reacting to its absence. He had always thought that drinking problems were serious character flaws, a weakness that had nothing to do with the physical addiction of the juice itself. Maybe that was true. Maybe the body ruled the mind at this point and not the other way around. Regardless, he knew that he could beat this, and just maybe he was in the right place to conquer it. Without the temptation in front of him at all times.

He continued up the ridge and came to a point where he could see even farther than he had earlier in the day. It was the best place for miles to get a signal. If there was a satellite somewhere on the southern horizon somewhere above the point where Norway, Sweden, Finland and Russia met, perhaps his SAT phone would pick it up.

Looking back down the ridge toward the helo, he hoped Anna and Kjersti were staying warm. His mind drifted for a microsecond about what Anna had said earlier. He knew she was kidding, but he also knew that she knew how to play with a man's natural thoughts.

He tried the SAT phone, angling it in all directions, hoping he could get any signal at all. Nothing. Yeah, the Aurora Borealis was playing with the satellites. They were beautiful but destructive.

Then he lifted the binoculars from his chest and scanned in all directions. He had no idea what he was looking for, but he knew that he couldn't go back to the helo at this time. It was tight in there and he would more than likely start to shake uncontrollably. Anna didn't need to see that, nor did Kjersti. Their confidence in him would be shot all to hell.

There! Nearly a mile to the northeast. A large figure and a smaller one lumbered across the glacial plain—a polar bear sow and her cub. They were vectoring away toward the east of their location. Better check for company. He quickly scanned in three hundred sixty degrees. Nothing.

He set the binoculars to his chest and took in a deep breath, when something green glimmered just thirty yards away. Then it was gone. Then again. He looked up at the Northern Lights and saw they were mostly green at this time. But something had reflected the light.

Pulling up the binoculars again, he couldn't tell what was causing the reflection. So he walked over there for a closer look.

As he got closer, he saw that the ridge had an overhang—an indentation like a half cave. He clicked on his headlamp and directed the beam of light lower. Then he saw it. With the warmer temps and the wind, snow had cleared from a trailer. Brushing further ahead, the trailer was attached to a snowmobile. The missing snowmobile.

His old friend, Captain Steve Olson, had to be close by. What would Jake have done? Steve had been either hiding or trying to find protection from the elements. The overhang would have provided some cover for both. And until recently, Jake guessed, the entire cave-like structure would have been covered in heavy snow. It was only because of the warm trend that summer that any of these things—the MiG and the snowmobiles—had been exposed.

Jake set down the rifle and moved to the deepest point under the overhang, got to his knees, and started digging with his hands. Moments later he hit something solid. Not rock solid, but something out of place.

It was a body.

Exhausted, he rolled to his side and something sharp stabbed him in the back. Damn it!

He dug to see what it was. His headlamp soon started shining back at him. Metal of some kind. He dug faster now and quickly uncovered a one foot cube metal box.

There was no doubt that the box had been a perfect fit to the foam hole inside the MiG. So his old friend had actually gotten the box, whatever it was, away from the Soviets. And he had somehow survived the shoot-out, escaping to this place. Jake imagined his old friend's face and tried to understand what had gotten him to this location. On top of the trailer, the item that had reflected the Northern Lights had been one of the old collapsible satellite dishes the military and the CIA had used back then for remote communications. Maybe Steve had also gone to high ground to call in their location, call in for extraction. But maybe he had been injured. Or maybe the weather had been severe. It had been October, an unforgiving time up here. Regardless, Steve had gotten the item from the MiG and now Jake had it.

He wiped snow from the metal box and saw the Russian symbols on the side. Although he couldn't read the words, he had seen the symbols before many times.

Biohazard.

Crap!

CHAPTER 7

Stockholm, Sweden

Colonel Reed had gone back to his hotel after being shot at during his meeting with Oberon at the café. He had sat for a while eating and drinking from the mini-bar, wondering what had happened and why. His mind flicked back and forth considering if the shots had been aimed at him or the Russian. But one thought stuck with him—the little Russian, the former KGB officer, had warned him just in time to save his life. Sure it could have been self preservation coupled with a natural inclination to help a fellow human being. Yet, Reed guessed it had been more than that. For some reason Oberon, or Victor Petrova, had wanted him to live. The why was the difficult conundrum. After all, they had been adversaries at one time. A time when spy versus spy had rules of civility—if that were even possible. You didn't kill your adversary just for the hell of it. You tried to use your opponent to gain some intelligence advantage, some piece of information you could exploit for your side. And maybe that had been the motive of his little friend.

Later in the evening, the colonel had gone to a section of Stockholm where he knew he could satisfy himself to make him feel alive. For he had survived the shooting, and that type of close-death activity had always led him to the arms of a woman. At first it had been his wife, who had come to almost enjoy those close calls just so she could benefit from a rough encounter afterwards. But they had been divorced for nearly fifteen years now, so his pleasure quests had to come elsewhere.

Although he didn't like to do so, paying for sex was the most efficient form of unsubdued intimacy, if he could call it that. With a hooker he didn't have to screw around pretending he was something or someone he wasn't, spending hundreds of dollars taking a woman out to dinner, to the movies, or some other expensive activities. And then when all that worked and he finally got to sleep with a woman, it was usually underwhelming. A flat on the back hair twirler, while he pumped away. No, a call girl was much more efficient. He got an experienced woman who would do damn near anything, within reason, and they could cut all the damn games and pretense. A business transaction. That's what he liked. And that's what he needed after being shot at.

Now, laying awake at zero three hundred, the tall blonde naked Swedish goddess snoring lightly at his side, Reed thought about his old friend Jake Adams, who was still up on Spitsbergen Island. He hadn't been truthful with Jake, and that did bother him.

Jake was supposed to call him hours ago for an update. When that call didn't come, Reed had contacted the charter helicopter service he had arranged for them. They had not returned to Longyearbyen yet, but that didn't concern them, since the pilot was experienced and they had brought plenty of warm weather gear, including sleeping bags that went down to fifteen below zero. They were also armed. Reed wasn't sure why the man had told him that. They both agreed to wait until noon the next day, this day now, before they would send someone out to look for them. The weather was clear and had been displaying amazing Aurora Borealis, which was strange for that time of year. They were far more prominent in the winter. But that had also made Colonel Reed understand why Jake had not called him on the SAT phone. The Boreal activity had probably wiped out the SAT communications. He was sure Jake was all right. A more capable man the colonel had not met.

The woman at his side rolled over, exposing her tight body to him, her perfect round breasts rubbing up against his arm. God, he would have never been able to get a woman that hot no matter how many dinners he had paid for—unless he was rich. He smiled thinking about having more money. More money than he would ever have dreamed possible.

A hand reached down and grasped his erection, stroking it gently.

"Someone's awake," the woman said.

What was her name? Who cared. It was fake anyway. Names were a pain in the ass.

"You were snoring," the colonel said.

With one hand she stroked a rubber onto him. Then she rolled onto him and with one smooth motion was filled completely by him. A real pro. That's what he liked. He grasped her breasts as she rode him with great enthusiasm and precision. And he held out longer than normal, thinking about the cold edge of Svalbard.

Oslo, Norway

McLean had gotten back to Edinburgh, cleared his travel with MI6 headquarters at Vauxhall Cross in London, and booked his travel. The only caveat was that he bring his associate, Velda Crane. He had protested, knowing that she had some kind of obsession with him, and that could cloud her judgment, but she had proven herself quite capable to Vauxhall. She also had friends and benefactors there who could send Jimmy to an assignment far less comfortable than his native land. That little halfpint had even suggested Turkey or Iraq—two places he had no desire to see again.

Their plans had changed late the night before, when McLean had gotten word that his contact, Gary Dixon, had purchased a ticket to Oslo—the red eye. Velda had hurried to Glasgow to get on the same flight as Dixon, and McLean had taken a different route, flying to London to pick up a diplomatic pouch and then going on to Oslo, getting in an hour before Dixon and his associate.

Sitting now near the arrivals gate for the Glasgow to Oslo flight, Jimmy McLean watched over the top of his newspaper as the passengers streamed out and down the concourse corridor, their eyes like zombies from the night flight. It wasn't hard for him to see Gary Dixon shuffle along, a carry-on bag over his shoulder. Bringing up the rear was Velda, her little legs doing their best to keep up, and her gaze catching McLean, who smiled at her.

McLean caught up to her and walked a few paces behind Velda. "Glad to see you made it."

"Crappy flight. Hot as hell. No air. We going to get some local support?"

"NIS says they can't spare an officer." NIS was the Norwegian Intelligence Service, the MI6 counterpart.

"Great. I gotta pee. Can you keep an eye on that little troll for me while I scoot?"

"Go ahead. Since he knows me, I'll stay back and track him on my Blackberry."

Her head nodded as she hurried off.

McLean went to the baggage carousel area and looked at the wall advertising hotels in Oslo. He could see Dixon's reflection in the glass. Seconds later he felt a nudge at his side.

"That was quick," McLean said, not looking down at Velda.

"You gotta go you gotta go. Time for me to move front and center."

"Put on the charm."

"You know me."

He thought about the alley encounter with her the other night. Yeah, he knew her.

The crowd was large enough now that Jimmy McLean could turn around and watch her work. She stood a few feet from Dixon and kept checking bags, not even looking at the man. But he had noticed her. Couldn't keep his eyes off of her. McLean walked farther away so he wouldn't be seen. Finally the bags stopped coming and the only two who had not gotten their suitcases were Velda and Dixon. Both of them went for help, two little folks without their bags. Of course, McLean had made sure both were confiscated—Dixon's to have a bug sewn into the lining, and hers to maintain the ruse and bring them together.

CHAPTER 8

Spitsbergen Island, Norway

The night had been uncomfortable for Jake. The back of the helo was small and the three of them were packed in tight, girl girl boy, with Anna in the middle. For some reason, maybe because of Anna's comment the evening before, he couldn't help thinking about the three of them together. It wasn't like he was dissatisfied with the sex that he and Anna had experienced over the past couple of years, but still. . .this was like having two Anna's.

But not only those thoughts had kept Jake awake. He also wondered about the box he had found with his old friend, Steve Olson. The one with the Biohazard symbol. What was in there? And, better yet, why had it been so important back in 1986 to send four KGB officers after it? Even more importantly, perhaps, was why they had not sent more officers to retrieve the box. What had changed? And why hadn't the old CIA sent someone to find Olson and Korkala? Too many damn questions.

Jake had told Anna and Kjersti about finding Steve and the snowmobile, but had left out the part about finding the box. No need to mention that. At least not yet. He had simply buried it again where he had found it. What if it was a biological weapon? What if the box leaked? Although the box looked completely solid, as if there was no seam or way to open it. How was that possible? It was as if the box had been formed around something. Or at least the top had been melted onto it.

Jake finally did get to sleep. He dreamt of a beast gnawing at the bodies, even though there wasn't much left of them.

He woke and it was almost light outside. Sitting up, he glanced out the window and saw something from his dream.

A huge polar bear rummaged about a few feet from the helicopter. A cub shuffled around the sow.

Not wanting to wake Anna and Kjersti, and knowing that was probably not possible, Jake unzipped his sleeping bag and put on his jacket. Then he pulled the rifle from his side and looked at the two women sleeping. Better to wake them with a nudge than a shot.

"Anna," Jake said, shaking her.

Her eyes opened. "Yeah?"

"Got a little polar bear problem."

With those words Kjersti woke also and sat up, her sleeping bag falling from her shoulders. She was completely naked, or at least from the top to the waist. Jake looked away as Kjersti put on her thermal underwear top.

"Don't shoot them," Kjersti said. "Just scare them away. Here, use my handgun." She handed Jake her .44 magnum revolver.

He slid the door open slightly, put his entire arm outside to keep down the noise inside, and fired off a round into a snow bank. The huge sow swiveled around and ran off, the cub at her tail. Jake closed the door and handed her gun back to her.

"Nice piece," Jake said.

Anna smiled at him.

They got dressed and Anna checked over the helo to make sure it was ready for flight, while Jake put a backpack over his shoulders and the 30.06 rifle over his right shoulder. He needed to take care of one more thing before they left.

"I'm going to hike back up to Steve," Jake said.

"Need some company?" Anna asked.

"No. Stay here and watch for those polar bear."

"Your loss," she mumbled.

Jake came closer to her. "What'd you have in mind?" he whispered.

"Thought you might be a little excited after seeing Kjersti's breasts."

"They were all right."

"Come on," she said. "They turned me on. She stripped down in front of me last night before getting into her sleeping bag. What a body."

Jesus. Why was she doing this to him? His body still felt like shit, although not as bad as the previous morning. He had a feeling things were moving in the right direction for him.

"Let's hold that thought until we reach the hotel tonight," he said.

She pouted her lips. "All right."

Jake reluctantly walked away toward the ridge where Steve's body remained, and would probably remain forever. When he reached the top he programmed in the location on his GPS. Looking around, the sun was rising. No wind. He could see the sow polar bear and her cub nearly a mile away already. See the clarity of the morning and that the GPS had picked up a number of satellites, Jake tried the SAT phone. A perfect signal.

Punching in the number, he waited.

"Jake, you there?" It was Kurt Jenkins.

"Yeah, we're fine. I tried calling last night but the Boreal activity must have been messing with the SAT comm."

"That's what my comm guy said here also." Pause and static. "What's your current situation?"

"Found the MiG yesterday. It's actually a MiG thirty-one, not a twenty-five. Initially we found five bodies and two snowmobiles. All looked like gunshot but with animal predation."

"Any sign as to what they were trying to find?"

Jake wondered how much he should tell Jenkins. He was the Network governor and should already know the answer to this. But maybe the Russians had not been as forthcoming as they initially seemed.

"Jake?"

"Yeah. No sign of weapons configuration on the aircraft. No external drop tanks, as far as I could tell, but those could have been jettisoned as the plane was going down."

"Anything else remarkable about the MiG?"

"Well, in eighty-six we knew just about as much about the MiG thirty-one as we did about the MiG twenty-five.

As you know, they were very similar. The newer model had some upgrades in avionics and engines. Both were screamers, yet far less capable as our initial fears. Most of what we knew came from that plane that landed in Japan. The one we flew to Wright-Patt, tore apart, and sent back to the Soviets in pieces. That was brilliant, by the way. I'd like to know who came up with that plan."

"That would have been former President George Bush, the senior, when he was director of the CIA."

What was his old friend not asking? "Anything else you need me to find out before I leave here?"

Quiet and hesitation. "You said five bodies? Could you identify them?"

"Initially we found five bodies at the crash site, four Soviets, I'm guessing KGB or GRU, but no identification. We also found the former Oslo man, John Korkala."

"Wow. He took out all four of them?"

"Well, he probably had help from our friend the Air Force captain."

"You found Steve Olson." A statement.

"Yes. He was a couple of hundred yards away, on the highest ridge in the area. I'm guessing he was wounded and went there to try to get a satellite signal. You know how the coverage was at that time?"

Jenkins laughed. "It's not great now, and they were using an ancient system back then, compared to today's equipment. Our own use back then was tracking the Soviet sub fleet. What about the MiG pilot?"

"Right, that would officially make seven," Jake said. He glanced down the hill toward the helo and saw Anna and Kjersti standing in conversation. Looked like they were laughing about something.

"What's your bottom line assessment, Jake?"

"Once you tell me the true mission of the MiG pilot, then I'll let you know for sure." His statement came across more callous than he wanted.

"As I said, we were told the pilot had defected."

"Right. Last time we talked you told me to be careful. Be careful of what?"

Silence.

"Well?"

"We heard about a possible plot to take out Reagan and Gorbachav during the summit. The hard-liners in the old Soviet government didn't want anything to do with Glasnost and Perestroika."

That was true, but also well known. "They would have been quickly cut down if they had done that. That would have been an act of war, and they knew it."

"That's what our analysts are telling us also," Jenkins said. "You sure you don't want to come back and work for us?"

Considering the times they had asked for his help over the years, it seemed like he had never left. "I hate D.C. And, no offense, but field officers don't make shit."

Jenkins laughed and then said, "Offer's always open. Anyway, back to this case. What was the mission?"

Did Jake tell him what he knew? What did he know for sure? There was a strange metal box with no visible way to open it, with the international symbol for 'biohazard' plastered on four sides. If there was anyone Jake could trust, it was Kurt Jenkins. He told him what he had found near Steve Olson's body, buried in the snow.

"Wow," Jenkins said. "Maybe it was true, then. Maybe they had planned on using some bio-agent to kill the two leaders. You say they had been carrying it in the fuselage somewhere?"

"Yeah, they had foamed an area inside an avionics bay, which saved it during the crash."

Silence on the other end. "Anyway of telling if they had modified the bay to run cold air into the cube? Something to keep the biological agent cold?"

Jake hadn't thought of that. "That wouldn't have been necessary unless they landed for any extended period of time. And the way they have whatever they have in this cube sealed, I'm not even sure hot or cold would do anything to it. Also, assuming the MiG flew above twenty thousand feet, the cube would have remained at temps below freezing."

"You could have an active agent in that cube."

Jake knew that. It's one of the reasons he had left it in the snow all night instead of bringing it into the helo. "Should I leave it here or bring it out with me?"

"I would bring it out, Jake." No hesitation.

"That's easy for you to say, Kurt. You don't have to sleep with the damn thing."

"You said there was no visible point of entry."

"True. But a biological can seep through some gas masks. All it would take is a damn pin-hole and I'm fucked."

"It's a risk."

"Why don't I just stick it out a couple hundred yards and blow the damn thing all to hell with my rifle?"

"You don't know what's in there, Jake. It could get into the environment, some bird gets it and we have a pandemic."

"The Butterfly Effect."

"Exactly. Or you could kill off some polar bears."

"I might have to do that anyway. Had to scare two away from the camp this morning."

"Is there much left of the bodies?"

"A little. From what I understand, until recently the area has been pretty much frozen since eighty-six. But it looks like all but Steve Olson had been chewed on a long time ago."

"Probably right after they died."

"Right," Jake said. "A polar bear can smell blood twenty miles away."

"You know this how?"

"Discovery channel."

Silence as Jake glanced down the ridge toward Anna and Kjersti, who still seemed to be laughing about something. Maybe they were talking about him. Anna telling stories.

"Anyway, Jake. Get the box out of there and we'll check it out. I'll have a jet sent from England to Oslo."

Jake agreed, ostensibly, with a grunt, and then he hung up. He thought about his next call to Colonel Reed. What did he want to tell his old commander? Since Kurt Jenkins had not even mentioned the colonel, Jake began to wonder if his old friend was even sanctioned on this mission. Or was something else going on? In the end, he decided the call to Colonel Reed could wait.

He went into the cave overhang where his old friend, Captain Olson still lay, frozen and nearly indistinguishable. Finding the box, Jake shoved it deep into his backpack and surrounded it with his spare clothes.

It was then that he heard the helo approaching from the west.

CHAPTER 9

Jake had a choice to make. He could either stay put and see who had come to them, or head down to the helo to be with Anna and Kjersti. In the end, time required him to stay put. From the west, flying in hot and fast, the green camo Bell 412 helicopter swept over a rise, banked hard right circling around their own helo, blowing snow in all directions, and hovered to a stop fifty feet above the MiG-31 crash site.

Confusion below as Anna and Kjersti scrambled into their helo.

Having no choice, Jake had hit the hard snowy surface, his 30.06 rifle propped onto his backpack. Now he aimed the scope at the hovering helo, trying to find out who was inside and what they wanted. When he noticed the side door open and what appeared to be a barrel pointing out, Jake shifted his focus to their helo. But he couldn't see either Anna or Kjersti inside.

It looked like a Norwegian Air Force Bell 412SP like those that had conducted training with some of Jake's units in NATO exercises. Yet, he was sure something wasn't right.

Suddenly the rotors started turning on their Bell 407, first slowly and then picking up speed with each revolution.

Jake saw the flashes and then heard the sound of gunfire echoing up the ridge toward him. He trained the scope on the military helo and had to make a split-second decision. He centered the crosshairs toward the middle of the cockpit and fired once, the bullet penetrating the windscreen and settling somewhere inside the cockpit.

The shot made the pilot immediately shove the stick to the left, sending the craft in a wide circle toward the east.

Jake popped open the magazine, shoved another round to replace the one he had fired, and then chambered a new round. He had five shots, plus five more left in his pocket. The rest he had left in the passenger compartment of their helo.

But Jake was stuck. It would take him too long to run the two hundred yards to jump inside their helo. But if they came to him. . . .

Just has he thought it, Kjersti lifted off the glacier and headed in his direction.

By now the green helo had circled around and was coming right after Kjersti and Anna.

Jake raised the rifle and prepared to shoot again. He needed to turn them around long enough for Jake to jump inside. This time Jake aimed to the second seat of the green helo and squeezed off a round. Whatever he hit, it worked, since the green Bell 412SP immediately broke right and swung around in a wide loop.

Now, Kjersti slowed and dropped down to the glacier

just feet from Jake. Simultaneously, Anna shoved the door open, Jake threw his backpack inside and then slid his body and rifle after it.

The door slammed.

"Go, go, go," Anna yelled.

Seconds later they were airborne and picking up speed.

Jake made his way to the cockpit, leaning in toward Kjersti. "Who the hell are those guys?"

"I don't know," she said. "But I can't outrun them. Even fully loaded, they've got about five knots on me."

She had pulled the helo to a couple hundred feet above the jagged surface, heading west southwest.

"How many shooters did you see?" Jake asked her.

"Isn't one enough?" The controls jerked around in her hands. "Two for sure. Maybe more."

"It almost looked like a Norwegian Air Force Bell four-twelve SP," Jake said, glancing back and seeing the other helicopter right behind them. "Tell me I'm wrong."

"It's a four-twelve all right, but not our air force version. It's private. Hang onto your pants."

She went maximum power and pulled back on the yoke, rising to four thousand feet in just a few seconds.

Before Jake could ask why, Kjersti said, "I gain a few miles per hour at four thousand feet. Plus, look what's ahead."

Approaching fast was a bank of clouds much like the day before when they had taken off from Longyearbyen.

"I hope you know the terrain ahead," Jake said.

Kjersti smiled. "Absolutely." Her smile turned grave as she checked her six. "They're moving up on us."

Jake turned and saw the other helo nearly even with them on the port side. He went to the back and found his rifle.

"What's her plan?" Anna asked, concern in her eyes.

"Gonna try to lose them," he said. "Strap yourself to that harness."

Without hesitation, she stepped into a harness that was clipped to the bulkhead. Jake got into a sitting position, the rifle aimed at the door.

By now the other craft was alongside them.

"Slide that door open a foot," Jake ordered.

As she did what Jake asked, the first salvo of bullets struck the side windows, shattering glass into the compartment. Anna screamed and hit the deck.

Jake took aim at the front man with the rifle and squeezed off a round. He saw the bullet strike the man's right shoulder, knocking him onto his back.

He cycled a round and fired.

Miss.

Another round.

Miss.

Two rounds left.

He aimed a little to the right and squeezed off another round. Hit. Dead center in the chest. The man dropped straight down and then rolled out of the helo, his body free-falling helter-skelter. The Bell 412 backed off slightly, but Jake had a feeling they'd be back.

Now, Kjersti had hit the fog bank. With the obscurity of the fog, they also had more turbulence, the craft bouncing up and down. Jake reached over and slid the side door shut. Then he sat down and reloaded the rifle.

"How you doing back there?" Kjersti yelled over her shoulder.

"I hit two of them," Jake screamed back. "One took a

dive out the side." He put a hand on Anna's back and said to her, "You all right?"

She turned her head up to him. "Just a little queasy from the flight."

"Stay right there. I'm gonna have Kjersti make a call."

He made his way to the cockpit and sat in the spare seat. Looking out the windscreen, he couldn't see anything but swirling fog.

"Hope you know where you're going," Jake said to her.

"We're out over water," she said. "I can smell the sea air."

"Great. A pilot who flies by smell."

She laughed. "Hold on." Pushing forward on the yoke, they quickly descended. When they hit only three hundred feet on the altimeter, she pulled back and Jake could see the water below.

"I believe you."

"I didn't do it to prove a point," Kjersti said. "Did I lose them?"

Jake looked back. "Seems so."

For the next half hour, she quickly changed altitude from five hundred feet to four thousand feet and nearly everything in between, at all times maintaining maximum speed.

"How's our fuel?" Jake asked her.

"Should be all right. We added fuel in Pyramiden, which was two hundred K from Longyearbyen. We have a six hundred K range. I was planning on giving you a scenic tour along some of the beautiful fjords, so even at max speed we should be fine."

"We've got less than half a tank," Jake told her.

"What?" She looked at the fuel gauge and tapped it.

"That's not right."

"They must have nicked a fuel line," Jake said. "Will we make it?"

She hesitated, in deep thought, running the calculations in her head. "I don't know."

Seconds later she had made up her mind, shoving the yoke forward.

"We're going down."

CHAPTER 10

Victor Petrova, aka Oberon, shuffled along the wet cobblestone sidewalk of Stockholm's old town, his footing maintained from his low center of gravity, while he talked on his cell phone. He had just gotten a call from one of his associates on his satellite phone.

"What you mean you lost them? How many damn choppers are flying around Spitsbergen at any given time?"

Oberon stopped and casually glanced behind him, as if he were lost, which he was surely not. He had a photographic memory and had never been lost in his life—not in the forests of the Ural Mountains, and definitely not in a damn city. No, he was checking for a tail. But all he saw was a dead rat that had been run over the night before. Not fast enough, he thought.

The man on the other end of the phone said, "Oberon, we'll find them." He stopped, collecting his words. "There was some gunfire."

He started walking again. "I don't give a shit if you shot

them outta the sky. Find them! And get me what they've found."

"Sir, how do you know they found it?"

Oberon stopped again, this time looking into the store window reflections for the tail he could feel somewhere behind him.

"Trust me. Jake Adams found it. Now you find him and what's mine pronto."

"Yes, sir." The man hung up.

Shaking his head, Oberon shoved his satellite phone into a fanny pack, zipped it, and swung it to the back of his waist. Then he walked toward his favorite coffee shop.

Two blocks back and across the street, Colonel Reed gazed around the corner of a brick wall at the entrance to a narrow alley. Keeping up with the little man was never a problem, but doing so without being caught was nearly impossible. It was if the man had a sixth sense about being followed, turning around like a spastic absent-minded professor who had lost his way. But Oberon's moves were all calculated. Reed knew that Victor Petrova had not only been highly trained by the old KGB, he had actually written the book for them on counter surveillance.

Now the little spy had ducked into his favorite coffee shop, and the colonel guessed he would be there for a while.

He was suddenly startled when one of his phones vibrated in his coat pocket. Right side. That would be his satellite phone. Only two people had that number.

Answering with a simple, "Yeah," the colonel waited.

"I was nearly killed today."

"Nearly? That's a weekly occurrence for you, Jake.

Where the hell are you?"

"How'd you know? Seems like hell has frozen over."

The colonel kept his eyes open for anyone near him. The streets were not super busy, but he still needed to stay at the top of his game.

"So, where are you?" the colonel repeated.

"Where you sent my dumb ass. Spitsbergen."

"What's that noise in the background?"

"The pilot is fixing a fuel line. Someone got a lucky shot. You don't seem surprised by this."

The colonel cleared his throat. "Where exactly are you? And did you find our old friend?"

"Yeah, I found Steve. He was dead just like we guessed. Of course he's been frozen solid for more than twenty years."

Their signal was starting to break up and the colonel guessed it had something to do with his proximity to the buildings. So he started walking toward a small park a block away.

"And then someone started shooting at you?"

"Yeah, I don't have much time for small talk. The shooters were in another helo. I've got the specifics. Remember this." Jake told him the tail markings, model and paint scheme.

"I'll check into it. Can't be that many helos on Spitsbergen." The reception had improved as the colonel reached the open park.

"Listen, colonel," Jake started and stopped, breathing into the phone heavily. "What have you failed to tell me?"

"What do you mean?"

"You know damn well what I mean," Jake screamed. "Tell me about the frickin' box."

"My God, it's true. Do you have it?"

"It had biohazard written all over it," Jake said. "Why the hell would I keep that?"

"You didn't leave it at the site."

"What's in it?"

The colonel swiveled his head around, hoping nobody had him under sound surveillance. "Tell me you have it?" he whispered loudly.

"I'm not a complete idiot, colonel," Jake said. "Do you really think I think you sent me all the way to Bumfuck, Norway to find a frozen friend? Christ, I might have been drinking too much recently, but that doesn't mean I'm entirely brain-dead."

"All right," the colonel said. "No bullshit. You have it right?"

"What's in the damn box?"

The colonel thought for a moment. Jake had a right to know what he was into, but what he didn't know might be as important as what he did know. "It's a weapon the old Soviets developed."

"What kind of weapon?"

"Don't know for sure. But I heard it was based on the nineteen-eighteen flu virus. Modified somewhat."

"Jesus. That killed millions."

"Between fifty and a hundred million. Over seventeen million in India alone."

"But don't we have a way to fight that now?"

"It depends on how they have modified the virus, or if they can catch it before it spreads too rapidly. But remember, back in nineteen-eighteen the main form of transportation for worldwide travel was by boat. Steam ship. It took a month to cross the Atlantic. Now, assuming best case, or worst case, depending on your perspective, the number of people traveling during any given week is astronomical compared to back then. More travel today in one day than traveled in an entire year back then."

"So, I should destroy it," Jake said.

"No."

"It's heavy, I could drop it into the ocean and it will sink like a rock."

"No."

"Or I could just leave it buried in a glacier," Jake said. "Tell no one where I put it."

"No."

"What is wrong with you?" Jake asked him. "This could be the most deadly virus in the world. Why would we hang onto it?"

Silence. Colonel Reed's eyes shifted around the small park for any sign of danger. Finally, he said, "Our government needs it, Jake. They want to try to come up with a vaccine. This is probably not the only sample of the virus from those old days. What if it gets into the hands of terrorists and they unleash it on the world? We need to have a way to ramp up a vaccine. If we have a head start." His words hung in the damp air.

"I'll bring it to Oslo," Jake said.

"Keep me informed along the way," the colonel said, and hung up the SAT phone, returning it to his right jacket pocket.

Looking around, Colonel Reed wondered what his little friend was up to now. He guessed that Oberon thought he was at least one step ahead of him, maybe two. But that would have been a false assumption. He smiled and stepped off toward a taxi. Time to leave Stockholm and the land of tall narcissistic blonde bimbos and head to Oslo. At least the women weren't so damn self-centered.

♦

A few blocks away in the coffee shop, Oberon sat at his normal corner table sipping a cup of cappuccino, swirling his cell phone around on the hard wood surface. He wasn't concerned about being in front of the window, because the last attempt on his life was only a ruse to impress his American friend. He needed to keep the good colonel on his toes and looking over his shoulder. The more he looked behind him the better chance he would not see something coming from the front or sides.

As the phone jangled an ABBA tune, he smiled and stopped the spinning.

"Yeah?"

"He followed you to the coffee shop. Then he had a long conversation with someone on his SAT phone in the park."

"Good work. Where is he now?"

"In a taxi a couple of cars in front of us. Looks like he might be heading back to his hotel."

"All right. Stick with him and keep me informed."

"Will do."

Oberon flipped the phone shut and gave it another spin on the table. Then he smiled again and finished the last of his coffee. A long talk on a SAT phone? He must have gotten an update from his man, Jake Adams. Which means his chopper didn't go down in the ocean off Spitsbergen. Time to take a more active role.

CHAPTER 11

Jake had just gotten off the phone when Kjersti closed the side panel below the engine. She had found a small leak, but enough of a hole to lose far too much fuel to allow them to return to Longyearbyen without repairing it.

Kjersti had expertly dropped the chopper down out of the fog bank, found a fifty foot ceiling above the icy ocean, and had expertly flown just above the white caps to a small glacial point at the edge of a deep fjord, setting down on the hard surface to find the fuel leak.

Anna had not found the flight particularly comforting, and had almost not made it out of the side before throwing up with great ferocity. Jake wondered how she even had that much in her, since they had only eaten power bars, smoked salmon and water over the past twenty-four hours.

While Anna lay in the helo and Kjersti fixed the fuel line, Jake had wandered off and made the SAT phone call to Colonel Reed. He was disturbed now with the revelation that the box likely contained a deadly flu virus, modified even more to kill with greater efficiency. How the hell could the Soviets do such a thing? And did the Russians still maintain a program and the virus somewhere in that country? Worse yet, perhaps, was the possibility that the American government wanted the virus for more than just defensive purposes. He didn't know who to trust. Colonel Reed had always been a straight shooter in the past, but he had sent him on this wild goose chase. Why hadn't he just told him the truth from the beginning? Why use the ruse of finding an old friend to entice Jake into going here? That was easy. If Jake had known he was going to Spitsbergen to find a deadly weaponized virus, would he have been so eager to go? Hell no!

So the good colonel had played him. But what about his other good friend, Kurt Jenkins, the current governor of the American Intelligence Network. He had to know there was more to this box of biohazard than he was saying. At least Colonel Reed final came clean. Christ, he should just dump the damn thing in the ocean. But then it would eventually decay and do who knows what to the marine life. Maybe they'd end up with a fish flu that would kill off the entire salmon population. Damn, he liked salmon.

"What's up?"

Jake turned and saw Kjersti standing ten feet away, her hands on her thin hips. "I called in and said we'd be late for dinner. Get her fixed?"

She swept some hair away from her face with the back of her hand and said, "Yeah. Good enough to get back to Longyear."

"Great. What about our friends?" Jake gazed out onto the misty ocean for a second. When he looked back, he was staring at a .44 magnum revolver.

Neither said a word.

"Let me guess," Jake said. "You work for them." That wasn't right or they wouldn't have shot at her. What the hell was going on?

"Who are you?" Kjersti asked him.

"We told you. We're just here looking for our old friend. We found him. Now we're heading back. Hella fun in the Arctic."

"You were CIA," she said, "and have worked with the Network many times over the past decade."

"You seem to know me better than I know me," Jake said, a cold edge to his words.

She continued. "And your girl friend works for Interpol."

He strained to keep his eyes on her. "So. We have day jobs. What's your point?"

"I want to know what you found back there," she demanded.

"You're just my taxi driver," he said. "I give you my locations and, if you don't piss me off too much, throw a tip your way. Now, with the gun pointed at me, you might kiss that goodbye."

"You're incredible."

"Anna seems to think so."

With her name mentioned, there was a soft whistle from behind Kjersti, who swiveled her head and saw Anna pointing one of the rifles at her back.

Jake stepped over and took the pistol from Kjersti's hand. "If you plan on pulling a gun on someone, make sure you have your back to the sun and nobody can sneak up on you. Since there's no sun to be seen, you only had one thing to remember. Didn't the Norwegian Intelligence Service teach you that?"

"How did you know?" Kjersti asked, her tone dejected.

"You just told me."

"You were bluffing?"

"Kind of. But we were tailed from our hotel to the Oslo airport. That was one of your NIS men. Then our hotel room, which I changed at the last minute, was bugged while we ate dinner. A man watched us while we ate, but I'm guessing he wasn't NIS. Nor was the bug. It was not the type your government purchased."

"How do you know?" Kjersti asked him.

"Because I consulted with NIS, the Swedish Security Police, SAPO, and the Danish Security Intelligence Service on covert communications a few years ago. I told them what to buy. This bug was good, but it was former East Bloc. About a decade old."

"They told me to watch out for you. That you were good."

"Why were you sent with me?"

"For that reason. We heard something was going down at Svalbard. When we found out the Network was sending you, we assumed something big was happening here. Since I had flown tourists here during my summers in college, I was the natural choice. We knew you'd need a ride."

"The Network didn't hire me," Jake protested.

Anna lowered her gun, took a few steps forward, and said, "So then your government has been tracking us by GPS the entire time."

"We've been trying," Kjersti said. "But, as you know, the Borealis that screwed up our SAT Comm has also messed with our GPS tracking."

"I noticed," Jake said. "Had to wait until this morning to get a good location on Steve's body."

"Can you tell me what the hell is going on?" Kjersti asked. "Why are these people trying to kill us?"

"I have a better question," Anna said to Jake. "Tell me about the box in your backpack. The one with the biohazard symbols and the Russian letters. What's up with that?"

Kjersti's eyes widened as her gaze shifted from Anna to Jake.

He didn't want to get either of them involved with this. Just wanted to get back to Longyearbyen, fly to Oslo, fly separate from Anna back to Austria while he took care of the rest of this case, but now that she knew about the box, there would be no denying her into this game. After all, this was her area of expertise at Interpol.

Jake explained what he knew about the biohazard box. When he was done, the three of them stood around like high school kids, kicking snow and wondering what to do.

Kjersti was the first to speak. "This is crazy. Why would the Soviets just leave it here? Why not come back? Especially after losing four KGB officers and a fighter pilot."

That was the burning problem stuck deep in Jake's gut. There had to be a reason to leave it there, but he still had no clue why.

Anna looked to Jake for answers.

"I'm not sure," he said. "The cover story is that the pilot tried to defect. We know that's probably bogus. But what if it was actually true? What if the pilot was part of some conspiracy to ship the virus out of the Soviet Union? Maybe the authorities were not entirely sure about his actions or what he was planning. When he crashed, they sent a sanitation crew to make sure he was dead." Jesus he wasn't sure he believed that scenario.

"I don't know," Anna said. "The old Soviets would have sent a second crew once the first crew didn't return."

"I agree," Kjersti said.

"Afraid I do too," Jake conceded. Then it came to him. "Unless someone with enough power cancelled the operation and destroyed all evidence of the event."

Kjersti shrugged and Anna nodded her head in agreement.

Jake continued, "Then the cover-up was on. If they sent another crew, that would have forced us to send another crew to counter them. But you forget about it, and like my friends at the Network told me, say it was simply a defection gone bad, then both sides can write it off as a horseshit op and move on. Besides, as far as we know, the actual location of the downed plane was never relayed back to Washington or Moscow. They would have had to start over from scratch. And, according to the weather reports from that time, it didn't stop snowing for nearly two months, completely encasing the MiG into the landscape. In fact, as you saw, the crash site appeared to have been undisturbed in more than twenty years."

"Except for the animal predation," Kjersti reminded Jake. "But it looked like some of that came years ago. Perhaps just after they were killed."

"Right," Jake said. He thought of his old friend, Steve Olson, and how he would probably become polar bear bait in the next few weeks.

Anna swung the rifle to her shoulder. "Where do we go from here?"

"Exactly," Kjersti said. "What do we do with the box?"

That was the problem still rumbling in Jake's gut. It would be irresponsible to simply leave it behind. If some bird caught the virus and then passed it on to another bird and then to a human, and that human passed it to another. He didn't want to think about him having unleashed a pandemic virus, with deaths in the millions.

Jake let out a quick breath and said, "We'll have to get a hold of some guanidinium thiocyanate to inactivate the virus before transport."

"What is that?" Kjersti asked.

Anna said, "It renders the virus inactive without killing its structure. So scientists will still be able to study it to possibly synthesize a cure or a vaccine to fight it."

"Why not just destroy it and call it done?" Kjersti asked, her gaze shifting from Anna to Jake.

"Just in case," he said. "In case the Russians still have a stockpile of the virus in some lab. We have to assume that this is only a small representative sample of the virus."

"I'm so stupid," Kjersti said. "I didn't even think about that possibility."

"It's why our military handles most of the testing and storage of these viruses. It's more for defense than offense. We never know what might get out there. I've been ordered to turn this over to the American government. Nobody else can properly handle this."

Kjersti's disposition seemed to fade. "Well let's get you two back to Longyearbyen as soon as possible."

"No," Jake said. "They'll be waiting for us there. We need a Plan B."

CHAPTER 12

Oslo, Norway

They had followed the little guy, Gary Dixon, all over the city, as he met with various contacts, most of equally diminutive stature. Jimmy McLean had stayed back now as his associate Velda Crane had taken the lead. But Jimmy didn't like laying back in the shadows. He wanted to be out front taking charge. Yet, he knew there were times when he had to give up control. He had taken photos of those Dixon had contacted and sent them to London for identification. Nearly all of them had records of underground activity, most of them jacked for petty crimes. But the disturbing fact had been their nationalities—everything from Norwegian to Swedish to Danish and even Russian. What did they all have in common, other than the obvious fact that most were also little people? Jimmy McLean had no idea there were so many small folks running around—especially with criminal records. Did he simply not see these people on the streets because of his own large stature?

Sitting in his hotel room on Karl Johan, McLean thought about how Velda had worked like a real pro. Not that she didn't in the past. But this was different. To Gary Dixon, Velda was a supermodel, and he had insisted she follow him around Oslo as arm candy. She had even changed into a more revealing outfit, with high heals that made her rise above her new friends. McLean had been able to listen to all of their conversations, knowing she had played the part of her life.

Now, he waited in his hotel room, glancing out the window at the busy street below, the major thoroughfare of Oslo, with the Royal Palace and the Norwegian Parliament a few blocks away. Thousands of pedestrians streamed by below, but he still caught a glimpse of Velda as she strut along the sidewalk and into his hotel lobby.

A few minutes later came a low knock on his door. McLean let Velda in and she smiled at him before taking a running jump and landing on his queen-sized bed, rolling onto her side and kicking her high heels to the carpeted floor.

"What a day of hiking," Velda said. "Haven't walked that much in months."

Jimmy McLean opened the mini-fridge and pulled out a couple small bottles of booze. "Will you look at this? Irish whiskey but not a drop of single malt Scotch."

"Ah, pour it on some ice and call it good."

He threw her one of the bottles, which she caught with her tiny right hand.

"Or we can drink it like this." She cracked open the bottle and took down half, not affected by the surge of warmth.

Jimmy McLean downed his bottle all in one stroke, letting out a hearty breath of air. "Just what the doctor ordered." He threw the empty bottle into the garbage can and pulled up a chair near the bed.

"Well, you gonna ask me?" she said.

"Ask you what?"

"If I slept with Gary."

With the exception of the last hour, he had directly monitored every conversation the two of them had made, but then they had gone into the little man's hotel two blocks away and she had called McLean off for a while. He trusted her and knew she could handle herself.

"What did you learn from him?" he asked, ignoring her baiting him into caring.

"I didn't," she said. "But it wasn't easy. He was all over me, like a fat girl on chocolate."

"But?"

"He showed me that, too. Yet, why settle for a lizard when I can have a dinosaur?"

"So now I'm old as a fossil?"

"You know what I meant, Jimmy."

He didn't want to go here. They had too much to consider. He knew something was going down, but he didn't want it to be Velda. At least not right now.

"Business, Velda."

She cocked her head to one side. "How about another drink first?"

He went and got her another bottle and threw it to her.

"Vodka," she said. "Now that's appropriate." This time she sucked down the entire bottle in one shot and set her empty onto the nightstand.

"What'd you find out?" he reiterated.

"I found out Gary Dixon, besides being a randy dog, is in to something big. Bigger than he's been involved in ever."

"He didn't tell you what?"

"No. He talked about a package. A box."

McLean had heard a little of that. "What do you think he meant by that?"

"I don't know. But it's worth a lot of money to someone. Right, the vodka. Some guy showed up at Gary's room. A Russian."

"A Russian? What did he want?"

"Don't know. They talked out in the hall. Gary came back more excited than normal."

"What the Russian look like?"

"You mean, was he also a little person?"

"Well, we didn't get a photo of him, since I came to the room."

"I saw him, though. And I never forget a face."

That was true. Her memory for facial details was quite amazing. "All right. We'll check on the computer and see what we can find."

"Hang onto your kilt, Jimmy. Gary Dixon has a dinner meeting with the man tonight. Maybe we should get a little rest before then." She patted her hand onto the bed, raised her brows, and smiled at him.

He knew it would come to this eventually. They had played around a little in the past—she placing his hand onto her breasts, and then the more recent encounter in the dark Edinburgh alley. The tension had been thick, and now he also felt the thickness in his pants. That's what she wanted, then that's what he'd give her—every centimeter.

Pushing the chair to the side, he stood before her and

slowly removed his pants and underwear. Standing before her in all his glory, her eyes got very wide.

"Now that's a T-Rex," she said.

American Intelligence Network Headquarters
Camp Springs, Maryland

Kurt Jenkins sipped a cup of green tea as he read an intelligence briefing, a Russian area analyst standing in front of the governor's mahogany desk and a stunning brunette sitting back on the sofa, her slim legs crossed. Jenkins had gotten off the SAT phone with Jake Adams an hour ago, immediately asked his analysts for more information on the old Soviet virus development, and had been somewhat surprised they had come through for him so soon. It was only a two-page brief, but quite thorough and in-depth.

The analyst, a man who looked like a computer geek right out of college, thick glasses and a bow tie, with a crumpled white shirt that looked like he had slept in it, alternated from one foot to the next like a stork. His dark eyes kept shifting to the side to catch a view of the pretty woman.

"Are you sure the Soviets were actually developing a modified version of the nineteen-eighteen H1N1 influenza A virus back in the 80s?" Jenkins asked the young man and then sipped more tea.

"Yes, sir." The analyst pushed his glasses higher on his narrow nose. "And as far as we know, they still have the virus frozen at their research facility."

"But no indication they have ever had any breach of security or theft of the virus."

"No, sir. But. . ." His eyes drifted again toward the woman and then back to the governor. "But we might never know for sure. As you know, the old Soviet Union collapsed around that time and security crumbled to a certain extent."

Jenkins didn't need this young man telling him that, since he had spent much of his covert life cleaning up messes in the former East Bloc.

"What about what Jake Adams mentioned," Jenkins said, picking up the briefing for reference, "this guanidinium thiocyanate." He struggled with the words and shook his head.

The man nodded and adjusted his glasses nervously again. "Yes, sir. That would render the virus inactive, but our scientists would still be able to study it and come up with a way to battle any release, inadvertent or otherwise." He cleared his throat.

"So you recommend we use this. . .stuff. . .before transporting?"

He nodded. "Yes, sir. Jake Adams was right on the mark with that."

"You know Jake Adams?"

"No, sir. Just heard about him. His work with the Joint Strike Fighter, Kurdistan, the Dolomites, China, and his more recent work in Austria."

"Sounds like you're a fan," Jenkins said.

The analyst smiled and nodded.

"That'll be all."

The man turned, checking out the woman as he did, and left the office.

When he was gone, the brunette rose from the sofa and took a seat in a leather chair closer to the governor. Toni

Contardo had recently taken on a special projects role at the headquarters after working in the field in mostly Europe for the past couple decades. She was in her early forties, but could easily pass for thirty-five. Some would say she was in her prime as a field officer, having risen to station chief in Austria and Italy. But Jenkins asked her to take on this new position and she reluctantly accepted. After all, she had not even lived in America for nearly twenty years.

"What do you think?" Jenkins asked Toni.

"I think your analyst has more ticks than a Tennessee coon hound," she said. "And he just might have a man crush on Jake."

"Are you jealous?" Jenkins knew all too well the history between Jake Adams and Toni Contardo.

"I'm so over him."

"If you say so."

"Besides, isn't he still shacking up with that Austrian Interpol whore?"

Jenkins smiled. "But you're not bitter."

"Can we get on with this? What kind of shit has Jake stepped in this time?"

My God she was still beautiful. But all business with him. Too bad. "All right." He briefed her on what Jake Adams had been up to from start to finish, leaving out nothing. When he was done, he waited and watched her carefully.

"And Colonel Reed is not working for us?" Toni asked, a face of incredulity.

"Not officially. We have not been able to reach him yet. But we have assets in the area looking for him. You know Reed, right?"

"Yeah. But just by reputation. Jake talked about him. He had nothing but good things to say about Reed. Jake also mentioned the death of Steve Olson. But that happened before Jake joined the CIA and before we met. So it was always past tense. I knew they had been good friends, though. Jake would have gone off to the Arctic to bring back his body, or at least find out what happened to the man."

"How'd you know I was going to ask you that?"

"How many years in the field? Besides, it's the question I would have asked. Why would Jake take off to the Arctic on a whim? And, perhaps more importantly, was Jake and Colonel Reed into something they shouldn't be into? You said the Interpol slut was with him?"

"Let it go."

"No, I'm just thinking she wouldn't have been involved in this if she didn't think it was important. Is she sanctioned by Interpol?"

"We haven't verified that yet."

Toni leaned back in the chair, her dark eyes settling on the ceiling tiles.

Jenkins had not been entirely sure he should have involved Toni with this, considering that she and Jake had been lovers for so many years—their relationship nearly highlighted in the agency manual as what not to do as covert officers. Yet, despite their relationship, it had never cost them a case. In fact, the two of them worked so well together, they might have to reconsider conventional wisdom on how close to get with colleagues.

"What you thinking?" Jenkins asked her.

She turned to him. "I'm thinking you haven't told me everything about Jake."

He let out a heavy sigh and shook his head. "I could never keep anything from you." He thought about if she needed to know this and decided she did. "Jake has gone through some rough times in the past three months. He's been drinking too much and hasn't taken on any new cases. Quite the mess."

She looked concerned. "I didn't know."

"Well, he isolated himself after his sister died in a car accident."

Toni shifted forward in her chair. "Jake has a sister?"

"Two sisters and a brother. How well do you know him?"

Slumping back in the chair, she said, "Not as well as I thought. So his sister died three months ago?"

"Four. It took his siblings a month to find him. By then his sister had been buried."

"Wow. He never mentioned any siblings. Anything else I should know? Parents? Children?"

"He told you his parents also died in a car accident when he was in college?"

"He told me that. He just left out the siblings."

"As you know, a lot of officers do that. Jake figured the siblings could be vulnerable if anyone knew about them. They could use them to get to him."

She lowered her head and shook acknowledgment. "Why do you need me?"

"I need you to fly to Oslo with our scientists and a an Army team to secure the virus. They'll inactivate the virus and bring it back to the Army lab."

"Why me?"

Jenkins swiveled in his chair. "Because I don't know for sure what Colonel Reed is up to, and I don't want Jake deciding to turn this over to him instead. He trusts the colonel."

"And you think he'll trust me more," she said. "Because of our background."

Jenkins shrugged.

"When do I leave."

"One hour."

"You know I just got married," Toni said.

He knew. "Three months ago. The honeymoon's over."

She got up to leave but he stopped her with a wave of his hand. "Yeah."

"Make sure Jake knows he'll be compensated for his efforts," he said.

She laughed. "You think Jake is motivated by money? He'd cut your balls off if he thought it would be good for the country. Money never concerned him."

With that, she left him, and he watched her every deliberate step and the shake of her hips. He saw what Jake had always known, and perhaps what had motivated him more than even national security. It was her security. An even better reason to send Toni to Norway.

Jake's drinking might have started with the revelation of his sister's early death, but then probably accelerated once he realized he had lost two women in his life forever.

CHAPTER 13

Norwegian Sea
One Hundred Miles South of Svalbard

The three of them had flown from their perch on the glacier due south to the town of Sveagruva, a Norwegian settlement of some two hundred people, where they topped off the fuel tank. While there, Jake had come up with a plan to bypass Longyearbyen, where he assumed they would have run into more trouble. He had made a few calls and Kjersti had done the same. Together they had found a direction.

From Sveagruva they had flown out over the Arctic Ocean into the North Norwegian Sea, a huge leap of faith considering the four hundred mile distance from the Svalbard Archipelago to the Norwegian mainland, and were now running low on fuel. The winds had picked up and the cloud cover made it hard to see too far in the distance.

Jake checked his watch and then his own hand-held

GPS. He guessed the ship had to be just over the horizon. Had to be. They were searching for a ship. Not any ship— a particular ship. He was sitting in the second seat in the front and Anna was laying in the back, her stomach still upset by the rocking craft jumping about in the turbulence.

"How much fuel left?" Jake asked Kjersti.

"Ten minutes. Maybe less. Where the hell are they?"

"Call in your Mayday," Jake prompted. "We gotta be close enough."

Kjersti didn't hesitate, calling an in-flight emergency, heading, and fuel situation. Almost immediately, she got a response in Norwegian, and Jake could only guess what was being said to her. Clicking off the headset, Kjersti adjusted their heading and elevation.

"How far out?" Jake asked her.

"They had changed directions slightly," she said. "Should be coming into view. . .now."

Off on the horizon they could see the Norwegian Coast Guard patrol vessel *KV Svalbard*, the largest ship in Norway's armed forces. Yet, even at 300 feet long, the ship seemed like a fishing boat as it cruised away from them. The large patrol icebreaker carried two helicopters.

"They gonna clear the deck for you?" Jake asked.

"One's in the hangar," she said. "And there's the other one."

As they got closer, they could see a helicopter airborne trailing the ship to the port side.

"Isn't that an NH90?"

"Yeah," Kjersti said.

They came alongside the large ship on the starboard side, slowing to the speed of the cutter. The ship had slowed somewhat to allow them to land.

With expert precision, Kjersti slipped her craft to the right and dropped her down in the center of the helo pad. They waited while crewmen scrambled to chock and tie the helo to the flight deck, and then Kjersti cut power.

"How much fuel we have left?" Jake asked her.

"Fumes."

Suddenly their helo was surrounded by sailors with automatic weapons pointed at them.

"This doesn't look good," Anna said from the back.

Jake leaned into Kjersti. "We can't let them search us. I hope like hell Norwegian Intel has some pull."

She smiled and pulled her credentials from a small backpack beside her seat. Then she got out onto the flight deck, her hands up with her ID pointed at someone who looked to be in charge. Rifles still pointed at her and the helo. The man went onto his radio and moments later a man appeared from the hangar bay door. An officer.

"What's going on, Jake?" Anna asked, moving from the back closer to him.

"She's explaining who she is. At least that's my guess." If she had wanted to, she could have simply told them the truth. Then they would all be quarantined until someone came and broke open the box, rendering the virus inactive. Maybe she was doing that. But Jake didn't think so. He had a feeling she wasn't that close with the military, and didn't trust that her government had the proper expertise to handle this type of virus. She had said as much on their flight. He just hoped she wasn't playing him.

Moments later the coast guard officer handed her identification back to Kjersti and they were all smiles. He even had his hand on her shoulder as they both laughed. Then the officer ordered his men to stand down and he waved for the helo to be refueled.

Kjersti and the officer came to the pilot's door, opened it, and the officer leaned in, his hand extended. They shook and the man introduced himself as Commander Berg.

"Nice to meet you," Jake said. "And thanks for the drink. Didn't think we'd make it."

"No problem," the commander said. "It's always nice to help the CIA, or the American Intelligence Network. I keep forgetting the change."

Jake hesitated, his gaze first on Kjersti and then back to Commander Berg. "I forget myself which organization I'm part of anymore. Thanks again."

"Good luck tracking those terrorists," Berg said before departing, shaking Kjersti's hand again, lingering longer than normal, and heading back toward the hangar bay.

Kjersti leaned in and looked at Anna. "I've gotta hit the head," she said. "How about you, Anna?"

"If that means going to the bathroom," Anna said, "that would be a big yes."

"Jake?"

"I'm good. I'll watch our gear."

Anna slipped by Jake, who pinched her on the butt as she scooted past him and out the pilot's door. She turned with her evil eye look, which was only mock disdain, and closed the hatch on him.

He watched the two of them saunter off on the pitching deck like twin sisters walking to school. What was that TV commercial years ago? Double your pleasure? Forget it, Jake. You've got a beautiful girlfriend.

While they were gone, Jake looked at a map of Norway, memorizing the terrain, the cities, the roads, the rail lines. They had to stay one step ahead of whoever wanted to grab the box from them. He had to assume it was the Russians, but not to their exclusion. It could have been just about anyone who wanted the virus for their own purposes or to sell on the open market. He had no clue how much something like that could be worth, and he also had no intention of letting the box get into the hands of anyone who wanted to sell it. The unspoken possibility, that which he could not say out loud or seriously consider, was that his old friend Colonel Reed wanted the virus for that exact reason—to sell to the highest bidder. After all, the colonel was not officially working for the Network. But there was no damn way the colonel would ever do such a thing. No way.

Finally, Kjersti and Anna came out of the ship and walked back to the helo. Instead of opening the side door, they piled back in through the pilot's door.

The flight deck crew pulled back the fuel line and rolled it onto a spool and they were almost ready to go.

"What we waiting for?" Jake asked.

In a second Jake knew, as a couple men came out, one carrying a heavy flight bag and the other with a cardboard box. Kjersti said something to them and they laughed. Then Anna opened the side door, they set the items into the back, and she slammed the door shut. The men waived at Kjersti and returned to the inside of the ship.

"What you say to them?"

"I asked if they took Visa."

"A Norwegian with a sense of humor?"

Kjersti smacked him in the arm, much like Anna would

do to him more than he liked.

"Hey," Jake said. "What they give you?"

"Some food in the box, and some weapons and ammo in the flight bag."

"How'd you convince them we needed that?"

"I gave the commander a blow job."

Jake smiled.

"I'm kidding." Pause. "Anna did it."

"I did what?" Anna said, leaning forward.

"Nothing," Jake said. "Can we get the hell outta here?"

Moments later Kjersti had the helo revved up, four-bladed rotors cranking, and they lifted off the deck. She powered the Bell 407 to maximum power and the craft rose to four thousand feet before leveling off and cruising due south toward the Norwegian mainland. Even at that maximum speed of 148 mph at that elevation, they would still have a range over 300 miles, and their destination, Tromso, Norway, was a little more than 200 miles away. They would be there by dinner.

"What you tell the coast guard commander?" Jake asked Kjersti through the headset.

"Told him NIS was working with the American Network chasing down some terrorists trying to ferry through our country. Said they had gone from Russia to Svalbard and were heading toward the mainland. We needed fuel to intercept."

"Good thinking."

She smiled but kept her eyes on the horizon. "It wasn't too hard to convince him, considering all the bullet holes in the side of my helo. Where do you think that other helo went?"

He wished he knew. "I don't know. But I get the feeling

we haven't seen the last of them."

"Why don't you go back and get some rest," she said. "I'll have us in to Tromso in less than two hours."

Jake didn't answer, but he did crawl back from the cockpit to be with Anna. She was laying down on her sleeping bag, headphones on and, no doubt, listing to techno. So Jake unzipped the flight bag to see what the Norwegian Coast Guard had given them. First he pulled out an HK MP5 submachine gun. He cycled the bolt and dropped the magazine. Nice. Then he found three Walther P99 automatic handguns, all in 9mm, in military spec with 16-round magazines. With all weapons in 9mm that would make it easy, not having to mess with different calibers. Since they were all German guns, he and Anna were quite familiar with all of them—even though she usually used Austrian Glocks and Steyrs. He spent some time loading each magazine with the 9mm rounds. When he was done, he lay down onto his sleeping bag next to Anna and wrapped his arm around her. Now he could rest.

CHAPTER 14

Oslo, Norway

Colonel Reed walked out onto the sidewalk in front of the arrivals area of Oslo International Airport and glanced at the taxis and buses lining the curb. He had told his Russian friend to meet him at precisely seventeen hundred. He checked his watch and saw that it was two minutes before that hour. He didn't entirely trust the Russian. How could he? At one time they had been fierce Cold War enemies. But he guessed the lack of trust went both ways. However, sometimes it was better to know your enemy instead of getting stabbed in the back by someone you thought was a friend.

Just then the black rental BMW, the one he had rented for two weeks on his last visit to convince Jake Adams to fly to Svalbard, came rolling to the curb in front of him— the Russian at the wheel and not looking too happy. Reed guessed the man was used to having his own driver in Russia. At least during the last few years of his government employment.

The colonel threw his three-day bag in the back seat and climbed into the front, settling into the plush leather seat.

The Russian pulled away from the arrivals area, his eyes concentrating on the road, and his ubiquitous mini-cigar hanging from the right side of his mouth. Neither said a word for a couple minutes.

Finally, the Russian said, "How was that little troll in Stockholm?"

Colonel Reed shook his head. "He calls himself Oberon now."

The Russian laughed. "We used to call him little Stalin. You know what Oberon means?"

The colonel shook his head.

"King of the Fairies."

"You mean like. . ." Colonel Reed flapped a limp wrist toward the driver.

"The other one. At least traditionally."

"Magical and fantastical."

"Right."

Leaning back in his seat, the colonel thought about what Jake had told him. About being shot at in Spitsbergen.

"By your silence, I'm guessing your man found the box at the crash site." The Russian sucked in and blew out smoke almost simultaneously.

"He was nearly killed," Reed said.

"Wasn't my guys."

Since the International Airport was nearly forty miles north of Oslo, it took them a while to get to the city. Now they drove toward downtown Oslo, the traffic lighter than normal for that time of day. The colonel had been in deep thought for much of the drive, observing the plush green hills, neither saying a word for miles.

Finally, the Russian asked, "Does he know what's inside the box?"

Colonel Reed hesitated. But not too long. "I told him."

"Good. Then he'll be damn careful with it. I got you your same hotel. Fourth floor. Street view, just like you asked."

"You'd make a good travel agent," Colonel Reed said.

"Don't need them any more with the internet."

Good point. "If you're going to smoke those things in my car, at least give me one."

The Russian reached inside his jacket, pulled out the little box of cigars, tapped the bottom on the shifter, bringing one out, and the colonel took it from him. He lit it with the car lighter and puffed hard to get the smoke rolling into his lungs. The colonel liked a cigar from time to time, but only when a mission was accomplished. He guessed this one was far from over.

♦

Toni Contardo stepped down out of the U.S. Air Force Gulfstream jet and collected her bag from a staff sergeant dressed in civilian clothes. The flight from Camp Springs, Maryland to Oslo included a refueling stop in Reykjavik, Iceland. She had not been able to sleep much of the trip, her mind drifting back to images of her and Jake Adams through the years. They had once been so close. And that also bothered her, because she had used their love-making as a barometer for subsequent affairs, and none had met that intensity, the same depth—including her recent marriage. Yet, she was happy, she kept telling herself.

A rental car waited for her on the tarmac, a charcoal BMW 5-series. A man sat in the passenger seat. A man who looked just out of college. Slight build, but chiseled features. Great. Babysitting. She set her bag into the trunk and got in behind the wheel.

"Thom Hagen," the young man said, reaching his hand to Toni. "Norwegian Intelligence Service."

She left his hand there for a moment before squeezing down hard on him. "Toni," she said. "Are you my tour guide?"

He didn't say anything, searching for his thoughts and trying to shake some life back into his hand.

She didn't wait for him. "So NIS is pulling from the middle schools now?" She cranked over the car and pulled away, squealing the tires and planting the man back into his chair.

Finding her way out of the airport, they drove for a while in silence.

"I'm twenty-nine," the NIS officer said. "Four years in Army Intelligence in NATO units in Mid-East wars, before joining NIS."

Toni shook her head and said, "I read your file on the flight."

"Really?"

"I don't work with just anyone," she assured him. "I demand professionalism and expertise with weapons. I will not baby-sit anyone. So if you want your hand held or your dick serviced, you can go elsewhere."

"I'm married with two children. And you're not my type."

Type? She guessed the guy's wife was on the demure side. "Stay the hell out of my way and we'll be fine."

The NIS officer slouched in his leather chair, his gaze straight ahead.

All right. A little harsh. "Listen," she said. "I've got nothing against you. It's been a long flight. I'm tired."

Still nothing from him.

She picked up the freeway toward Oslo and gunned the gas, sliding into traffic. Her passenger grasped the door handle with a death grip.

Time to get to work. "Where are they?"

"You mean your old friend, Jake Adams?" the man asked.

"And your old friend, Kjersti Nilsen?"

He swiveled his head toward her. "How did you. . ."

"I told you. I leave nothing to chance. So I knew you were more into blondes. I also knew that you and Miss Nilsen were lovers while she was an Army pilot and you worked intel with her unit. You both only got written reprimands for your affair. You shouldn't have gotten that, since you were both junior officers and there was no reason not to have a sexual relationship. But your commander had his own desires toward Kjersti, which he had tried to act on but she said no. Tell me when I get something wrong."

His head lowered to his chest. "Sounds about right. But I didn't know about our commander."

"All right," she said. "Let's get to work. Where are they? And I mean Jake, Kjersti and Jake's girlfriend, Anna."

"Right. They flew from Svalbard to Tromso by helicopter, refueling on one of our coast guard ships half way there. The coast guard captain gave them some weapons, but he was not given any information on their true mission." He went on for a while giving great details on what they knew about the activity in Svalbard, including the shoot out. He mentioned the virus in passing and without much concern.

"You never found the other helicopter and the shooters?" she asked him.

"No. As far as we know, they're still on the island of Spitsbergen. But we'll find them. What's our plan to bring them in from the cold?"

Great. This guy's been watching too many spy movies.

"We get them to Oslo and pick up the box," she said. "It's as simple as that." However, she knew it was never a simple task. Something always went wrong. She continued, "We have scientists on their way who will render the virus inactive and bring it back to America."

"You can have it," Hagen said.

Forty-five minutes later, they drove into downtown Oslo and Toni found her hotel without asking for directions, pulling into the underground parking garage and finding a spot. She had studied the maps on the plane during her sleepless flight.

The two of them agreed to meet first thing in the morning for breakfast in the hotel. She needed to get some sleep. He walked off to catch a cab and she checked into her hotel on Karl Johans Gate.

In her room, she took a long, hot shower, which woke her up considerably. She dressed in black, from spandex pants to the skin-tight Under Armor long-sleeve shirt that accentuated her perfectly-large breasts and fit torso.

Then she checked her equipment. Secure cell phone. GPS enabled secure SAT phone. Wireless PDA with tracking. Stiletto. And more.

She quickly lifted out a Glock 23 handgun in .40 cal, slapped a magazine into the handle and cycled a round into the chamber. She aimed the gun around the room, feeling the weight and balance and visualizing targets and eventual recoil. Setting that gun aside, she pulled an identical handgun from the bag and went through the same process. When she was done, her mind in the proper place, she strapped a holster under her left arm and shoved a gun into it. To conceal the gun, she put on a black zip-up jacket, but left it open most of the way. To finish off the outfit, she put on quiet black athletic trainer shoes.

Now she would wait. But not long. She had sat on the bed for only five minutes when the cell call came in with a vibrate. She listened and hung up. Time to move.

She walked down the hotel corridor to the stairway and went down one flight to the fourth floor, checked around the corner, and continued down to room 425. Listening against the door, she smiled. Then she took out her PDA in her left hand and her Glock in her right hand. She punched in some pre-programmed numbers, pointed the infrared beam at the electronic key box and the light turned green.

Quietly, she opened the door, could hear the voices in the room better now, and gently closed the door behind her. Only a small floor lamp lit the back corner of the room.

As she stepped lightly toward the bed, which was moving up and down with great ferocity, the woman voicing approval as the headboard slammed against the wall, she stopped at the corner, her Glock ready. Wait for them to finish? She smiled as she peered around the corner. Give them that.

Even more gently now, she took a seat on a chair at the foot of the bed and crossed her legs, the gun on her lap. They were doing it on top of the sheets, the man on top of a woman with dark hair, stroking in and out of her.

Finally, the man finished with a final thrust and pulled out, a condom full and drooping from the end of an unremarkable penis.

As the older man rolled off the beautiful brunette with the perfect body, she saw Toni first but could not even get a squeak out of her mouth.

Toni smiled at her, the Glock pointed at the couple on the bed.

"Hey," the woman said, tapping the man and then pointing at Toni.

Turning his head toward Toni, the man was shocked to see her, pulling the sheets over his body.

"Who the hell are you?" the man said.

She ignored him, pointing her gun at the woman. "You. Put on your clothes and get out."

With no words, Miss Perfect Body stood up, not concerned that Toni saw her, and started to get dressed. When she was done, she hesitated until Toni trained the gun on her.

"You have a question?" Toni asked her.

"I was hoping for a tip."

"Right. Here's a tip. Find a new profession." Toni waved the gun for her to leave, which she did, with lips pouting.

After the door was securely locked, Toni cast her gaze on the man in the bed, her Glock pointed in his general direction.

"Who are you?" the man asked. "And what the hell do

you want?"

"Your memory is as short as your dick," she said, trying to be as serious as possible under the circumstances.

He said nothing, waiting for her.

"You don't remember me?" she asked. "I'm hurt. Well, Colonel Reed, I remember you."

"Shit! Network."

"Before that," she said.

His mind was working overtime. Then it came to him. "You were with Jake Adams. Your hair was different."

Her hair had always been long, black and curly—the benefit of her Italian father and mother. "Close enough. You sent Jake to Bumfuck, Norway on a fool's errand."

Colonel Reed propped himself on his elbows, but didn't say a word.

Toni continued, "You should have mentioned something to the Network before going off like this."

He shook his head and released air from his nose. "You think I'm some rogue officer."

"What should we think? You no longer work for us, yet you send one of our former agents into harm's way to secure one of the most deadly flu viruses to ever strike planet Earth."

The colonel sat up now, but kept his lower body covered. "It's not what you think."

"You'd be surprised what I think."

"Can you put the gun away? It's Toni, right? Toni something Italian."

She waved the gun toward his clothes thrown to the floor haphazardly. "Get dressed, colonel. We've got a long talk ahead of us."

CHAPTER 15

Tromso, Norway

They had made it across the ocean with plenty of fuel, landed at a small airport near Tromso, the city called the 'Paris of the North,' which Jake wasn't buying, and rented a car with cash. Tromso was far more beautiful than Paris, with the snow-capped mountains ringing the town and the ocean-front fjords that ran through the area like a spider web. He had come to hate the crowded big cities of Europe. Although Vienna didn't seem big to him, the traffic could be a nightmare. Rome was worse and Paris perverse. No, he missed living in Innsbruck. Tromso might have been in the running if it weren't for the cold winters and the bug-filled summers. Not to mention the strange lighting—long summer nights and nonexistent daylight in the winter.

Now, the three of them were together in more confined space, having transferred their gear from the helo to the rental Volvo sedan. They had just grabbed dinner, decided it would be better to keep moving, so they would drive through the night in shifts. Jake had taken the wheel first, with Anna at his side, and Kjersti sprawled out in the back sleeping. It was closing in on midnight, but the sky was still a strange glow of light. The Land of the Midnight Sun finally made sense to Jake. Most of the night would be in that weird glow. The highway they were driving resembled a tunnel as it wound along a river, the canyon walls periodically steep and narrow.

According to the map, they would reach the border in a few miles. They were at the top of the world here, with Norway, Sweden and Finland coming together in a narrow stretch of land. Not far to the northeast and they could have crossed into Russia. Traffic? In the past fifty kilometers they had come across only two other cars.

"Are you sure we cross into Finland?" Anna asked Jake, her voice quiet and confused.

"Yes," he said. "But for only about a hundred and twenty kilometers. Then we head south into Sweden."

"Wow. I had no idea they all came together like this. Where do we go from there?"

Jake looked into the rearview mirror at Kjersti, whose breathing indicated she was in deep sleep. "We continue south and eventually work our way to Oslo."

"Why the crazy route? We could have flown and been there by now."

They had been over this before. Jake was tired and didn't want to explain it again, but he also knew that Anna was finally feeling better. She had been constantly sick while flying on the helo. Not to the point of throwing up all the time, but she had lost her lunch a few times in the last couple of days. So, considering the circumstances, she might not have heard everything he told her.

"We couldn't bring the box on a commercial flight," he said. "I couldn't trust placing it in baggage. And there was no way they would have allowed it in carry-on. This is the only way. Plus, the bad guys could easily pick us off at commercial airports."

"What about crossing the borders? We have enough firepower for a small army."

Jake had thought about that. "You have Interpol credentials and Kjersti is with Norwegian Intelligence. That should give us enough clout to pass through without trouble. Besides, Kjersti said the border crossings up here are not very heavily controlled."

"I guess we'll find out in a minute."

They passed a sign saying the border was ahead. As Jake slowed and collected the passports, he looked for any sign of human activity as he powered the window down. Only one small building sat between the two lanes of traffic. No gate. He slowed even more and a man appeared from a door, his hand up. Jake stopped and handed the passports to the older man. So this was where border patrol agents went to retire, Jake thought.

The man asked him something in a language he didn't understand. English, German, French or Italian, Jake asked the man.

"I speak English," the border agent said. "I mentioned to you this was a strange group of passports. American, Austrian and Norwegian." His disposition turned from confused to dubious. "What's the purpose of your visit to Finland?"

Jake saw Kjersti wake in the back seat.

"We're tourists," Jake said. "Just passing through."

"It's after midnight," the guard reminded Jake.

"Yeah, I know. I can't get used to this light at night. How do you do it?"

"Please step out of the vehicle." All serious now.

They didn't have time for this. But he had their passports. Reluctantly, Jake did as the man asked.

"Jake," Anna said, her hand reaching to him.

"It's all right. I'll take care of it." He smiled at her and got out. As he did so, another man, a man in his early twenties, came out of the door, an automatic rifle in his hands across his chest.

The older man stepped toward the back of the car, giving Jake some room.

"Please open the trunk," the older guard ordered.

"Why?" Jake asked.

"Inspection."

"For what?"

"Contraband. Drugs. Maybe a bomb. You could be terrorists."

Jake shook his head. This was crazy. He was trying to save all of their asses from a deadly virus. Sure, they didn't know that. Damn it!

Hesitating, Jake twirled the keys in his hand and threw them up in the air. As the old guard's eyes followed the keys, Jake punched the man in the sternum, taking his breath away and bending him over. The young man backed up, his rifle coming around. Suddenly the back car door opened, hitting the young man in the legs and swiveling him toward Jake again. With a sweep, Jake took the young man off his feet and into a sleeper hold. But as the man struggled, his gun discharged three rounds into the trunk of the car. Jake thrust his knee up into the man's kidney, making him drop the rifle and come to his knees. A second later and he had passed out.

Kjersti grabbed the rifle and pointed it at the old man, who had started to recover and grab for his handgun on his side.

Jake took the gun from the man's holster and retrieved their passports. "Watch them," he said, and then ran into the building, the gun pointing in all directions. Nobody else there. He came outside again.

By now Anna was out of the car. "What the hell, Jake."

Jake grabbed the young man and dragged him inside the building, while Kjersti escorted the old man inside. He hand-cuffed and tied both of them.

"Get in the car," Jake ordered. "Grab the keys out there," he said to Kjersti. "You drive."

When the two women were gone, Jake got close to the old border guard and said, "We are all officers of our respective governments. I'm sorry we had to do this, but we are tracking international terrorists from Russia. I will drop your guns precisely two kilometers down the road. I could have killed the both of you. We must get to Helsinki by tomorrow afternoon to intercept the terrorists. Do you understand?"

The man nodded his head.

"You didn't see us. You understand?"

Head nod again.

"Good."

Before leaving, Jake turned off the lights and then locked the door behind him. He jumped into the back seat and Kjersti gunned it, squealing the tires as they pulled away. Checking his watch, Jake realized the entire event had taken less than five minutes. They were lucky no other cars had come along.

In exactly two kilometers Jake had Kjersti pull over and, after wiping down their prints, he dropped the guns along the side of the road in tall weeds.

Back in the car and driving down the highway, Kjersti glanced at Jake in the rearview mirror. "I had heard you were crazy, but I didn't expect that."

"All we needed was someone there calling in our location. He should have just let us pass."

"Trust no one?" she said, smiling.

"Something like that. Can you go a little faster. We need to get the hell out of Finland before those two break free."

"How far for our turn?" Kjersti asked.

Anna looked at the map. "Little over a hundred kilometers. At this rate, assuming we don't hit a herd of reindeer or an elk, perhaps forty minutes."

"How do I explain bullet holes in the trunk?" Kjersti asked.

They had rented the car in her name. Since it was her country, it was the best choice. "You took out the insurance, right?"

"Of course. But somehow I don't think that covers bullet holes."

"Blame hunters. Crazy Finns."

They traveled through a couple of tiny towns along the way. In less than an hour they turned south at Kaaresuvanto, Finland, a border town across the Konkamaeno River from Kaesuando, Sweden. They crossed into Sweden without even a nod from the border patrol. The word had not gotten out on them. Either the men were still tied up, or they had decided to let the incident go. Better to save face and not admit to someone getting the jump on them and tying them up.

Safely in Sweden, they continued south at the speed limit until they reached Gallivare, some two hundred ten kilometers from the Finnish border. Kjersti had kept the wheel for that entire stretch.

"Kjersti," Jake said from the back seat. "Pull over up ahead on that road."

She didn't hesitate, pulling over on a remote side road on the outskirts of town.

Anna and Kjersti both turned around, wonder in their stares.

Anna said, "What's up?"

Jake had a feeling they weren't going to like this. "We need to split up."

"Why?" Kjersti asked.

"Just in case those two at the Finnish border decide to call us in. The Swedes could also be looking for us."

"I don't think so," Kjersti said.

"You don't think they'll be looking for us," Jake said, "or you don't think we should split up?"

"Both." Kjersti looked disturbed and concerned. "Besides. . .this is my case and my territory." Determined now.

"She's got a point, Jake," Anna said, her expression of disappointment in him obvious.

Jake had anticipated them not wanting to comply, so he had a back-up plan. The real plan, in fact. But he needed to sell it. "Listen. There's no need for the two of you to be exposed to this virus. Anna, perhaps you should go with Kjersti back to Oslo."

"What?" Anna was pissed now, like she had been finding Jake drunk on the floor at the Oslo hotel. "This is my case as well. If anyone should go back to Oslo, Jake, it's you. You're a private citizen."

Cold but true, and part of his plan. See how determined they were; then break in with the real plan. "I was paid to go to Svalbard," Jake reminded Anna.

"To find an old friend."

"You think I really believed that story Colonel Reed was selling?" Jake shook his head, playing it up big-time. "And now the Network is involved. I've essentially been ordered by the highest intelligence source in the world, a man who takes his orders directly from the President of the United States, the leader of the free world, to bring this virus to Oslo so the American scientists can render it inactive and save the entire world from this deadly pandemic." Too thick? Maybe.

But the two women simply stared at him. Then they broke out in laughter together and didn't stop until tears came to their eyes. Jake sat back and crossed his arms until they were done, his poker face not revealing anything to them.

"You done?" Jake asked.

They both nodded to him.

"So I guess we're a threesome," he said.

"You wish," Kjersti said.

"Yes, he does," Anna chimed in.

Finally Jake got out and went to the driver's door, opened it and reached down for the trunk release.

"What you doing?" Anna asked him. "Come on, I know you can take a joke."

"I need to grab something. The SAT phone. See if I can get a call through."

He went to the trunk and opened it, glancing out onto

the main road as a car passed. But they were concealed by a strip of thick trees, so they would not be seen. When he looked into the trunk, the first thing he saw was a bullet hole in his backpack. The border guard's shots had entered the trunk, passed through and through, and one had crashed into his bag. He thought about stepping back or throwing the bag into the woods, but if the bullet had struck the metal box, chances are the flu virus would have released into the trunk over the past four hours. He could be infected already. No, he probably needed direct contact with the virus. Just look, Jake. He had to know for sure.

Carefully and slowly unzipping the bag, Jake tried his best to look inside. But he couldn't see anything. Without further thought, he reached his hand down and carefully felt the side of the metal box that had faced the driver's side of the car. Then he felt it. A hole. Crap!

From a side pouch, Jake found a mini-flashlight and turned it on, looking deep into the bag. Something wasn't right, though. There was a strange color as the light hit the hole. Yet, the color changed when the light went slightly off center. He shone the light into the bottom of the back-pack and saw something else. Something that should not have been there.

"Colonel Reed, you bastard," Jake whispered. Then he looked around and found a pencil. He shoved it into the hole in the box as deep as it would go, then he broke it off. That would have to do for now. Looking down at his right hand, he noticed a slight tremble, as if early Parkinson's had set into his body. His body needed a drink. The only thing keeping him from stopping now and grabing at least a beer was Anna. Her and the rush he got being back in the game. He couldn't decide which was a stronger fix for him. Taking a deep breath, he closed his eyes an willed the shake to stop. Opening his eyes, he was steady again.

He quickly zipped up the backpack and found three bottles of water to bring back to the car. He slammed the trunk shut and went to the back seat.

"Water anyone?" Jake asked them.

They each took a bottle from him.

"Everything all right?" Anna asked.

"Yep. Kjersti, how good is the insurance on this car?"

"You checked out the bullet holes?"

"Afraid so. I think we should dump it and catch a train. Once we get down the track a ways, we'll call in the car stolen." Jake's true reason for coming this crazy way in the first place. Passenger service in Sweden started in the little town of Gallivare, just a kilometer away.

"All right," Kjersti said. "But let's grab some breakfast, check the train schedule, drop off the bags, and then dump the car."

"Sounds good," Jake said, even though he already knew the next train heading south would depart at 11:19. They had a few hours to kill. Jake had been reluctant to take the box on the train for fear of exposure to more people. But that fear was gone now. That bastard.

CHAPTER 16

T oni Contardo spent most of the evening just talking with Colonel Reed. She had a hard time thinking of him as a bad guy, or even someone who would do something bad. After all, he had been a respected military officer for decades, and after that had worked for the old CIA, just like Jake Adams. The only difference was that Jake had gotten in and out of both endeavors much sooner than the colonel. But Jake had also stayed in the game since leaving the CIA, working for himself as a consultant and in private security. She had no idea how involved the colonel had been over the past ten years. His Network file, which she had read thoroughly on the flight from Camp Springs to Oslo, had been spotty over the recent years. So those are the years she concentrated on first. He had mostly been retired, traveling to places he had not been able to see when his security clearance had restricted certain areas. As this became more of a travelogue, she suggested they have a beer from the mini-bar, which she had gotten for them. It was easy to drop the drug into his beer, and he was out cold in a few minutes. Then she had tied him to the bed and had gotten some sleep in the chair.

Now, as the sun seemed to be close to making an appearance, she kicked the bed and watched as the colonel's eyes opened, his expression changing from erotic dream to bound reality.

"So, it's come to this," Colonel Reed said.

She shrugged. Her gun was in its holster under her arm. "You told me a bunch of crap I wanted to hear last night. Now you're going to tell me the truth about why you sent Jake to Svalbard. First of all, how did you find the MiG crash location?"

He told her about the snow having melted and someone seeing the wreckage from the air.

"But how did you get involved?"

His eyes shifted to the ceiling. "Can I take a piss? I really gotta go."

"Go ahead. Who's stopping you?" No smile.

"Wow. You're cold."

She simply stared at him.

"All right," he said. "A guy approached me. He knew I knew the captain who never returned from there."

"Steve Olson."

"Right."

"How'd he know you knew him?"

"He. . .was in the game years ago."

"At the time of the crash."

"Right."

"Russian." She was guessing.

He hesitated and she got her answer.

Toni was still confused, though. "Tell me about the

virus and why this former KGB officer would want to get you involved."

"I didn't say he was KGB," he reminded her.

"KGB, GRU, military officer. But this sounds like KGB. Why'd he need you?"

"He has no former resources."

"And you do."

"Well, he knew I had military and Network contacts. Figured I could help because of that."

Something was not adding up here. "Why didn't the Russian just send a crew to Svalbard to get what was there?"

"I'm trying to tell you," the colonel said emphatically. "He needed my resources."

"Bullshit! He's still under surveillance by the Russian Foreign Intelligence Service. How high up was he?" She knew by name, face and reputation most of the old guard from the KGB and the newer SVR.

He let out a deep breath of air and shook his head side to side. "Jake mentioned how relentless you were." He hesitated and then said, "He was in the First Chief Directorate."

"Which department?"

"A."

"Let me guess. The disinformation department. And you believed anything that came out of his mouth?"

"He wasn't trying to sell me a damn bridge. I knew the man. And I checked him out. What he knew was confirmed by my sources."

Who in the hell was feeding Colonel Reed information from the Network? That wasn't important right now. For now she needed to find out what Jake was into. "Tell me what you know about the virus."

He explained all he knew about the virus, including how it had been modified by the Soviets. As far as he knew, the Russians still had other samples of the virus in labs outside Moscow. Didn't know how secure those samples were, though. While he talked, Toni could tell one thing for sure—the man was telling the truth.

"So you were just going to turn this deadly virus over to the Russian?" she asked him.

"Of course not. I knew that Jake would find the metal box if it was there. I bet on it. I also bet that there was no way Jake would turn over the virus to anyone but the American Intelligence Network. Why the hell do you think I chose him to go there?"

She leaned back into her chair, her eyes concentrating on his, but her mind spinning. Damn it! The guy made sense. If you had to choose a man you could trust, then Jake was that man. He couldn't and wouldn't turn it over to anyone. She thought about possible Russians who could know about this from the old First Directorate. Time to play a little poker.

"When's the last time you heard from Jake?"

"Yesterday. We talked by SAT phone."

"While you were in Stockholm?"

"Yes."

"So you saw Victor Petrova." A guess, but an educated one, since she had heard the little dwarf had retired there years ago. Judging by his reaction, she was right.

"How the. . ."

"Hello. Who the hell do you think I work for, Colonel Reed? So that little midget hired you. What's Victor up to these days? About three feet?"

"About that."

They stared at each other for a minute, neither saying a word, but Toni considering what to do with the good colonel. She felt like sticking him on a damn plane and flying him back to Camp Springs for debriefing.

♦

Jimmy McLean and Velda Crane had spent the last evening keeping track of Gary Dixon, who had not left his hotel since he got there. He had eaten dinner there with the Russian, an expensive steak from the money on the debit card Jimmy had given him, and then three pints of Guinness at the hotel bar before locking himself in his room. All of this was verified by Jimmy on his laptop. He loved it. Everything was electronic. Nothing was secret anymore. There wasn't a hotel in Europe that still used the basic key and lock. Jimmy had been able to get a digital photo of the Russian and had sent it to London for possible identification. Of course Velda had also planted a bug in Dixon's room, which had produced hours of snoring and farting and not much else.

Now, Jimmy clicked through his computer looking for any information that would help him understand what that little troll was up to in Oslo. So far nothing. There was a knock on his door just as his cell phone rang. Looking through the peep hole and seeing the top of a head, he let in Velda and then flipped open his phone and gestured for Velda to take a seat.

"Yeah?" Jimmy said in the phone. It was an analyst at MI6 headquarters. He listened for more than two minutes without saying a word.

"Are you sure?" He smiled at Velda, who had taken a flying leap onto his bed.

"We'll stick with him," Jimmy pledged. "Thanks. We will." He clapped the phone shut and threw it to a chair.

"What's the word?" Velda asked. "The muckity mucks have a plan?"

Jimmy plopped down into a chair. "They identified that man from last night eating dinner with Dixon. The Russian. He's a guy named Victor Petrova, a former KGB officer in the First Directorate."

Velda scooted her little legs over the side of the bed. "Department A?"

"Yep. Disinformation."

"Wonderful. Where do we go from here?"

Jimmy rolled his eyes up in thought, recalling the conversation. "There's more. London decided they needed to coordinate with the Americans. Make sure we weren't stepping on toes. International coordination."

Velda seemed to sense what was coming, her head shaking side to side.

"It's complex," Jimmy said. "They have some assets in place. This is big. Really big."

Suddenly an alarm sounded from the laptop and Jimmy turned to look at the screen.

"Dixon is on the move. Let's go."

CHAPTER 17

The train slowly pulled out of the Gallivare, Sweden station. Jake and Anna sat together in a second class section, with Kjersti facing them and across the aisle six rows forward. They had decided to split up. They were all dead tired. Kjersti was already dozing off and Anna had her head against Jake's shoulder. The train was less than half full, so the two of them had no one else across from them or directly behind them.

He squeezed down on Anna's hand, wanting to tell her what he had found out about the box. But this was not the right time or place. At least he was no longer shaking. Perhaps he had simply been tired and his body was reacting appropriately. But he had to admit that, at the time, he thought it had been some kind of reaction to the old Soviet virus.

She brought her face up and kissed him on the cheek. "What you thinking?" she whispered to him in German. It was more likely someone there spoke English than German.

"Maybe we should have just flown down to Oslo and get rid of this damn box." His eyes rose to the overhead compartment that contained his backpack and the metal box before settling on her again.

"This is safer," she assured him. "It's more logical to be safe and make sure we don't expose too many people."

"We could have just kept the rental car."

She shook her head. "Not if the Finns had reported us. What's bothering you?"

Should he tell her? Not yet. He had been taken in by Colonel Reed, and by extension so had she. And that torqued his jaw. When he caught up with his old friend they would have more than words.

"Let's get some sleep," Jake said, sticking with the German. "We have about two hours to Boden, our next stop, and then another three or four to Umea."

"Is that where we switch to the sleeper car?"

He nodded his head.

The two of them rested their heads together, holding hands, and drifted off to sleep.

Jake opened his eyes and the first thing he saw was the Swedish police officer standing next to Kjersti, his right hand on the butt of his gun and the left looking at her passport and ticket. Anna was still sleeping, her head against the window now.

Kjersti tried not to look at Jake, but she was concerned. He could tell that much.

He slowly rose and stretched with the rocking train. Then he made his way up the aisle toward Kjersti, stopping because the police officer blocked his way.

The police was speaking English to Kjersti. Something

about a rental car. Crap! They had already found it.

"Why didn't you report the car stolen, then?" the police-man asked Kjersti.

She needed to come clean with the police and tell them she worked for Norwegian Intelligence. Or not. How could she explain running an op in Sweden without coor-dinating it with the Swedish Security Service, SAPO? No. She was right to not tell them. It was never a good idea to run something in another country without the home team knowing about it.

Jake got uncomfortably close to the police officer and shoved a thumb into his kidney, pushing him forward to the train window. The policeman dropped Kjersti's pass-port while Jake rushed to the front of the car and through the door toward the next car.

Time seemed to stand still for a moment as the police-man and Kjersti were both caught off guard by Jake's action. The policeman recovered and started after Jake.

By now Jake was in a sleeper car. He had to hurry. He rushed into a bathroom at the end of the car and waited.

When he heard the door between the car swish, he timed his exit and swung the door open with great force, smash-ing it into the cop's face. He went down to his knees and Jake swept his foot up into his crotch, bringing the man to a rolling ball on the floor.

Quickly, Jake took the man's gun and radio. He hated to do this. The guy was only doing his job. But Jake could-n't let him stop them. Not now.

As the man held his nuts in a fetal position, something started to happen. Something that gave Jake an idea. The train was beginning to slow for their stop in Boden.

At that exact moment, the door opened and Jake turned

to see Kjersti standing there, her mind obviously conflicted.

"What have you done?" Kjersti said.

The policeman got to his knees and Jake swiftly
wrapped him in a sleeper hold. Seconds later the man
passed out and Jake lay him on the ground.

"Jesus," she said. "What do we do with him?"

"How long is our stop in Boden?"

"Five minutes. No more."

"Good."

"Go swap seats with Anna. I need Interpol for this."

Kjersti left immediately.

While she was gone, Jake took off the man's clothes,
leaving him only in his underwear. He shoved the clothes,
the gun and the radio and other gear into the closest sleeper unit, keeping only his handcuffs and the key.

When the door opened next, Anna entered and then
stood there with her arms crossed. Jake was crouching
over the near-naked man and it looked like he was trying
to have man sex with him.

"It's not what it looks like," Jake said. "Help me get him
to the end of this car." He explained his plan to her and she
shook her head and helped him.

Jake cuffed the man behind his back and dragged him to
the front of the car. By now the train was almost stopped.

"You think this will work?" Anna asked him.

"Yes. He has no clothes." Then his plan got even more
interesting. "Go get those sleeping pills of yours and those
two little bottles of whiskey you took from the room in
Longyearbyen."

"They're a sleep aid," she corrected, and then hurried
off.

By the time she got back, the train had stopped in the station and Jake was between cars with the man.

"How many should we give him?" Jake asked her.

"Two knock me out." She opened a bottle of water.

"Give him three."

"He's out cold," she protested.

Jake lifted the man up to a sitting position, cranked his head back, and pulled the man's mouth open. "Shove three in."

She did it and followed them with the bottle of water. Jake shoved the man's mouth closed and held his hand over it. The man tried to choke, but finally got the water and pills down. The activity woke the policeman, though. He moved his head from side to side.

"Now the whisky."

"It could kill him," she said.

"Bullshit. He's a big guy. He can handle it. Besides, I don't care if it all goes down. He just needs to smell drunk."

"But the pills will take fifteen minutes to react."

Crap. He hadn't thought of that.

The man came more to life and Jake could feel his muscles tense beneath him.

"Get a baggage cart," Jake ordered.

Anna looked concerned, but she did what he said.

When she was gone the man tried to struggle free, so Jake elbowed him in the head. That just made him more mad. He hated to do it, but Jake put him in another sleeper hold until the man passed out. He knew it could be dangerous making the man pass out twice in such a short period of time, but he had no other choice.

Jake dragged him outside the train onto the cart Anna

had brought. People stared, wondering what was going on. Jake pushed the cart inside to the first police officer they could find. He was an older man. Anna showed her Interpol identification, which impressed the local cop, and explained that the man had been drunk and obnoxious. This kind gentleman with her had helped her subdue the drunk. But they had to get back on the train. She was tracking a possible terrorist. A real pro, Jake thought, as the two of them hurried back to catch the train. They just got aboard and the doors closed. The train pulled away from the station.

"Great job," Jake said. "He should be out cold for about eight hours."

"Will that be enough time?"

"No. But it'll be the middle of the night. He'll tell a story and it will take them a while to check into it. Probably until morning. By then we'll be to our stop in Falun or Mora. Go back to your seat. I'll get rid of the cop's clothes, gun and ID."

She smiled at him. "This is all too natural to you. Are you sure you worked for the government?"

He put his hand behind her head and kissed her on the lips. They embraced and she finally pulled away.

"Sure, change the subject," she said as she wandered off through the sleeper car.

Alone now, Jake went into the sleeper compartment where he had stuck the cop's gear. First he made sure he had not left any fingerprints on the man's gun, and then he pulled a pillow case from a pillow and shoved everything inside. Then he looked at the window. They opened. Great.

He watched as they reached the countryside between

Boden and Lulea. They were traveling at least sixty miles per hour.

The window propped inward about six inches maximum. Squishing everything in the bag as tightly as he could, he jammed the pillowcase and gear through the narrow opening. It got stuck halfway. He shoved it harder and it finally released, falling down toward the tracks below. He pushed the window shut and took a seat on the bed. How the hell had it come to this? Whatever happened to simply flying from Vienna to Oslo for a little vacation? Drink a few beers, some wine, maybe a martini or two. But no. He had to go off on some wild-ass goose chase to Bumfuck, Norway, some Arctic islands that most couldn't even find on a map, get shot at there, and fly back to the mainland, only to run into overzealous Finnish border guards and a super-vigilant Swedish cop. What next? That was his problem. He knew it would probably only get worse. Especially once he confronted Colonel Reed about the contents of the metal box. That was one helluva deadly flu virus, he quipped to himself. Time to get back to the lovely ladies. Damn, he could use a stiff drink right now.

CHAPTER 18

Oslo, Norway

Jimmy McLean spent most of the day traveling around the city, trying his best to not be seen by the little man, Gary Dixon. Something was going down, Jimmy was sure of that. Dixon stopped a dozen times to talk with various people, many just as small as him, and kept checking his watch. It was as if he was on a strict time schedule. Like he had to hurry to contact all of these people before a certain deadline. There were too many of them. Jimmy had Velda in the car calling in photos and names to their headquarters. Some had been easy to ID, since they were owners of small businesses. Others they might never identify, though. At least not without a lot more manpower then the two of them. And that was the problem. With the Russians and the Chinese running so many spies inside of the U.K., most of their assets were keeping track of those thousands of operatives. Not to mention those dedicated to the war on terror. They were strecthed too thin in all directions. It was amazing to Jimmy they had dedicated he and Velda to this cause.

Now, Jimmy pulled over to the curb in front of Dixon's hotel. The little man had just scooted out of his cab and into the lobby.

"What you think Gary is into?" Velda asked.

"Who knows. It's hard to believe he could be into any-thing dealing with international terrorism. The guy can barely keep his own shoes tied. And everything he has ever done involves thievery of some sort. The guy started out in a pickpocket crew in Aberdeen. Then he moved onto ripping off tourists in Edinburgh and Glasgow. All before the age of eighteen."

"But he's never done more than a few days in jail," Velda reminded her colleague.

"True. But it wasn't from being too slick to get caught. He's been snitching for years."

"Maybe for both sides."

That was a distinct possibility. But did that matter at this point? Suddenly the little guy was associating himself with a heavy Russian player. A former KGB officer with criminal activity, supposedly, from Moscow to London and all points between. According to their MI6 briefing, Petrova had built one of the largest gang of thieves in decades. But word also said that Petrova worked out of greed, not ideology. The guy had even sold his own sperm on eBay—touting it as that from a genius former Cold War KGB officer. He hadn't lied. And he had gotten bids past five thousand Euros until the website shut him down. A true entrepreneur.

♦

They had followed the tall man and the little woman all over Oslo, with Colonel Reed behind the wheel and Toni Contardo in the front seat researching on the fly. She had gotten word from the Network about the Scottish man, a dwarf by the name of Gary Dixon, saying he was involved somehow with the Russian, Victor Petrova. Just as she and the colonel had gotten to Dixon's hotel, the little man came shuffling out the front door. Then Toni spotted the other two following Dixon at a safe distance. She suspected the Norwegian Intelligence Service was running some surveillance on the little man, but had called her NIS contact, Thom Hagen, and he had confirmed they had nothing going on.

So the chase was on. The little man, Dixon, went from place to place talking with others of his stature, and even some standard size folks, while the tall man and the little woman followed him. And then Toni and the colonel kept their distance, changing places with Thom Hagen, who had caught up with them after about an hour of playing that game.

But now the little man had gone into the hotel and the cat and mouse had come to an abrupt stop. On the other hand, as far as Toni could tell they had not come across the Russian, Victor Petrova, who was now using the name Oberon.

Toni set the laptop on the car floor, checked her gun inside her jacket, and said to Colonel Reed, "All right. I'm gonna go up and see who the hell we've been following all day."

"Is that a good idea?" Reed said. "What if they're associated with Petrova?"

She considered that and had to admit he had a point. But she still didn't completely trust the colonel. Not after how he had sent Jake to the Arctic like that without telling him the truth. "Then we'll know."

Toni got out of the rental car, glanced back a block, catching the gaze of NIS officer Hagen, and then stepped down the sidewalk. The car was a block ahead.

She would stroll along, as if just out for a casual walk. Nobody to concern them. As she got closer to the car, she angled to the edge of the sidewalk to be out of mirror view, then cut a direct line toward the open passenger window, drawing her gun at the last second and pointing it directly at the little woman's head.

Both inside the car startled when they saw her.

"What the hell?" said the little woman.

The man instinctively swept his hand into his jacket.

"I wouldn't do that," Toni said. She reached inside the car and unlocked the back door, then hurried into the back seat. "Who the hell are you two?"

The man spoke first. "MI6."

She switched the gun to her left hand and leaned forward, putting her hand into his jacket and collecting his 9mm handgun and passport. She got her phone and said, "Jimmy McLean with MI6." She flipped her phone shut and reached up for the woman's purse. Inside she found a little Walther P22, just right for her tiny hands. Then her passport. "Velda Crane. You also claim to be with MI6?"

The woman nodded her disproportionately large head. "Who are you?"

Jimmy McLean took this question. "This, Velda, is Toni Contardo with the American Intelligence Network. Why else would I have told her we were with MI6?"

Toni glanced at McLean in the rearview mirror.

"We heard you were in Oslo," McLean explained, "but had no way of knowing how to contact you. Camp Springs said you were out in the cold. Hadn't heard from you in a while."

Her phone rang and she picked up and listened, before flipping it shut with force and shoving it into her jacket pocket. Toni handed their guns and passports back to them. "Sorry about that."

"No problem," Velda said. "How long were you with us?"

Toni put her gun in its holster. "All day. What was that little dwarf. . .no offense. . ."

"No problem," Velda said.

"What was Gary Dixon up to today?" Toni finished.

"That's what we've been trying to discern," McLean said. He explained what they knew about Dixon's activities, and how they had followed the man from Scotland to Oslo.

Toni's story was much less revealing. She wasn't one to give up information freely, and didn't trust just anyone. Hell, she didn't even trust Colonel Reed, who had been an Air Force officer and CIA and Network operative.

"That has to be the biggest crock of shit I've heard in a long time," Jimmy McLean said. "Couldn't you give us a little more information than that? What ever happened to cooperation?"

Velda chimed in. "This Victor Petrova is a bad ass mad genius. A frickin' puppet master."

"Halfpint is right," McLean said.

"Halfpint?" Toni asked.

"Has nothing to do with her size," he explained. "She

always orders a half pint of beer."

"Okay. She's right about?"

"Petrova," he said. "Our intel says the man orchestrated so many crazy-ass schemes for the KGB, he could have started World War Three if he wanted to during the Cold War. He was that good. Now he's made millions off his criminal activity. He runs a massive organization throughout Europe."

"And is headquartered in Stockholm," Toni said. "I got the same briefing." What's he up to now? That was the question of the hour. Yet not one of them could come up with a good answer.

◆

Sitting in the passenger seat of his rental Volvo, Victor Petrova smiled as he listened through his ear piece as the three intelligence officers lavished praise and hatred for him and his criminal activity. His driver had reached each location Gary Dixon had gone, knowing where and when the man would be at each location. By doing so he had accomplished two goals. First, the Scotsman had delivered messages to men with mostly clean records—men who themselves would not do a damn thing for him, but who would pass the word to those who would act soon. And second, he had collected all the players in this grand game of his, from the two Brits to this new Network woman. He had heard of Toni Contardo from his days in the KGB. She was more than a little capable. No match for his intellect. But then few were. So she had teamed up with Colonel Reed in some way. Disturbing, but not completely unexpected. Still, the colonel had served his purpose, sending Jake Adams off to the Arctic to do his work for him. Sure he could have sent his men to accomplish the same task. But there was no reason to involve the Russian Foreign Intelligence Service. Sure the SVR was no KGB, but even the blind hamster finds his way up the actor's ass once in a while. Maybe he was the puppet master. He smiled.

CHAPTER 19

Jake stretched his legs out in the sleeper car—the very same car where he had thrown the police officer's clothes and then dumped them out the window. Anna was asleep on the upper bunk and Kjersti was alone in her compartment next door to them.

They had traveled for hours along the Swedish coast, passed through the seaport cities of Umca and Sundsvall, and at nearly one in the morning were at least an hour away from Gavle, some hundred miles north of Stockholm.

He had had plenty of time to think about this case during the ride. They had been lucky the Swedish police had not invaded the train at one of their stops and hauled them all in. He couldn't let that happen, though. The box he carried with him, with the Russian words and the international symbol for biohazard stamped prominently on four sides, would put him in jail faster than he could consider. Sure he could have his friends at the Network get him out, assuming they would be willing to do so. But with what he had discovered before getting on the train, they might not be willing to help Jake in any way. He needed to contact the Network and Colonel Reed. But first his friend at the Network.

He reached into his backpack and found the SAT phone.

When he turned on the phone, he saw that he had missed thirteen calls. Ten from scrambled Network numbers that would lead to pizza places in New Jersey and Chinese restaurants in Portland, Oregon. The other three were from the untraceable number from Colonel Reed. A number that when punched in by anyone else finding the phone, or stealing it, would be picked up by a Swiss sheep herder—which Jake was sure would piss that guy off to no end.

Jake called Jenkins at the Network, who picked up on the second ring.

"Where the hell are you?" Jenkins asked hurriedly.

"Come on, Kurt," Jake said, his voice barely a whisper. "This is a GPS-enabled SAT phone, which I'm sure you broke the code for during our first call. Even with the phone turned off, you can track me."

"Why do I even try?" He stopped and said, "Okay. You're traveling at a steady one hundred thirty kilometers per hour at sea level. So that would put you on the night train heading toward Stockholm."

"I could be driving," Jake muttered.

"I don't think so, Jake. I know your driving. It's not that steady. Plus our people have tracked your stops in each city. Also, we got a report about some cop getting his ass whipped. When they sent out the description, it sounded like you."

"You take care of it?"

"Yeah. First we altered the description, and then we wiped it from their system. Made it go away."

"Thanks. That's why I didn't dump the SAT phone. Thought you could be of some use."

"Glad to help. But aren't you taking a risk traveling on a train with that deadly virus?"

Crap. He had a feeling Jenkins would bring that up. It's why he really didn't call in his actions. He was hoping to finish the train travel before he had to explain his actions.

"I know what I'm doing," Jake assured him.

Anna rolled onto her back and started to snore. She had taken a sleeping pill, so he knew she would sleep through the night.

"What's that noise?" Jenkins asked.

"Nothing." He struggled with his thoughts of what he should tell his old friend. Could he explain that he had been duped? They all had been suckered.

"What's wrong, Jake?"

"Nothing. Do you have your people in place in Oslo?"

Now Jenkins took his time to answer. "We have assets in place there, with more to come. It's taken us a while to get a team of scientists together with the expertise needed to inactivate the flu virus. You understand."

Yeah, he understood. He understood that his friend's efforts would be nothing more than a drill—an exercise— for possible future breaches of security. Maybe the American government would be able to work out better protocols because of this. Right. That was a fantasy.

"No problem. Make sure they get there within twenty-four hours."

"One question, Jake."

"Shoot."

"Why the crazy route? Why not just a direct approach to Oslo?"

"Well, that was smart on my part wasn't it," Jake said, sarcastically. "Your people aren't ready for me anyway. I'd be sitting in Oslo holding my dick waiting for your scientists to arrive. Besides, some bad-ass folks seem to want this. . .virus even more than us. And I have a feeling they're willing to do damn near anything to get their hands on it. Anything else you can tell me?"

"We've tracked down Colonel Reed."

"Yeah?"

"He's in Oslo. It took us some time, but we backtracked some calls he made to your SAT phone."

Great. Did Jenkins know more than he was telling him? "I was just going to call the colonel."

"No need," Jenkins said. "He's with. . .our people there in Oslo."

"So you're on the same page. Did he explain anything about his contacts?"

Jenkins explained everything they knew, including the involvement of the Russian, Victor Petrova.

"I'm familiar with Petrova," Jake said. "He was one of the most manipulative bastards in KGB disinformation. And that's saying a lot."

"We tried turning him in the height of the Cold War," Jenkins admitted. "He strung us along like Gepetto. Then pulled the rug out from under us and a couple of our agents were killed."

Jake remembered that. It happened right around the time he had switched from being an Air Force officer to joining the old CIA. "What's he up to now?"

"Mostly running one of the most successful criminal

organizations in Europe. Headquartered near you in Stockholm."

"Right. I could run down there and have a little talk with the little man."

"No use. He's not there. We've been checking into he and his men since we heard Colonel Reed had been in contact with him, but they've all disappeared. Poof. Gone."

In Oslo, Jake guessed. Waiting for him to deliver his package.

"Sounds like we're running right into him. You want me to keep going to Oslo?"

"It's as good a place as any to stop this."

"Not really," Jake said. "Might be better to go to some remote military site or isolated airfield. Less exposure there."

Hesitation on the other end. Heavy sigh. "You might be right. But for now we're going where the players are. I'll let you know if that changes."

Jake hung up and thought for a moment. He didn't have to play by their rules anymore. Maybe he should just scoot off somewhere. Change the plan to suit him.

In the bunk above, Anna's snoring had calmed. Must have rolled to her side. He looked at the SAT phone in the near darkness and wondered if he should call Colonel Reed. No. He was too pissed off at the man. He'd probably go off on him and wake Anna.

Instead, he got up and went to the door. The train rocked gently back and forth as he turned to look at Anna sleeping in the upper berth. Then he slipped out the door and locked it behind him. He considered going for a drink, but the bar would be closed by now. Maybe he needed a drink.

Needed to understand what was going on. Perhaps he should tell Anna what he had discovered. No. She shouldn't know at this time. His discovery could make this case even more dangerous, for greed had always brought out the worst in people.

Jake found himself wandering down the aisle, shifting with the rock and roll of the train. As he came back down toward his berth, he noticed the door next to his cracked slightly and then Kjersti appeared before him, wearing only a long shirt that barely covered her bottom. She nodded her head for him to come inside, which he did.

What the hell was he doing? He was with Anna, but now he found himself in a sleeper car in Sweden with a beautiful intelligence officer from Norway. He couldn't say he wasn't turned on by her—she was as hot as they came—and he had already caught a quick glimpse of her breasts as she woke in the chopper on Spitsbergen. In fact, she and Anna were so similar in physique they could have easily passed for twins. But something had pulled he and Anna apart over the past few months. The drinking had been part of it, he was sure, but there was more. Her work had become a problem, making her take sleeping pills just to be able to get enough rest to function the next day. So was her taking of pills any different from his drinking?

He glanced between the drawn curtains at the countryside. But they were so close to the ocean, all he saw was the lights of a large ship in the distance.

"What's keeping you awake?" Kjersti asked.

Jake turned to see her sitting on the lower bunk, her bare legs crossed, shoving her shirt even higher on her thighs. She wasn't leaving much to the imagination. And Jake had always had a vivid imagination. It must have been more chilly than he thought in the sleeper car, because her nipples were as hard as that metal box in the other compartment.

"I don't know," Jake said. "How 'bout you?"

"Everything. Nothing." She smiled at him and turned her eyes away coyly.

Jake moved and leaned against the bathroom door. "What's the matter?"

"I'm just waiting for the Swedish police to haul us off."

"Not gonna happen." Jake explained how his unnamed friends had made sure that nobody was looking for them.

"Wow. You do have friends in high places. Anna said you were well connected." Her eyes went from his eyes to his groin area and then back again. "What's going on in Oslo?"

He wasn't sure how much to open up to her. "Well, our scientists are on the way. Hopefully they'll get there before us and we can get rid of this damn box. Part of me wished we had just left it up in the Arctic. But I know that someone would have gone for it and found it. If the money is right, or the ideology, then almost anything is possible."

She uncrossed her legs and Jake could see she was a natural blonde. Moving to the edge of the bed, she stretched her legs out toward him. "Can we stop this?" she asked breathlessly.

"Stop what?"

"This pretense. This playing around the issue. This cat and mouse game. I need a man, and you are all man. Just fuck me and do it fast. I am so hot for you."

"What about Anna?"

"God. If she was here, I'd do the both of you. I'm not

trying to steal you from her. I just want your cock. Just tonight." She pulled the shirt over her head, exposing a perfectly naked body.

Jesus, was he being tested now or what? She was going to finish with or without him, as she played with her breasts with one hand and put the other between her legs.

Unsure what to do, Jake heard movement out in the hallway. Since the policeman incident, Jake had armed himself with one of the 9mm handguns. He thought about pulling it now, but instead went to the door and peered through the peep hole. Nothing.

"What's up?" Kjersti said. She had gotten out of the bed and now stood behind Jake, her bare breasts pressing against his back. "I was hoping something was." She reached around to the front of his pants and he turned away from her.

"Something is going on," Jake whispered. "I'm sure of it. Someone is checking compartments down on the end, working their way this way. Get dressed."

Disappointed, Kjersti did as he said while he watched through the door peep. Nobody was in view yet. But someone had a pass key and was checking each compart-ment. He was stuck. He couldn't go next door to Anna to warn her or they would see him.

Quietly, he unlocked the door.

"You have a small mirror in your purse?" Jake asked her.

Without answering, she produced a small round mirror, which Jake used to check the hallway. Two men. Down the end of the sleeper compartment. One man quietly entered a room, while the other kept watch on the hallway, switching his gaze from one end to the other, a pistol in his hand. Jake closed the door quietly and told Kjersti what was happening.

"Are they police?" she asked him in a whisper.

"No. They aren't announcing themselves. They're looking for us, though. Have to be." Jake thought about the box in his compartment, stuffed in his backpack. And Anna in her pill-induced state would not hear them enter.

They had just a few minutes to come up with a plan. The men were getting closer. Based on their progress and their pattern, they would check Jake's room first. He pulled his gun and handed it to Kjersti. Then they listened and waited.

Just as the first man opened Jake's door, he opened Kjersti's door and rushed the men, pushing one man into the other and the three of them crashing into Jake's compartment. In the chaos, the man dropped his gun and flailed at Jake.

Kjersti followed the scuffling men, Jake's gun pointed at all three of them.

Jake smashed his fist into the gunman's face, knocking him out, his body going limp. By now the man with the pass key had recovered to his knees and pushed his hand at Jake, catching him on his right side and bringing a sharp pain.

A knife.

Standing a few feet apart, the man made another lunge for Jake when he suddenly dropped to the floor at Jake's feet, a knife sticking out of the side of his neck. Jake thrust his foot into the man's face, sending him crashing backwards into the outer wall.

With quickness now, Jake and Kjersti pushed the knocked out man into the compartment and closed the door. His adrenalin raced through his body. The man against the outside wall spasmed in concert with the spurting blood from his neck. Jake swiftly pulled a plastic bag from the garbage can and wrapped it over the head of the stabbed man to contain some of the blood, then pulled the knife out of his neck and wiped it on the guy's shirt. But the room was a mess, with blood all over the place.

Anna, still in a daze, rolled to her side. "Jake, what's going on? Who are they?"

"That's what I plan on finding out. You two get the bags and put them in Kjersti's room. Stay there while I clean up this mess and find out what this asshole knows."

They both did what he said within a couple of minutes. Kjersti stepped back in and handed Jake his gun, which he shoved into the holster under his arm.

Alone now, Jake sat on the bed and thought it through—figuring out the approach he would take with this man.

First, he bound the man's hands behind his back and his feet together, then strapped a line from his hands to his feet. He shoved a wash cloth in the man's mouth. Then Jake clicked on the overhead light, found two towels in the bathroom, wet them down and soaked up the blood. It took many trips back and forth to the narrow shower, washing out the towels and soaking again until the majority of the blood was gone.

When the bound man started to stir, Jake hurried and pulled identification from each of the men. He read the passports and driver's licenses; both men were from Stockholm. He turned off the light, leaving the room lit only by a small reading lamp on the lower bunk.

The man's eyes opened and gazed up at Jake, who loomed over him. "Wakie wakie time, motherfucker,"

Jake whispered loudly.

Grunting something through the rag, the man tensed his muscles against the restraints. He was strong, but Jake had him bound tight.

"This can go one of two ways," Jake said. "You tell me what I want to know, or you die like your friend there."

The man twisted his body and saw his friend's head in a blood-splattered plastic bag with more dark blood soaking down the man's clothes.

"You understand your situation?"

The man nodded his head.

Jake pulled the rag from the guy's mouth and said, "Good. Now. . .who sent you?"

"Fuck you!" he said. Too loudly.

Jake punched him in the sternum, taking his breath away, and shoved the rag back in his mouth. The man gasped for air and finally settled down.

"That wasn't very nice," Jake said. "I asked you a simple question and you say that to me. What happens when we get to more difficult questions?"

The guy's eyes shifted wildly at Jake. He wanted to kill him, Jake knew that much. Good. The feeling was mutual.

"Answer my question," Jake said, and then took the rag out of his mouth again.

"We were looking to rob some people," he finally muttered, his English perfect.

"Come on. The couple down on the end have a shitload of money and the woman more jewelry than a movie star. You have no bag of goodies collected. You were looking for someone. And I'm guessing that was me."

The man glowered at Jake but said nothing.

"Okay." Jake shoved the rag in and then rolled the man to his stomach. He found a point under the man's right ear and applied pressure, bringing excruciating pain to the man. He struggled beneath him until Jake let go. As the guy relaxed, Jake knuckle struck him in the right kidney, making him gasp for air.

While the man squirmed in pain, Jake thought about their current route and situation. The train wouldn't stop for another hour, until they reached the port city of Gavle, Sweden. Then they would have another three hours until Falun. Plenty of time.

"We've got plenty of time before your friend starts to smell," Jake said. "Now you will tell me who sent you and why. The body can only take so much pain, and I can deliver more than you can handle. I'll guarantee you that much."

Jake went from pressure point to pressure point, bringing just enough pain, but not enough to make the man pass out. He pulled the man's pants down and even threatened to cut the man's balls off, poking the tip of the knife that had taken his friend's life into his scrotum. That got him. Always did. Every man thought they would rather die than lose their balls or penis. This guy held out a little longer, until Jake found a glass coke bottle and shoved it up the man's ass and said he'd break it off inside him if he didn't talk. That worked.

The bound man nodded his head, so Jake pulled the rag from the guy's mouth and waited.

"Some Russian guy," the man forced out.

"And you don't know his name? Hard to believe."

Hesitation, and then, "Goes by the name of Oberon."

Jake guessed that much. So Victor Petrova had sent his

men to get the box before Jake could turn it over to Colonel Reed in Oslo. He also had to assume that Petrova had sent the men in the chopper in Spitsbergen. But how in the hell had they found them on the train. That was disturbing. Jake would have to work that out in his mind. But first. . .

There was a light knock on the door. Jake got up and looked through the peep at Kjersti before opening it.

"Everything all right?" she asked, her eyes catching a glimpse of the man on the floor. He still had his pants down around his ankles, the coke bottle sticking out of his butt.

"Just great. We're getting to know each other."

"I see that."

"It's not what you think," Jake whispered.

"Never is. We're about ten minutes out of Gavle."

Jake checked his watch. "Already?"

"Time flies when you're having fun."

"Right. It's a five minute stop. Lock yourself in your room. Keep your eyes open. They could have a back-up team."

She nodded compliance and left.

Jake stuffed the rag into the man's mouth until they passed through Gavle. Then he had a longer talk with the man, getting as much information as possible. When he was done, Jake was sure the punk had given up everything he knew. He ripped the coke out of the guy's butt, pulled up his pants, and punched him in the left kidney just for the hell of it. Then Jake shoved some of Anna's sleeping pills down the guy, followed by the rag, and made sure his bindings were nice and tight before leaving him with his dead friend.

He locked the door behind him and crossed the hall to Kjersti's room. Anna was asleep again on the upper bunk. Jake took off his leather jacket and went to the window, looking out through the curtains. He thought about being in that room a while ago, with Kjersti naked and waiting for him to make love to him. The situation had gone from a moment of sensuality to a man dying and another having to be persuaded to talk. The contrast was not lost on him.

Suddenly, Kjersti gasped behind him.

Jake turned and saw horror in Kjersti's eyes. "What's the matter?" he asked her.

She pointed at his side. Jake looked down and saw that blood had drenched his T-shirt, soaking out from a slice in his side. The man's knife had caught him, but only now did the pain start to come. His side ached and Kjersti pulled away the shirt to check on the wound. He had lost a lot of blood, and that loss made his head light, his knees almost buckling beneath him. Kjersti helped Jake to the lower bunk and went to work patching him up.

CHAPTER 20

Oslo, Norway

The four of them made an odd group. Jimmy McLean was a tall man in his thirties, a Scotsman with an no-nonsense attitude to life and his work with MI6. Serious. His colleague couldn't have been in greater contrast. Velda Crane was a hip-height voluptuous woman, with a fun-loving disposition. Yet, Toni quickly realized that she also had a serious side to her. Then there was Colonel Reed, the gray-haired uncle figure, at times serious and other times his eyes would wander disturbingly at Velda's overflowing breasts. He probably would have looked at Toni's as well if she hadn't been wearing discreet clothing. Then there was the quiet Norwegian Intelligence Service officer, Thom Hagen. Toni had no way of knowing what he was think-ing, if he had a thought. The man was stereotypically stoic. And how would Toni describe herself at this point in her life? That was the problem. She had no idea. Although she had been married only a few months, she had also only seen her husband a few weeks during that time. She couldn't control her husband's overseas assignments any more than she could control her own.

The five of them had gone to the MI6 hotel, starting out in the bar, and not being able to talk freely, had retreated to Jimmy McLean's room. They had talked for hours over drinks, trying their best to understand everything that had happened and everything they needed to accomplish in the future. The facts? Jake Adams had found a metal box that the old Soviet guard had lost in the Arctic. A box containing one of the most deadly flu viruses to ever spread throughout the world. A pandemic virus modified in some way. But to what end? And now Jake was to deliver the box to scientists that were currently somewhere over the Atlantic on their way to Oslo.

She watched as the other four of them bantered about the room, finishing off all the alcohol from the mini-bar. Velda had already raided the little bottles from her own room, but now they were dangerously low and in fact running out. That was good. Toni hadn't gotten much sleep on the flight over the pond, barely slept the night before in the colonel's room, and it was well past two in the morning. She was getting too old for this type of late night.

Toni's secure cell phone went off and she picked up, moving into the bathroom. She recognized the number as that from the Network.

"Yeah."

"Is that any way to talk to the governor of the American Intelligence Network?"

"Sir. It's zero two twenty here and I feel like I'm babysitting." She told Kurt Jenkins about how they had caught up with the two MI6 officers, and how the three agencies were now working together.

"How's the NIS handling this?" Jenkins asked her.

"Just the one officer. An odd fellow."

"There's also the woman with Jake," he reminded her.

"Well, we haven't met yet. But so far I'm not that impressed."

"They're working in the background, providing us some great intel and helping keep Jake out of trouble. Which reminds me. . ." He stopped and the line went dead for a second.

Toni glanced around the bathroom, noticing that Jimmy McLean kept a low profile. Tooth brush and paste and razor and small can of shaving cream. Speed stick. That was it.

Jenkins came back on the line. "Sorry about that, Toni. Had to deal with something. What was I saying?"

"Something about Jake."

"Right. He'll arrive in Mora, Sweden at zero eight forty by train."

"How far is that from here?"

Jenkins asked the question to someone on his end and came back. "About two hundred kilometers by air. Longer by road."

"How's Jake traveling?" she asked.

"No idea. He wouldn't say."

She smiled. That sounded like the Jake she knew. "Let me guess. He doesn't want to get into Oslo and sit around waiting for the scientists."

"Exactly."

She couldn't blame him. With a deadly virus like that, she was surprised he had even gotten on a train. "What's the ETA on the scientists?"

Jenkins hesitated as if he was asking the question, but he never left the line. "Be there by noon. They stopped off in Iceland to refuel."

Toni calculated how long it would take Jake to drive two hundred fifty to three hundred kilometers. Depending on the roads and traffic. Never. There was no way he would drive the virus to them. He had another plan. She was sure of that.

The Network governor broke her thoughts. "Do you have any idea what that little madman is up to now?"

"Jake?"

"No. Victor Petrova."

"No. We think he's in Oslo still, but can't verify that. We suspect he'll strike when Jake gets close. We plan on checking out of our hotel this morning and moving out toward the airport."

"Good idea. The scientists will be landing on the Royal Norwegian Air Force Station at Gardermoen, just across the runway from the Oslo Airport."

"I just landed there yesterday."

"That's right."

What the hell was the matter with him? "Are you all right? Sounds like you're having a stroke."

"No. I mean yes. I'm fine. I just can't let this virus get into the wrong hands. Not under my watch."

Now that was the man she knew. "Don't worry," Toni said. "Not gonna happen as long as I'm around." And Jake, she thought.

They both hung up at the same time and she went back out into the hotel room. She'd have to split up this slumber party in a hurry. She needed them fresh by noon.

♦

Victor Petrova woke to the sound of his cell phone playing Tchaikovsky's Dance of the Sugar Plum Fairy. He was
staying in the most expensive hotel in Oslo, registered
under the name Vladislav Petrenko, his newest alias. He
rolled over in the darkness and waited for the song to
recycle. He loved the Nutcracker, watching all those lithe
people jumping around in tights. He imagined them now.

Finally he picked up the phone. "Yes," he said, and then
listened carefully to the man speaking English, the only
common language he had with some of his men. He was
expecting good news from Sweden.

But the man on the other end didn't have good news.

"What do you mean missing? You're their back up
crew," he reminded the man. "Find them. You're talking
about two women and a drunk."

He listened longer now to excuses, wanting nothing
more than to reach through the phone and grab this man
by the throat. He hated working with the Swedes. They
had a damn excuse for everything.

"Just do your damn job or I'll send someone to do it for
you." He meant do them as well, and the man would
understand without him actually saying it. Then Victor
slapped his phone shut and set it on the nightstand. He
knew he should have used Russians. They were so condi-
tioned to having nothing, they rarely complained. At least
those who had worked in the government.

Maybe he had underestimated Jake Adams. No. The
game was early and he had a lot of moves. After all, he
had found out the other players, played the old colonel

like a pawn, and would soon take their queen. Not long for mate and one step closer to checkmate. He rolled over in his bed and went back to sleep almost immediately.

CHAPTER 21

They had locked up Jake and Anna's room, not wanting some wandering drunk or porter or both stumbling onto a dead man and another drugged and tied up like a pig. But Jake was disturbed by the men finding them on the train. Who knew they were there? The Network. The Norwegian Intelligence Service. Perhaps Interpol, if Anna had called in their position and travel plans. But he doubted that. As far as he knew, and she had said, her last call had been from Spitsbergen, where she had told them about the virus, against Jake's better wishes. Yet, they were traveling in Sweden, Victor Petrova's new home base. He could have had eyes and ears on all transportation routes, heard recently about the police officer on the train, the abandoned rental car, and done the math. After all, Petrova was a bona fide genius with years of experience in the field and behind the scenes. That wasn't it, though, and he knew it. Regardless of how they had been found, the fact was that they had been discovered, and they would have to do something to change that fact.

They had two choices. They could split up or change their transportation again.

The train ended in Mora, Sweden. They could take a bus, not a good choice, catch a commuter flight, a possibility, or go by car. Not long to decide, either. They were a half hour out of Falun, a ten minute stop in a former mining town, before an hour and a half final leg to Mora. Maybe their best choice would come to him.

The three of them were together in the sleeper car next door to the one with the two men who had attacked them. It would be difficult now to explain this to the Swedish police, especially if they were able to tie them to what had happened to their man farther north.

Anna was sleeping soundly on the upper bunk, and Jake and Kjersti shared the lower bunk—Jake sitting up on the end waiting for a possible second team to attack, while Kjersti lay in a fetal position taking up the rest of the bed. But Jake could tell she wasn't getting much rest. She was tossing and turning for the past few hours, occasionally kicking him in the process.

Now she sat up onto her side and stared at Jake. "What time is it?" Kjersti whispered to him.

"Almost six thirty."

"Should be to Falun soon," she said, pulling herself from under the covers and sitting closer to him.

"Yeah. I'm thinking we should get off there."

"They have camera security on the train," she said. "When they find our friends next door, they'll review the digital files and see we were involved."

"I know. But if we get off at Falun that'll give us at least an hour and a half head start before we have every law enforcement agency in Sweden after us."

She ran her fingers through her hair, pushing it away from her eyes. "Not to mention the bad guys. I've been laying here trying to figure out how they found us."

"I know how." Jake reached down to his backpack and found his SAT phone. The one Colonel Reed had given him to use. "With this." He turned the phone in his hand.

"I thought you disabled the GPS by turning it off," she said, her face concerned.

"No. This is a newer version. Doesn't have to be on to track the GPS chip inside."

"But why? Why not throw the SAT phone away a long time ago if you knew this?"

"I needed to know who our friends were and who might come for us."

He could tell her mind was reeling, trying to understand Jake's actions.

She said, "You knew they'd come for us. You expected it."

"Yes."

"And what does that tell you?"

"That depends. It depends on whether my good friend Colonel Reed had been tracking us or if Victor Petrova had been."

"What's your gut say?"

That was what had kept Jake awake the past few hours, even more than the possibility of a second crew coming for them. He didn't entirely believe that his old commander, a former Air Force colonel and CIA and Network officer, had actually sold him out. Couldn't believe that. The more he thought about the box, the purported virus within, and the colonel's reaction to Jake discovering it, the more Jake guessed Colonel Reed had not fixed their location and given it to Petrova. After all, the colonel knew that Jake would know about the GPS tracking function, active or passive.

Jake finally said, "My gut tells me that Petrova provided the SAT phone to Colonel Reed to keep track of my progress. He planned all along to cut us off at the pass. Not let us get to Oslo with the virus. He assumed I wouldn't take the biohazard on a commercial flight, and would do everything within my power to get it to my government. Which meant I would either drive or take a train. Perhaps a boat, but that would have been ruled out because of the time and distance. He knew that we could either pick up a train in Bodo, Norway or Gallivare, Sweden. They probably had a team waiting at both, and once they saw we had flown to Tromso and were driving south into Sweden, they shifted their people this way."

"Makes sense," Kjersti said. "But if they were waiting for us in Gallivare, what took them so long to come for us?"

"I don't know. Maybe they were under orders at that time to just follow. Or perhaps they figured we weren't going anywhere. Remember, we could have switched trains last night in Gavle and gone to Stockholm. They probably didn't want us to get lost in the transfer."

"But they still had the GPS."

"Right," Jake said. "Which I could have sent on a ride by itself on the Stockholm train. Or, left it on this train and jumped onto Stockholm without the SAT phone. Who knows why they came when they did." Well, Jake had a better idea, knowing what was really in the metal box he had found at the Svalbard MiG crash site. "Time to get going."

He got up and shook Anna awake. She reluctantly got up rubbing her eyes and yawning.

"Where we going?" Anna asked.

Jake quickly explained that they would be getting off at Falun instead of going all the way to Mora, and what they would do once off the train. They packed all of their carry-on into their backpacks, their only luggage, and headed out of the sleeper, planning on jumping off the train as soon as they stopped. Overhead, a soft woman's voice said they would be in Falun in five minutes.

Outside, Jake opened the compartment next door and saw that the man was still sleeping on the floor, but the berthing area smelled like iron from the dried blood. He guessed it would soon start smelling like rotting flesh.

The three of them split up and made their way through the dining car and into the regular seating area, taking seats separate.

The train stopped in Falun and the three of them got off and walked slowly with the others toward the terminal.

Jake would have to find them transportation. But first he had to make sure they were not being followed. He would stop and change directions. Stop and pretend to tie his shoes. Watch behind him in glass reflections. Finally, as the train pulled away behind them, he was certain they had not been followed off the train.

Now inside the terminal, he observed people coming from the small parking area, spotted a possible target, and followed her as she went to the ticket booth. The woman, in her early thirties, bought a ticket for Stockholm, which would leave in half an hour. Perfect. As the woman turned with her ticket, she bumped into Jake, who excused himself, and caught the attention of Anna across the terminal.

The woman also excused herself, smiled and walked away.

The ticket agent asked Jake where he would like to go, but Jake felt for his wallet and said he had left it in his car. Jake walked around the corner and turned to see the action.

First, Anna walked up to the woman, discreetly showed her Interpol credentials, and had the woman move over to the side wall. The woman showed Anna her identification, her ticket and looked quite concerned. Then the woman handed her purse to Anna, who made a quick pass through the purse and handed it back to the woman. Anna smiled and waved the woman away. The entire encounter lasted perhaps two minutes. Maybe less.

Kjersti now walked through the terminal carrying Anna's pack and her own. She caught up with Jake at the doors but didn't acknowledge him. Moments later, Jake walked out to the parking lot, followed back a ways by Kjersti, with Anna trailing even farther back.

Jake stopped at the rear end of a new silver metallic Saab 9-3 sport sedan. Kjersti came and set the bags next to Jake, and then Anna showed up and opened the trunk remotely.

"Nice ride," Anna said. "When do you suppose she'll realize her keys are gone?"

Jake loaded the bags into the back. "Four days from now. Around the time she tries to open her car after returning from the big city."

"That's when she returns?" Kjersti asked.

"Yep."

"Who's driving?" Anna asked.

Jake took the keys from Anna. "It's only a short drive.

Five or six hours. I'll drive, you navigate. Kjersti can sleep in the back."

Nobody complained. They all just piled in and drove off like it was their car.

Inside the car, Kjersti asked, "What you do with the SAT phone?"

"Set it into the woman's open bag when I bumped into her," Jake said. "It'll soon be on its way to Stockholm. Might fool them for a while." In retrospect, he probably should have simply hidden it on the train and let it go to their original destination, Mora. But he didn't want the men and the phone found at the same time. Besides, it was possible they could have changed directions.

Jake drove south toward Borlange. There was no good route from Falun to Oslo. Most roads led to Stockholm, but there were smaller roads that wound through little villages to the west, and Jake would have to decide randomly which one to take. About fifteen miles down the road, after passing through Borlange, there was a sign for the airport. He pulled over onto a side street and stopped the car, the engine still running.

"What's going on?" Anna asked him.

He turned off the engine and looked into the rearview mirror at Kjersti. She looked perplexed also.

"We need to split up," Jake said.

Kjersti said, "Why?"

Time for him to come clean and explain what was going on. "It would be safer for us to split up. The two of you should fly to Oslo, go to NIS headquarters and explain what has happened."

"What about the virus?" Anna asked. "We have a stake in this also." Meaning Interpol.

"Truthfully," Jake said. "Not your division."

"A biohazard, a bio-weapon. That is my business," Anna reminded Jake.

Jake reached into his pocket and retrieved an item that had fallen from the metal box when it had been shot in Finland. Between his thumb and forefinger, he lifted it to show them. The early morning light shone onto the oval-shaped one carat gemstone, changing it quickly from a brilliant burgundy-red to a dark shade of green.

"What is that?" Kjersti asked, scooting forward to get a closer look.

Anna tried to take it from Jake, but he pulled his hand back.

"This, my friends, is the flu virus everyone wants to kill for," he said, closing the gem into his hand.

"A ruby?" Kjersti said. "We went all the way to the Arctic for a ruby?"

"It's not a ruby," Jake said. "Watch this." He opened his hand and the gem was a beautiful red and turned swiftly to the dark green again. See that change in color?"

"What kind of trick is that?" Kjersti asked.

"Anna knows," he said. "Remember that jewelry store we visited in Zurich?"

Anna thought and then nodded her head. "Yes. But I don't remember the name of it."

Jake handed the gem to Anna, who played with the color change for a moment and then handed it back to Kjersti, who did the same thing.

"That's amazing," Kjersti said, handing it back to Jake. "What is it?"

"It's called Alexandrite," he said. "Named after the Russian Czar, Alexander the second. It's one of the world's rarest gems. This one, because of the color clarity, brilliance and cut, is probably worth about seven to eight grand."

"You're kidding," Anna said, her interest suddenly more intense.

"Wait a minute," Kjersti said. "How did you get it from the box?"

Jake didn't answer. Instead, he got out and went to the trunk, returning with his backpack. He pulled the metal box from inside and showed them the hole in the side, closed off now with the broken pencil. "A bullet strike in Finland," he said. "The lead is still inside here. This one popped out before I plugged the hole, but I could see that the box was full of them." He put the box back in the backpack and zipped it shut.

"Let me get this right," Kjersti started. "The old Soviets filled this box with these Alexandrite gems, sealed it, marked the box as biohazard, and flew it out of the country in nineteen eighty-six on a MiG, which proceeds to crash on Spitsbergen Island. The Soviets send a crew of KGB to find it. The Americans send the CIA after it, thinking it's something it isn't. They all die and are lost under the snow for more than twenty years. Until we go up there and find it."

Anna twisted her head to the side, her version of misunderstanding. "But why wait so long to go back after it? Especially if it's not the virus, but precious gems."

That had also bothered Jake. "I believe the pilot thought the mission was something else. He thought he was doing something for his country. Perhaps the KGB officers were equally motivated. They were sent to simply clean house, destroy any evidence of their mission."

"Which was?" Kjersti asked him.

Jake had spent much of the trip down the Swedish countryside wondering that as well. But he had a few theories, based on who was involved. "I think the old Soviet guard were flexing their muscles. Gorbachav was on his way to Iceland for a summit with Reagan. Any deal, they felt, would weaken the Soviet Union. They thought Gorby was giving away too much of the Soviet state. As it turned out, the old guard was right. They were about to lose power. Anyway, I think that our good friend Victor Petrova, who was at the time in charge of the Disinformation Department in the KGB's First Chief Directorate, came up with the ruse. Petrova must have somehow stolen the Alexandrite stones from the mines in Russia's Ural Mountains, had them cut, and then came up with a way to ship them out of the country by flying them out on a MiG. By then the Alexandrite mines were almost dried up. They're still finding some there, but in much lower quantities and size."

"Wait a minute," Anna said. "Why doesn't Petrova go back for the gems in the past twenty years?"

"Why send you now and not his own men?" Kjersti chimed in.

Jake had already thought this through as well. "First, he had no idea where the MiG had crashed on Spitsbergen. We checked on that. They only had a general idea of the crash site back then. The KGB found a local to help them find the crash. That man went missing at the same time, and we suspect the KGB killed him. Our two men found them, but were not able to call in their position before being killed. They had one of the old SAT phones back then, and coverage at the time was only a fraction of what it is today. And you saw I was having a problem with my current SAT phone because of the Boreal Activity. Records show they had similar activity back in nineteen eighty-six. So, if our guys couldn't relay the crash site position, the KGB must have been similarly hampered."

"So Petrova thought he had lost the gems forever," Anna said.

Jake nodded. "Until recently. And by now Petrova is calling himself Oberon and a dozen other names, running one of the largest crime syndicates in Northern Europe."

"Sill," Kjersti said. "Why have you go to Svalbard to get it for him?"

"Ah. That's the mad genius at work. He's the king of disinformation. The master of manipulation. He's still being watched by the SVR. If he goes to Svalbard or sends his own men, they might realize he's not going there for vacation."

"I'm still confused about the original MiG mission," Kjersti said.

"Me too," Anna said.

"The old Soviet guard thought that Victor Petrova was shipping the modified flu virus to Iceland during the Reykjavik summit between Reagan and Gorbachav. They were going to release the virus in the capital a day before the summit. It would quickly spread to all the major players, killing both Reagan and Gorbachav and setting back any peace process decades. The Soviet Union would remain strong."

"How high did the plot go?" Kjersti asked.

Jake smiled. "It was limited to an Air Force general and a few Politburo members, who all ended up dying mysteriously in late October of eighty-six."

"Compliments of Petrova?" Anna asked.

"Right. So Petrova is the only one who knows about this through the years. We believe the pilot never knew either mission, nobody at the KGB knew, nor did anyone else in the government. Petrova floated the cover story—the man had tried to defect with a MiG and crashed in the Arctic."

Anna shook her head side to side. "That's amazing. But what about Colonel Reed? How was he involved?"

The jury was still out on the colonel, but Jake would find out that for sure soon. "I don't know," he said. "I'll have to ask him that question."

Kjersti asked the obvious question. "What now?"

Jake shrugged. "Like I said. We split up. The two of you head to Oslo. The NIS and Network are working together there. Meet up with them across the runway at Gardermoen Air Station. The scientists will be there, but of course they aren't needed now. Explain what happened, just as I've told you."

Anna put her hand on Jake's leg. "I don't want you to leave me, Jake."

"Listen," he said, his eyes concentrating on Anna. "There's no need for you to get shot at again. Petrova will stop at nothing to get this box of gems. I can't even imagine how much they're worth, assuming this box is full."

"What about you?" Anna asked, squeezing down on his leg, a tear coming to her left eye and rolling down her cheek.

He wiped away her tear. He can't remember her ever crying. She had always been as tough as steel.

"I'm not sure," Jake said. "I don't want you to know. Either of you. It's better if you don't know."

Jake got out and put his backpack in the trunk. He

thought about all the guns and ammo he had inside the packs, and decided he would have to keep them. The two of them couldn't fly with them. He slammed the trunk and got back behind the wheel.

"We're going with you," Anna said defiantly.

He turned to Kjersti.

"That's right."

He didn't say a word. He simply shook his head and drove away. In a couple miles he turned into the airport, which was a small, regional terminal with commuter flights to Stockholm, Goteborg and a few other smaller Swedish cities. Jake pulled to the curb but kept the engine running.

"We're going with you, Jake," Anna reiterated.

"No, you're not. Get the fuck out. Now!" He had never raised his voice to Anna. Not even during the last three months while he was drinking himself to sleep each night. They had argued quietly and respectfully. Part of that was due to not seeing each other much, Jake knew. The anger in his voice even surprised him somewhat. But he had to at least appear pissed off.

"You have no standing at all," Anna said to him, her jaw tight. But another tear appeared now.

Kjersti was quiet in the back, her disposition uncertain.

"You too," Jake yelled, his eyes cast on Kjersti in the rearview mirror. "Get the fuck out."

Reluctantly, they both opened their doors almost simultaneously. Kjersti slammed her door and crossed her arms over her chest.

Anna leaned back inside the car for a second, tears in both eyes. "Why are you being such a dick?"

"Maybe this is me without alcohol," he said. "Close the

door." He felt like a monster dick now.

She hesitated. "I'll wait for you in Oslo. The same hotel."

Jake gazed straight ahead. "Are you sure you still want me?"

"Now you're being a royal dick." She slammed the door as hard as she could and went away toward the terminal.

As he drove away, his eyes drifted to the right and he saw Kjersti with her arm around Anna. Maybe he had been too rough on them. But he didn't think so. He knew Victor Petrova. The man was relentless and would not stop coming until Jake stopped him. And that's exactly what he planned to do.

CHAPTER 22

Victor Petrova, still in his Elvis pajamas in the posh hotel, slammed his cell phone shut and threw it over his shoulder onto the bed. He had just gotten off the phone with one of his men in Sweden, who had explained what happened to he and his partner on the train the night before. Somehow Jake Adams and the two women had gotten the best of them, killing one of them and beating and humiliating the other. Shoved a Coke bottle up his ass? Jake had gone off the edge farther than he had realized. And the second crew waiting for them at the Mora train station had monitored everyone coming off the train, not seeing the women or Jake.

He scurried back to get his phone and punched in a number, then waited for his people at his Norwegian mountain estate to answer.

"Yes, sir?" came the response on the other end.

"Where do you have our friends right now?" Petrova asked.

"You must be a mind reader, sir. I was just going to call

you. We have them almost to Stockholm. Looks like on a train, according to the couple of stops they made."

Petrova did the math in his head and said, "Almost two hours since they changed direction, and you were just going to call me now?" He'd pay the price for that. But not right now.

Let's see. They weren't in Mora and the GPS had them near Stockholm. Jake Adams was better than he thought. They got off the train in Falun and somehow put the SAT phone on the Stockholm train. Good idea. Especially with incompetent fools working for him, those who couldn't see a feign move to save their ass.

His man on the other end didn't even try to explain his actions, he just remained silent. His best move in weeks, Petrova was sure.

"Forget tracking the SAT phone," Petrova ordered. "Get the word out to all our friends. Operation Huldra."

"Yes, sir. Anything else?"

Yes. You're ugly. "No. What else is there?" He snapped his phone shut. Time for a bath and a drive. He guessed Huldra wouldn't come for another few hours, perhaps a day. Jake Adams had forced his move much quicker, which meant he knew. He knew what was really in the box. Jake would now eschew any federal responsibility and come directly for him. He cackled with glee at that thought, stripping his silk Elvis pajamas from his body and shuffling to the bathroom, his naked pendulous structure sloshing side to side.

◆

Toni had barely slept all night, and now her cell phone

woke her, jarring her to her side. The room was still dark, but the clock read zero nine ten.

She checked the incoming number and said, "Yeah."

"You sound asleep." It was Kurt Jenkins calling from Camp Springs.

"I'm awake. What's up?"

"Our friends have changed directions. Looks like they switched trains in Falun, Sweden and are almost to Stockholm."

"Maybe they'll catch a flight from Stockholm to Oslo," Toni said, sitting up in bed and running a hand through her long, dark hair.

"With the virus?"

He had a point, she realized. "Something you're not telling me?"

Hesitation. "They found a man stabbed to death on the train when it came into Mora."

Her heart skipped a beat and then almost stopped. "Jake," she muttered.

"A Swede from Stockholm. Criminal background. Another man was found bound, gagged and drugged. Looks like someone worked the man over with great enthusiasm."

Now that sounded like the new Jake Adams. "You think that was Jake."

"I'm guessing. But whatever information this man had, Jake now has as well. Which probably sent him to Stockholm."

Toni got out of bed and peered out the window at a solemn, damp Oslo morning. The sun had risen, but the clouds and rain kept it hidden behind a shroud. She thought about Jake and how he would react under those circumstances. He had to know they were monitoring the SAT phone by GPS. In fact, he had counted on it. But he also must have guessed that someone else had tracked them the same way, and was trying to throw them off his track for a few hours—until they realized, like her, that he was nowhere near Stockholm. No, Jake had something else in mind. But why?

"You still there?" Jenkins asked.

"Yeah. The scientists set down in a couple hours?"

"Right. You'll meet them."

She didn't think so. "I need to think this over. Jake isn't in Stockholm. He probably got off the train in Falun, but they didn't change directions. They changed mode of transportation."

"How do you know?"

"Because that's what I would do. Someone had found them. Jake had to assume the only way was by the GPS SAT phone, so he dumped that onto the Stockholm train and found a car."

"You sure?"

"Yeah." But she had no idea where he was going.

"Will he still bring the virus to Oslo?" Jenkins asked, concerned.

Something had changed. But what? "Jake will do the right thing. You know that."

"I know. So I guess you get to the airport and wait for the scientists and Jake."

"I understand," she said. Not an actual promise. "Have you found Victor Petrova?"

"That was next," he said. "We believe he checked into the Grand Hotel on Karl Johans Gate."

"That's only a few blocks from here. What name's he

using this time?"

"Vladislav Petrenko."

"Keep it simple. Same initials."

"Right."

"I think I should stick with him. He doesn't know me. You can send someone from the embassy to meet Jake and the scientists. But I have a feeling Petrova is the key here. Better to keep an eye on him."

Heavy sigh on the other end. "You're right. I'm glad you're over there, Toni. All right. I'll make it happen."

"One more favor?"

"Shoot."

"Could you make sure our NIS friend, Thom Hagen, escorts our embassy folks to the meet?"

"Why?"

"He's a stiff and I don't trust him."

"No pulling punches with you, Toni. That's what I like about you."

They both hung up and Toni quickly went to her computer and scanned Victor Petrova's file one more time, making sure she knew everything there was to know about the man. Then she grabbed her things and went to check out of her room.

CHAPTER 23

Jake had mixed feelings as he had driven through the remote Swedish countryside, the trees lining the twisting road and broken only by fields of hay and well-kept farm houses. He had been too hard on Anna, he knew, but he also had no time to play games. He had to make up time and get to Mora as soon as possible. As it turned out he had gotten to the town just after the train had pulled into the station. When he saw the police arrive shortly after, he knew a porter had swept through and found the two men. Jake guessed the man he had questioned was a small-time criminal, but the police would suspect he was the victim this time and let the man go after a brief stop at the local hospital. That's what Jake was counting on anyway.

Since Jake had anticipated the cops bringing the man to the Mora hospital, he had gone there in advance and had found the two men waiting outside in the black Volvo.

He sat now in his acquired Saab and waited, spending the time looking over information on Victor Petrova on his laptop. He was even able to access the internet with the hospital's wireless network.

His phone buzzed in his pocket and he flipped it open. "Yeah."

"Where the hell are you?" It was Kurt Jenkins, the governor of American Intelligence.

"Stockholm," Jake said, his eyes still on the two douche bags in the Volvo across the parking lot.

"Ah, no. Some lady found the SAT phone in her purse and turned it over to the police in Stockholm. They traced the card to one of Victor Petrova's front companies."

"How'd you find out about that?"

"We've been intercepting all of their unsecured communications. It doesn't matter. Can you just tell me what the hell is going on? We understand you ran into a little trouble on the train."

"No big deal."

"You have the package?"

"Of course." Jake thought about telling Jenkins about the true contents, but that might keep him from helping him. And Jake could use his information.

"So, where are you?" he asked again.

"Have those scientists take a nap," Jake said. "Better yet, you might want to get them a room. This could take a while."

Hesitation. Silence.

Finally, Jenkins said, "You're going after Victor Petrova."

The man who had attacked them on the train suddenly appeared at the entrance to the hotel, looked around until the brain trusts in the Volvo flipped their lights on and off, catching his attention. Then he adjusted his pants, pulling them away from his buttocks, and wiggled down the side-walk like an old man. Coke bottle, Jake thought with a smile.

"Well," Jenkins said.

"Listen. I've gotta go. I'm going to be following three Nobel laureates. I'll get back to you with my plan as soon as I know it." With that he flipped the phone shut and cranked over the engine.

The three men in the Volvo were not hard to follow. In fact, he had a feeling he knew where they were going. Only time would tell if he was right.

They headed North immediately, but turned off onto a smaller country road in fifteen kilometers, heading west. An hour later they crossed a small frontier border station into Norway. Jake didn't get much more than a nod at the border from the disinterested old guard, and would have had a lot of explaining to do if they had looked in the trunk and found the guns and gems. Or even looked under his left arm, where his 9mm automatic hung in its holster. Especially without Anna or Kjersti pulling credentials.

Shortly after crossing into Norway, Jake's hunch about their direction was confirmed. He saw the signs for Hamar, Norway, 110 kilometers, and started to back off the Volvo. No need for them to entirely engrain the Saab in their mind. He knew where they were going.

While he drove the remote country road, Jake ran through his mind how he wanted to proceed. First, he would need to do a little house cleaning. He found an isolated area far from the nearest town and farm, pulling off on a tiny road that headed north. He drove for a while and parked the Saab on the side of the road. This road was nothing more than a logging access, but looked like the

Norwegians had not cut trees here in ten years or more. That was good. It meant they probably wouldn't cut again for twenty or thirty years.

He got out and went to the trunk. Found his handheld GPS, turned it on and took a reading of his location, and rendered the reading to his memory, speaking the numbers over and over in his mind until he would never forget it. Then he purged the location from the GPS memory.

Looking around, Jake saw what he was looking for—a rock with a large tree behind it. Swinging his backpack over his shoulder, he went to that spot and found a stick. He set the pack down. The ground was moist and mostly moss and lichen, which he ripped back like a thick blanket at the back side of the rock. Then, digging with the stick, he finally had a hole deep enough for the box. He set the box inside and covered it only with the thick moss. Satisfied with his work, he flipped the lighter pack over his shoulder and went back to the car.

Anything else, he thought. He would need the guns. No. Should be good. While he was there, he relieved himself on the side of the road, then took a bottle of water from the trunk before closing it. He got back into the car, turned around, and drove back toward the main road, running the GPS location through his mind again. Without all those millions in Alexandrite gems lingering around, he felt a lot better. Now he could go have a discussion with that little Russian troll and see why he had devised such an elaborate scheme involving Jake.

♦

Anna Schult was conflicted. She knew that her departure from Jake had not gone as smoothly as it could have, considering their abrupt split at the Borlange airport. She had fought back tears on the short flight to Stockholm, during the short layover there, and again during the one-hour flight from Stockholm to Oslo. Her emotions were all over the place, and that bothered her. Why couldn't she just get over it? Jake was always intense, especially when he was working on a case. And she had to cut him some slack, since he had also not had a drink in days. She could only imagine how that was affecting him.

Now, Anna and Kjersti Nilsen wandered along the concourse after just having gotten off the plane.

"Are you all right?" Kjersti asked her.

"Yeah."

"You're wondering about Jake."

Anna stopped against a concourse wall. "I know he thinks he can handle almost anything on his own. And he has in the past. You'd be amazed at the things I've seen him do, the adversity he's overcome so many times."

"But?"

"I'm afraid. Afraid he might go too far this time."

"Why do you say that?"

They started walking again, this time slower, at their pace and not that of commuters rushing for the baggage claim.

Anna said, "This colonel friend of his. They go way back. Decades. If he deceived Jake, for whatever reason, it will throw Jake into a. . .funk of introspection. He'll start to question everything. He might even start—" She stopped herself, not wanting to think those thoughts.

"Drinking?" Kjersti finished.

"Yeah." Her head looked toward the ground at the

strange pattern of ceramic tiles in front of her.

Kjersti took Anna's hand and said, "Jake will be fine. I've heard nothing but good things about him. He will always do the right thing."

That was true. Jake had always done the right thing, even if it wasn't popular or easy.

"Here we go," Kjersti said, her head nodding toward an approaching man.

The two of them stopped a few feet from the tall, well-dressed man who Kjersti introduced as Thom Hagen, an officer with the Norwegian Intelligence Service.

"Thom works mostly out of Oslo," Kjersti explained.

The man was nearly expressionless as Anna introduced herself. All he said was that he had a car just outside. He turned and led the way.

"A bit exuberant," Anna whispered to Kjersti, who held back a laugh.

They piled into a dark Volvo sedan, Anna in the back and Kjersti in the front passenger seat.

Kjersti said something in Norwegian to the driver.

"Hey. No fair," Anna said. "Don't make me pull out my Tyrolean."

Kjersti laughed. "I'm sorry. I just asked him how his wife and kids were."

In French, Anna said to Kjersti. "I thought he might be gay."

Hagen looked at Anna in the rearview mirror. Still no significant emotion. "I also speak French," he said in that language.

"I guessed that," Anna said. "Just seeing if I could pull a smile out of you." She waited and then mumbled, "Guess not."

"Changing the subject," Kjersti said to her colleague, "what's going on?"

He briefed the both of them as they drove from the civilian commercial side of Oslo airport to the Gardermoen Air Station across the runways.

"The American scientists are where?" Kjersti asked.

"The operations building."

Anna chimed in. "You mentioned an American Network officer was with Colonel Reed. Where are they?"

The NIS officer went through the secure gate flashing his ID, and then slowly drove toward the operations building.

Finally, he said, "You'll get briefed in a moment on the operation."

Anna leaned back in her seat. Dickhead. She guessed she and Kjersti could brief this guy a lot more informatively than the other way around, considering what Jake had told them just before he dropped them at the airport that morning. In fact, if anyone should be lead on this case it was Interpol.

They got to the operations building, parked, and piled out, the NIS man walking in front of them.

Kjersti slowed Anna with her hand and whispered. "I know you'd like to strangle him. But he has small children and a good wife."

"I feel sorry for them."

"He's a good guy," Kjersti informed her. "Just no personality."

"Remember what we discussed?" Anna said.

"I do. Jake still has the virus."

Anna smiled and mouthed the word 'thanks' as they got to the door.

Their backpacks were checked and then they were brought through a security door to a conference room, which consisted of a large wooden table with chairs around two sides. A large LCD screen was mounted on the wall at one end. The three of them took the only empty seats.

A tall black man, a U.S. Army colonel in woodland digital camo, stood at the head of the table. He introduced his team of scientists and then dimmed the lights, clicked a remote, and went into his briefing on the flu virus, possible modifications, and the projected results of exposure and dispersal. While he talked in the semi-darkness, Anna thought about what Jake had told them and shown them. She could stop all of this if she wanted, but then she guessed they would either not believe her or, perhaps worse, believe her and then stop helping them and Jake would be in trouble.

Next, the Army colonel sat down and their NIS escort stood and went to the head of the table. He sequenced the PowerPoint to another file and a photo of a man appeared.

"This is Victor Petrova," Hagen said. He went on to give background information about the man, including what he currently controlled in the criminal world. Even if the man was not trying to acquire and sell a deadly virus, and this was only about precious gems, this man had to be stopped. For who knew what he would buy with the money he got from the gems.

Hagen then went through a sequence of photos of men and women that were part of Petrova's organization.

"Hold it," Kjersti said. "Go back one."

The NIS officer did what she said, returning to the previous slide.

"He's dead," she said.

"Are you sure?" Hagen checked his notes.

"Dead certain. Anna stabbed him in the neck last night on the train."

A man and woman held back laughter across the table from them. They were a strange pair. A man at least six four, and a woman half his height, her head barely above the table. They were the only two the Army colonel had not introduced.

Anna raised her hands in protest. "Hey, he was trying to kill us."

Hagen scribbled something in his note pad and then continued with the PowerPoint show.

Another familiar face appeared and Kjersti stopped the NIS man again. "He was with the guy Anna killed."

"But he's alive?" Hagen asked.

"Kind of. Jake Adams interrogated him with great prejudice last night. He probably wished he was dead."

Anna squeezed down on Kjersti's leg.

"Yeah, he's alive," Kjersti added.

The NIS officer stopped and the large man across the table got up and took the remote from Hagen. He opened a new file, showing first a little man.

"For those of you who don't know, I'm Jimmy McLean with MI6," the man said, his Scottish accent flowing freely. "And that's my colleague, Velda Crane."

The little woman waved around the table.

"The man on the screen is a low-level Scottish thief named Gary Dixon. He's been an MI-5 informant for years. Velda and I were working undercover for MI-5 when we discovered something was going down in Norway. Dixon wouldn't tell us what, and we suspected that was because he really didn't know. But then we coordinated our efforts with the Americans and the Norwegians and also followed Dixon to Oslo. It was apparent that something was going down."

McLean went through a long sequence of photos, mostly of little people in Scotland and then from the last few days in Oslo.

Anna raised her hand and said, "What do they have to do with Victor Petrova?"

"They're all thick as thieves together," Jimmy explained. "We suspect Petrova will use these people to spread the virus around the world."

Kjersti broke in now. "Not to actually spread the virus, though. I'm guessing Petrova has some kind of monetary incentive—like international blackmail. He doesn't seem like a terrorist without a Euro symbol."

"Good point," Jimmy said. "We discussed that at great length last night and came to the same conclusion." He flipped to the next photo. "This is Colonel Reed, a former American Air Force officer and with the old CIA and the Network. He was hired by Petrova to collect the virus in the Arctic. Reed, in turn, hired this man." A photo of Jake Adams filled the screen.

Anna took a deep breath as she watched the photo of Jake. He was standing in Tiananmen Square in Beijing, China. He was so handsome, she thought.

"I'm sure most of you know of Jake Adams," Jimmy said. He went on to brief the others about Jake's career. When he was done, he said, "That pretty much brings us up to date. Oh, yeah." He went to the next screen and added, "This is Network officer Toni Contardo. She is running the operation here in Norway now; however, she is currently with Colonel Reed following Victor Petrova and will brief us by phone in a moment. But first we need to be briefed by the two of you." Jimmy McLean lay his right hand, palm up, out toward Anna and Kjersti.

When Anna saw Toni's picture, she couldn't believe it. Jake's former lover was running the op. A woman who had haunted her relationship with Jake for two years.

"You all right?" Kjersti asked.

"Yes. If fine. Could you brief them?"

Kjersti nodded and got up. While she ran through everything that had happened to the three of them over the past few days, Anna stared at the last picture that remained on the huge screen. Damn it. It had to be a beautiful photo of Toni also. Why couldn't it be one with the woman's hair all messed up?

CHAPTER 24

Travel by car was Jake's favorite form. He had near-complete control over his actions and was not dependent on others. It also allowed him to clear his mind and run everything through, including possible scenarios. Traveling alone was even more cleansing, since he wasn't required to keep up inane banter. It wasn't that he was sick of traveling with Anna and Kjersti. They were both great conversationalists and comfortable associates. Christ, what was the matter with him? Now he was thinking of Anna as an associate? She was much more than that. He knew he loved her, even though he had a hard time bringing the words to his lips first. Perhaps he should be more responsive and feeling. He even knew in his heart that he had been a royal pain in the ass the last few months. And why? Hell, he was no shrink. Didn't believe in them. If a man couldn't grow a set and straighten himself out, then he didn't deserve to take up space on this planet. Suck it up! That had always been his mantra. You drink too much; stop the damn drinking. You gain too much weight? Don't eat so damn much and get the hell off the sofa. Easy to think and easy to say, but not always that easy in practice, he knew. Maybe part of a man questioned if he should live anymore. What was the point? Did he have a purpose on Earth? Without a case to work over the past three months, Jake had fallen into that questioning mode. Wondering if he had anything else to give society. He was tired of playing the game of life. Exhausted by living life on the cold edge of reality. He didn't even want to consider how many people had died by his hands. And why? Because someone had determined them to be the enemy. Not someone. Society. But still. . .what kind of man loses count of how many people he has killed? Was the number too high? Was it too much for his conscience to consider?

He contemplated all of these things as he drove through Hamar, Norway and on to Lillehammer. He had never been to this Olympic site, but had heard great things from Anna and seen her photos of her Olympic experience on the Austrian Biathlon Team. The two of them had talked about going to Lillehammer on vacation, but never had. When you live in Austria, the skiing capital of the world, it's hard to justify going anywhere else, especially an inferior site, just to do the same thing.

When he finally got to Lillehammer, he was reminded somewhat of Austria, although the surrounding mountains were nowhere near as dramatic. Still, the place had it's own charm. It was late afternoon.

He went directly to downtown and pulled over to the curb in front of a restaurant. Food. That's what he needed.

As he ate a late lunch and early dinner, he watched people pass by outside. When he saw a little person shuffling along, his mind immediately went to the recent photo of Victor Petrova. But it wasn't him. This man was younger and had blond hair spiked up by jell. He finished his meal and drank a cup of coffee. Then he saw another little person walk past. This one, a bald man, was mumbling something aloud, just like the first one had. He didn't want it too, but his mind considered the possibility that a circus was in town.

After dinner, Jake drove to the outskirts of town, near the Olympic ski jump, and paid for a room at a small B&B with cash. He still had plenty left from cash advances at ATMs along the way in Sweden. He couldn't use any cards from now on, though. All cash.

He lay down on his bed and rested, knowing he would be up late that night. He crashed immediately into a deep sleep.

Hours later, he startled awake, coming out of a dream. He had dreamt of he and Anna together in a cabin in the Tyrolean mountains, a fire burning in a river-stone fireplace. Anna walked across the hardwood floors in her nightgown carrying something in her arms. And then the windows burst in with gunfire and Anna fell to the floor, dropping what she was carrying. Jake couldn't respond soon enough to save her. What kind of man was he? Not even able to save the woman he loved in their own home. Their home?

He rubbed his eyes and yawned. It was dark outside. He lit his watch and saw it was an hour from midnight. Time to move out.

Dressing in black clothes, from his military tactical boots to a long-sleeve black Under Armor shirt, he strapped his 9mm auto under his arm and slipped a Gortex jacket over that. He checked the gear in his backpack. Extra magazines. Binoculars and Night Vision Goggles. Handheld GPS. Digital camera. He checked his cell phone and saw it was still turned off. No need to check for messages. He might have one from Anna and another from Kurt Jenkins. Maybe Colonel Reed. Digging deeper into the backpack, he found a lock pick kit and a couple of tools, including a hex-head screw driver, which he shoved into his back pocket. Then he locked up and left.

First he drove back to town and found a car parked in a large hotel parking lot. It was a Saab like his—same year and color. It was also from Sweden. Perfect. In less than a minute, he had swapped the plates from his car to the other. Nobody checked their own plates. Hell, most people didn't even remember the numbers and letters from their own plates.

Then Jake drove out of town to a remote lake, where large houses sat on the banks, their wealthy occupants saying to anyone looking: "Hey, I've got a shitload of money, and you don't."

At the far end of the lake, the most impressive place sat on a hill back into the forest, with a long strip of grass leading down to the water's edge. Jake knew there was a gate ahead that would need a code or buzzing in from someone inside. But he didn't get that far. Instead, he found a little road that pulled off toward the mountains, where Jake found a place to park.

Getting out, he checked his watch. Just about midnight. He was thankful the midnight sun had passed this far south. A month earlier and it would have still been light at this time.

He hiked through the woods above the road for a half

mile until he came upon a high metal fence with razor wire topping that. Looking more closely through his NVGs, he saw it was also electrified. Great. What was Victor Petrova hiding behind the wire?

Now, Jake could get through the fence, but that was just the first obstacle. He guessed Petrova would also have motion sensors, perhaps dogs. He could handle the dogs. He had brought some treats for them, and bullets if they decided Jake would taste better. But that would also give up his position, because he didn't have a silencer for the 9mm. His biggest fear, though, was the motion sensors. Because if he didn't know where they were, he couldn't avoid them. It wasn't like the movies, where huge lights would come on and an alarm would sound. Victor Petrova was smarter than that. He would have the motion sensors in synch with cameras, which would pinpoint the movement and silently record. Sure an internal alarm would go off, allowing a security agent to check the monitors and either release the hounds or send those with guns.

Think Jake. What would that little gnome do?

♦

Toni Contardo and Colonel Reed had followed Victor Petrova from his hotel in Oslo, past the airport and toward the north. She knew where they were going as soon as they passed the airport. They had a good deal of information about Petrova's estate outside of Lillehammer. It was probably more secure than most Norwegian military installations. And why? Norway was one of the most crime-free countries in the world. Most people in the country wouldn't even lock their doors. But she knew that

Victor had a lot of enemies, including those in the Russian government, former KGB officers, and even those in the current SVR. Not to mention those in the criminal world who wanted a piece of his action. No, Victor Petrova was right to be paranoid. Well, not paranoid. Paranoid meant you thought people were out to get you. Petrova knew for a fact people wanted him dead.

Once they confirmed that Petrova had gone to his estate on the lake, Toni had checked into a small B&B on the outskirts of Lillehammer, with cash, her in one room and the colonel next door.

Past midnight now, she flipped open her phone and called a number from memory on her secure cell.

"Yeah, we're in place.," she said.

"Jake never showed in Oslo," Kurt Jenkins said.

"What? Why not?"

"We don't know for sure."

"Did you talk with him?" She got off the bed and started to pace the room.

"Earlier in the day. He split up from the two women. Sent them by air to Oslo."

"So where is Jake?"

A long delay, followed by, "We think he's going after Victor Petrova."

Great. "What about the virus? What has he done with that?" Jake would never compromise the safety of so many people unless. . .

"We don't know," Jenkins reiterated brusquely.

Jenkins was getting upset, she could tell.

"Does he know about this place?" she asked.

"Of course," Jenkins said. "He knows what you know."

"He knows more than that," Toni said. "He knows

Petrova from the old days. Knows how he'll react."

No reaction.

"You didn't know that?" she asked him. When he didn't say anything, she continued, "Petrova was heavily involved with the INF Treaty verification process. So was Jake. Their paths crossed many times—in the Ukraine and Russia."

"How'd that go?"

"Jake never really discussed it. I just came out of the conversations thinking Jake was both impressed and frustrated. There was respect on both sides, but something had happened that Jake wouldn't discuss with me. Said it was need-to-know."

"Understand," Jenkins said. "Yet, there's nothing in the official record."

"I think it was more personal."

Neither said a word for a while.

"What's the plan?" she finally asked him.

"We've got nothing on Petrova. Not officially."

"We have Petrova hiring Colonel Reed, who hired Jake, to go to the Arctic."

"Right. To find his old friend."

"But. . ." She knew Jenkins was right. They weren't even sure the colonel had told them the truth. It could have all been a ruse of some sort. A grand bit of disinformation. Petrova's specialty. "But if Jake has the virus and a link to Petrova that goes back to the 80s, then we have something on the guy. We can stick the guy in one of our prisons until the little man drops dead."

"But until then," Jenkins said, "we need to hold back. Sure we have him on possible attempted murder charges, but the local courts in Norway and Sweden would have to fight each other for jurisdiction—if they could even tie Petrova to the shootings in Svalbard and the attack on the train. You need to find Jake."

She agreed and flipped him shut. But that might be harder than it sounded. If Jake didn't want to be found, she wouldn't find him. She lay onto the bed and thought about her old friend. They had been on some dangerous missions in the past with him. Both almost getting killed too many times to count. Now things had changed between them. She was married and he was living with a younger woman. A beautiful blonde Austrian.

CHAPTER 25

The Bell 407, almost identical to the helicopter they had used in Svalbard, cruised in the darkness at four thousand feet, Kjersti behind the stick and Anna to her right. Behind them sat a strange group: the MI6 officers, Jimmy McLean and Velda Crane; Norwegian Intelligence Service officer, Thom Hagen; and two beefy men with the Norwegian Police Security Service, the PST. An additional SWAT unit from PST was driving north in their mobile command post and would reach Lillehammer by morning.

It had not taken a great deal of convincing on Anna's part to get officially involved in the case. She had made one phone call to her boss in Vienna, who had called the Secretary General himself at Interpol headquarters in Lyon, France. By the time word had traveled back to Norway, Anna was not only sanctioned to help with the operation, she would become the lead investigator. She didn't want that kind of responsibility, considering the possible release of a deadly pandemic flu virus worldwide, but then she also had the advantage of knowing there was no virus—a fact she had failed to reveal to her boss in Vienna and would take to her grave. Regardless of motive or effect, Victor Petrova was either a purveyor of a possible weapon of mass destruction, or a criminal mastermind who was looking to fund his operation for the rest of his life with the theft of precious gems. And who knew what he would do with the money he got from those Alexandrite gems? Besides, he had crossed the line by sending his men to kill her, Jake and Kjersti. Twice. Attempted murder would put Petrova away for the rest of his life. But she wanted more. Petrova was a bad guy and they needed to bring him down.

All of this ran through her mind as the helo flew north.

"What you thinking?" Kjersti asked over the mic.

Anna looked over at Kjersti and said, "I don't know. I don't know if I'm ready for this responsibility."

Kjersti nodded her head. "Nobody's ever ready, Anna. I'm sure Jake would tell you that."

She was right. Jake probably had told her that. "But he seems to handle these situations so easily. He's a natural."

"I could tell. He definitely knows how to take charge."

That could be part of the problem. Would he let her take over? She had a feeling there was something Jake wasn't telling her about his relationship with Victor Petrova. It all seemed too personal.

"Does he take charge in the bedroom?" Kjersti asked, a smile on her face. "I'm sorry."

"It's all right." Anna knew she was only trying to loosen her up, relieve the tension. She smiled back and said, "No complaints."

"I'll bet. We'll be at the Lillehammer airport in ten minutes. You said you spent some time there, right?"

"Yeah, during the Olympics. But that was years ago."

"Well, we're right over Mjosa Lake. At a hundred kilometers long, it's the largest in Norway. Have you heard of the Mjosa Monster?"

She remembered the narrow lake that stretched along the rolling mountains for many kilometers between Hamar and Lillehammer, and had heard about the purported Loch Ness-like beast that locals had swore seeing for the past four hundred years. Somehow Kjersti had managed to take her mind off the case for a short while. She took in deep breaths and tried to relax, despite her angst over flying in a helicopter. Yet, at least this time she didn't feel like throwing up. She hoped that bug had passed.

Moments later, Kjersti circled around the resort town of Lillehammer, before setting down the chopper at the tiny regional airport. Large SUVs waited for them and drove them to a large hotel in town, where they would wait for the SWAT unit.

♦

Jake had circled the entire compound fence by the time he heard the helo swoop down around the town of Lillehammer. It sounded just like the chopper they had flown in Svalbard.

His recon mission had not found a chink in the little bastard's armor. Jake was sure there was no way in without being discovered. He might have an advantage in the dark, assuming Petrova didn't have huge flood lights that would blind him in his NVGs. No, maybe the day would be better. Petrova would assume a strike would come at night.

Moving back through the forest, Jake found his car and started back toward town. On the entire drive, he thought not of Petrova, but of his girlfriend Anna. He had felt sorry for how she had felt during the past few days. She had been miserable and he hadn't been the most support-ive. He could blame his coming down off the alcohol that had consumed him so thoroughly in the past few months, but he knew that wasn't the only problem. Petrova had been like a nagging wart that wouldn't go away. He had made Jake's life during his last year in the Air Force a nightmare. He might have been a contributing factor of Jake leaving the service. And then when Jake had joined the CIA, the man had come up again on one of Jake's first cases in Germany during the fall of the Berlin Wall. They had come close to killing each other more than once. Yet, something had held them back. Was it respect? Was it some professional understanding? Who knows. Regardless of those times, that was the past. They were both private citizens now, and for some reason their paths were crossing again—either by some polar force or unknown desire.

He got back to his room and went right to bed. But he lay in the dark, his mind confused. Something close was-n't quite right. Danger? Maybe.

♦

Victor Petrova, Oberon now to his friends, sat back in his plush leather chair viewing a 50-inch LCD screen in the media room of his estate outside of Lillehammer.

There had been no word of Jake Adams coming for him. He had also not heard from Colonel Reed, but he guessed the man had finally come to his senses, as expected, and was now back to working with the Network. Did Jake Adams know the virus was not really a virus? Perhaps. If so, what would he do with all of his Alexandrite gems? Mister Do Good would probably turn the damn things over to his new friend, the Grand Master of the Teutonic Order in Vienna. Or some other charity of the minute.

On the screen he watched Elvis shaking his hips on the beach with a bunch of women who today would be on Weight Watchers or Jenny Craig or some other diet plan. Chunky women. Nothing wrong with that. Made their tits bigger.

Victor switched screens to an array of cameras around the outside of the estate. Infrared images mostly of trees and some strategically placed open areas, including the stretch from the lake to the estate. Then he went through the cameras within the estate, where he saw his night shift security guard, who watched the same cameras, except for the one watching him, his feet up on the desk and his finger so far up his nose he appeared to be tickling his tiny brain. Joseph Stalin, it was hard to find good people in Scandinavia.

He clicked back to Elvis, who was now strumming his guitar, and finally switched off the DVD. Time to get to bed. Jake Adams would come within the next twenty-four hours, guaranteed. He was too predictable to not come. Victor expected nothing less.

Scooting down off the chair, he waddled to the adjoining bedroom, a huge grin on his face.

CHAPTER 26

Anna and Kjersti had shared a hotel room, talking in the dark like sisters until they both finally slept out of complete exhaustion. With everything that had happened, it had been a long week for the both of them.

In the morning Anna woke first. Her stomach had suddenly lurched and forced her to run to the bathroom, where she threw up everything inside her. Twice. She thought the bug had returned, but guessed now that it could have been nerves. She used to throw up a few hours before each biathlon, forcing her to suck down water and an energy bar closer to the start of the competition to avoid dehydration.

Then Anna took a shower and was toweling down in front of a mirror when Kjersti came into the bathroom naked and sat down to pee.

"Hope you don't mind," Kjersti said. "I really have to go."

Anna continued with the towel. "No problem." She ran

her hand across her belly. She must be getting her period, she thought. A little bloating. Either that or she needed to work out. It had been quite a while since she ran.

Kjersti flushed and came to the mirror next to Anna. Washed her hands. "You all right?"

"Suppose you heard me throw up again," Anna said. "Nerves."

"Yeah, that's probably it." Kjersti smiled and wiped her hands. "I'll take a quick shower and we'll go fill that belly of yours again."

Anna watched Kjersti in the mirror as she got into the shower. No belly on her. Perfect body. She left her friend alone and went to get dressed. She wished she could call Jake and see what he was doing right now. She missed him. He was a stabilizing force for her, even though crazy things seemed to happen with him. Should she try to call him? Would he even answer? She got as far as putting on her panties and bra when the shower stopped.

Seconds later Kjersti came out, her body dry but toweling her hair still. "Remember what we talked about last night?"

They had talked about a lot of things. Anna shook her head.

Kjersti said, "I either need a man to screw me hard or I need to kill something. My God, I'm horny as hell." She wiggled and sat on the end of her bed, the towel still working her hair.

Anna couldn't keep her eyes off of the woman. If she ever had feelings for another woman, then it was now. But she didn't go that way. She loved Jake and desired only what he had to give her.

Throwing the towel on the floor, Kjersti said, "I didn't

mean to suggest that we do something. I mean, you are beautiful and have the cutest body I've ever seen. But. . ."

"I wasn't thinking that," Anna lied. "I was just admiring your body. That doesn't make me a lesbian does it?"

"I wouldn't know," Kjersti said, embarrassed now. "I've never done it with a woman. I mean. . .if I ever was going to do it with a woman, you would be my first choice. I'm rambling. I'm sorry. I really didn't mean to suggest we should do anything. I was just saying what I was thinking. I haven't had a man in a while, and I could really use one right now."

Anna took a deep breath. "I've never considered doing anything with a woman. Although Jake made a joke about doing the both of us, and that actually sounded interesting."

"Wish you had told me that," Kjersti said. "I would have done it. Your man is hot."

Anna covered her eyes and looked away, then took a seat on her bed. "Don't tell Jake that. Now I'm embarrassed."

Kjersti giggled. "Maybe we should get dressed and find some breakfast."

Anna looked up at Kjersti. "Good plan."

Without saying another word, the two of them hurriedly got dressed, locked up, and went down to the hotel restaurant.

◆

Jake lingered in bed until around eight-thirty. The B&B was one of those mountain lodge type places with feather beds, the room somewhat chilled with the window cracked all night. He took a quick shower and went over his day in his mind. Too bad he didn't have a few friends to help him. Victor Petrova's place was protected by high tech and low tech. While he had circled the complex, he had heard a few dogs yelp. Although he could bypass many electronic systems, well-trained dogs rarely acted like they did on TV, where someone drops them a raw steak or dog treats and the dog eats it, rolls over, and falls to sleep. That was nice for the tube, where they didn't want to piss off dog owners by actually killing them. But, of course, it was okay to twist some guys neck. Humans were fine to kill.

Jake went downstairs and ate a hearty meal of various meat, including pickled fish, eggs, juice, and strong coffee. The older woman who ran the place kept pushing more coffee on him. When he was done, he went outside and took in a deep breath of fresh air.

A heavy fog wrapped itself around the entire town, and a light mist trickled down on Jake's head. He got into his acquired car with the new plates and drove off to the downtown. He had a few things to pick up before he went back out to Petrova's estate.

♦

Toni had slept in longer than she wanted. After her shower and changing into tight, dark clothes, she had found Colonel Reed in the room next door and they went downstairs for breakfast. She looked out the windows and saw only the fog and light rain. Perfect. Couldn't have asked for better weather. They were the only two in the breakfast room.

"You sleep all right?" Colonel Reed asked Toni, as the both of them took seats at a thick wooden table.

"Not bad. I love the feather bed."

"What time is our briefing?"

The older woman who ran the place came with a carafe of coffee. "You just missed another American," she said with perfect English. "Is he a friend of yours?"

Toni shook her head. "No, we're here alone."

"Oh." The woman glanced at Colonel Reed.

"We're not together," Toni said. "We're colleagues."

The old woman smiled and walked away.

"I don't think she believes you," Colonel Reed said. "That's flattering."

Not for Toni. The colonel was old enough to be her father. "Can we get back to the subject. You asked about the briefing."

"Right. At the airport. Do you expect Jake to show up at some time?"

"You can bet on it." She knew that Jake was far from predictable, but he was most passionate when wronged in some way. Victor Petrova had not only done that to him in the past, he had made it more personal now. Jake wouldn't stand for it. But she had already discussed this with Colonel Reed on the drive from Oslo. "You better hope Jake has a forgiving side."

"I've told you," the colonel said. "I was planning on turning everything over to the Network once I knew for sure what we were dealing with. I had no idea it was a deadly virus. If I had, I never would have sent Jake to find it."

"You didn't," she reminded him. "You sent him to find the body of an old friend."

"Right."

"But you knew that wasn't his real reason to go there."

"Right. I knew that if Victor Petrova wanted it, then it must be important. I had no idea. . ."

Time would tell if he was telling the truth. Toni only hoped Jake would give the man a chance to explain himself. Jake was better than anyone she knew at determining if someone was lying to him. Which made her wonder why he had gone to the Arctic in the first place. Was it because his mind was clouded by alcohol? Or maybe he suspected all along that the colonel was sending him there for some other reason. She'd have to ask him that when she saw him again. It would be the first time they saw each other since Jake found out she was married. Didn't sound like fun to her, but she couldn't help feeling something for the man she had loved at one time.

"Let's go," Toni said. "Briefing in a half hour."

The colonel sucked down the last of his coffee and they left the B&B.

CHAPTER 27

The fog was still as thick as Norwegian fish soup when Anna and Kjersti got to the airport. Anna was still not feeling great, even after a light breakfast and coffee. Maybe she should have had the tea.

They were at a small operations building near the air traffic control tower, not wanting to roll into town with the SWAT mobile and have one of Petrova's men see them coming. They could have also conducted the meeting at the local police station, but didn't for that same reason. The local police would only be told once they rolled on the estate. They would be used to cut off the highways.

Anna watched all the entities stream into the small conference room. There would be standing room only. When she finally saw Colonel Reed and Toni come through and take a seat at the table, she had mixed feelings. The colonel had set this whole thing in motion. Had brought her and Jake from their comfortable yet complex life in Austria to Norway, to the Arctic, and back. She didn't know if she should shoot the colonel or hug him. Jake knew him. Maybe she'd let him decide. And Toni. They had worked together a few times in Austria, while she was the station chief in Vienna, especially on that strange Teutonic Order case a couple years ago.

Toni wasn't looking at her. What did that mean?

Everyone in place, Anna started the briefing. With Kjersti's help, she showed them satellite photos of Victor Petrova's compound, building plans, although not up to date, since the man had made his modifications over the past few years, and what they knew about the security systems. The Norwegian Police Security Service captain briefed them on their roll, and then a Norwegian Air Force colonel explained how they would block all air traffic. With the roads and air cut off, there would be no flaw to their plan. Even the lake would be cut off. Questions were asked and answered. Yet, during the entire briefing, Anna noticed that Toni didn't say a word. She only sat and listened.

They would strike at three p.m. Petrova, if he suspected they would come for him, would think they'd wait for dark.

Everyone strolled out of the briefing to prepare for the mission.

"Toni," Anna said. "Could I speak with you and the colonel?"

Looking somewhat disturbed, Toni reluctantly returned but didn't sit down, indicating she wasn't going to stay long. Colonel Reed did sit down, his disposition somber.

Kjersti took a seat in a far corner.

Anna leaned against the conference table and said, "You didn't have any questions."

Toni hunched. "You have a good plan."

"But?"

"You didn't mention Jake," Toni said. "He might get caught in the crossfire."

"We don't even know if he's here," Anna assured her.

Toni huffed out a breath. "He's here."

Anna glanced at the colonel. "You think so?"

Colonel Reed nodded.

"Why did you send us to Svalbard if you knew there was a deadly flu virus involved?" Anna asked the colonel.

"I didn't know," he said. "You've gotta believe me. I would've never sent Jake into harm's way if I'd known that. Does he know that?"

They had discussed it some on the trip back from Svalbard, but Jake wasn't sure. "Jake said that people can change for the good and the bad." As she watched the colonel shake his head, she considered also how Jake had changed over the past years, especially in the past three months, and how he seemed to be changing again. Yet, he had stopped drinking. Then their last encounter flashed before her, how he had brusquely dismissed her at the airport in Sweden.

"I must talk with him," Colonel Reed said. "Let him know we must talk. I can explain myself to him. Make him understand."

Maybe he could.

"Are we done here?" Toni asked. She looked like she wanted to rip Anna's head off.

"Yeah," Anna muttered. "See you in a few hours."

Toni and Colonel Reed left the room.

Kjersti came to Anna and put her arm around her. "You all right?"

Anna put her hand over her mouth. She wanted to throw

up again, but willed herself to settle down.

"Yeah, I'm fine."

"That was Jake's ex?"

"Yeah."

"She might have been pretty at one time," Kjersti said, "but she just seems old and bitter now. You're much hotter."

A smile crossed Anna's lips. "Thank you."

"Hey, what are friends for?" Kjersti pulled Anna toward the door. "Let's go find us some brutal weapons."

CHAPTER 28

J̶ake had gone to a sporting goods store, which was-
n't hard to find in Lillehammer, and he found some
gear he needed. Then he went down to the lakefront
and rented a boat with cash, with enough gas to let him
run all day if necessary.

Now he chugged along in the sixteen-foot canoe, shoving the control arm from side to side to stay perpendicular
to the foot-high waves. He couldn't figure out how the
wind was blowing so hard, yet the fog was still so thick,
not allowing him to see very far ahead. But he had taken
the GPS readings out at Petrova's estate the night before,
and an arrow was now pointing him in the right direction.

He had piled two backpacks of gear in the bow to offset
his weight. The GPS had him at four hundred meters out,
but that was only accurate to about thirty feet, since he
had taken the reading about that distance from the water,
back in the woods where the fence ran right into the water
and was toped with buoys with warning signs to keep the
hell away. Jake guessed the fence probably ran right
around the front of the water.

Twisting the throttle, the electric trolling motor slowed. There wasn't much noise even at full throttle, with the exception of the waves slapping the bow. He couldn't have asked for better weather. The weather folks on the radio had said the fog would last until evening, and maybe beyond that. It could go on for days. That would make Petrova's cameras less effective. But it wouldn't stop the motion detectors or any kind of traps he might have for Jake. Not to mention the dogs. They didn't give a crap about the fog.

GPS read one hundred meters. He slowed more and looked through his binoculars toward the shore. Couldn't see that far. Damn that was thick.

Checking his watch, he saw he was behind his schedule. He had wanted to reach the estate by noon, but it was twelve-forty now. Still, he suspected Petrova wouldn't guess he would make a run at him in daylight. Nor did the little troll have any idea today would be the day. But he would be looking over his little shoulder for Jake, he could bet on that. Had probably not only predicted the outcome, but orchestrated it himself like a series of chess moves. So why was Jake falling right into his trap? That's what kept running through Jake's mind. He could have just flown to Amsterdam and have a couple of the Alexandrite gems examined for quality and price. Then he would slowly feed them to a discreet contact, collect the money, and load up his retirement fund. After all, who really owned the gems? Jake had found them in a glacial wilderness with the dead body of his friend.

Peering through binoculars, the trees along the shoreline finally appeared, so Jake cut the motor and let the canoe glide. Quietly he picked up a paddle and feathered the stern to keep the canoe running straight. The waves were so high, though, he didn't have to stroke once to reach shore—only J-stroke and rudder. He could hear a rubbing sound to his right.

Moments later the bow ran aground onto a patch of grass and tall weeds to the west of the rocky beach. Only now did Jake notice the dock to his right with a speed boat tied to it, the hull gently squeaking against rubber bumpers. He tilted the electric motor up and then worked his way to the bow, trying not to fall out of the canoe.

Once ashore, he quietly pulled the canoe into the weeds and then farther up into thick alder bushes. Satisfied the canoe was out of view, Jake slipped on one backpack and lifted the other from the canoe. Then he moved to the west a couple of steps, stopped, a couple steps more, stopped. He continued this pattern until he was fifty yards into the compound. So far so good. Unless Petrova had already detected him with silent motion sensors.

Suddenly he stopped. He didn't know why. Looking down to his left, he saw a sensor. Motion. Without moving, his eyes roamed higher on the trees until he saw the flood light. The sensor would flick that light on, so he wasn't busted yet. Pretty low tech, Victor.

Wait. He knew Jake would find that. It would make Jake move around to the right or left. Shit! Was he second guessing everything? Right, left or straight ahead? Think, Jake. What would he do?

The sensor was too obvious, he thought. Move straight ahead. Taking a deep breath, Jake stepped lightly forward and stopped again.

Wait a minute. Would Victor guess that Jake would guess that this was a ruse to get him to go right or left?

Then when Jake moved forward the light would go on and set off an alarm inside. You little bastard.

Jake felt the 9mm automatic under his left arm and wanted to simply pull it and run toward the estate. Screw the damn alarms. Just move forward.

Stepping forward, Jake crossed the path of the motion sensor and stopped beyond its range, cringing, waiting for the light that didn't come. But maybe the sensor still sent a silent alarm inside. Screw it, Jake. At this rate, he wouldn't get inside until Christmas.

He cautiously moved forward through the thick underbrush that made the estate almost invisible from the lake or the road. Petrova really liked his privacy.

Finally, Jake came to the edge of the grass that led to the estate. Twenty yards of grass surrounded the huge three-story structure, built in the Georgian style, with tall columns rising two stories to a portico with metal-railed balconies on each window, with, Jake was sure, a splendid view of the lake on days not like this one.

How the hell was he going to cross the grass without being viewed? He sat down into the tall grass among the bushes to contemplate this conundrum.

As he watched in a daze, mostly from the lack of sleep over the past week, a man finally appeared around the right side of the main building. A little man, but Jake could see it wasn't Victor Petrova. This guy was early thirties with spiked platinum hair, and looked like he pumped iron. He reminded Jake of a midget wrestler from the days before WWF or WWE. But this guy was different. He had an MP5 sub-machine gun strapped over his shoulder. Based on his trajectory, he would swing right in front of Jake. He had to move fast.

He left one bag there, camouflaged among the ferns, and scooted around to his left, making his way around the opposite perimeter of the house. Moving slowly, with purpose, he could now hear talking toward a garage structure. When another man, a near clone of the first, only with dark, curly hair, appeared around the edge of the garage, Jake stopped in his tracks and slowly sunk to the ground among the bushes. This little man would swing around and probably tag-team the other guy about halfway around the house. Jake couldn't take out one without the other seeing him do so.

Then, from the garage, came a large man with a shaggy Black Russian Terrier leashed and trying to pull him forward. This dog could have eaten the other two guards for lunch. The handler, who yanked on the leash and almost took the dog's neck off, also had an automatic pistol clipped to his belt. Now Jake could be in trouble. He needed to stay still.

When the man unleashed the dog, it pranced around the yard marking its territory. At one point, it came within ten feet of Jake as it sprinted in front of him along the edge of the yard. Then it finally stopped and took a massive dump, rubbed its feet in the grass, and ran back to the man, cowering as it got a couple feet away. He clipped the dog to the leash again and wandered back to the garage.

Jake needed to get rid of the dogs first. He hated to do it, but knew they were also trained for one thing—to rip into anything or anyone who wasn't supposed to be there. Maybe they would make it easy for him.

Just as the two little guards met near Jake's last position, he got up and made his way behind the garage. Hidden from view from the house and the two guards, Jake peered through a back window into the five-car garage. There were only two cars inside. A vintage MG midget, classic, and a new black BMW 7-series. Along the back side of the far end were kennels for four dogs. The big guy was putting the dog back into the end unit, and then he plodded off through the open garage door toward the house. He left the door open. Finally, a break.

Moving casually around the edge of the garage, Jake entered the door as if he worked there. The dogs immediately stood and took notice, but didn't bark. Jake had come across this breed while stationed in Europe. The old Soviets had used the Black Russian Terriers as guard dogs at some of their nuclear sites. They were strong and extremely loyal, yet somewhat submissive unless provoked or unleashed on someone by a handler.

Looking around the garage, Jake found a chair and pulled it up next to the cages. He put his back to the dogs, took off his pack, and sat down—ignoring them. Reaching into the backpack, he found some beef jerky he had purchased at the sporting goods store and started opening them. He took a bite out of the first piece, looked around behind him, and threw the jerky into the closest kennel. The dog immediately chomped onto the jerky. Jake did the same thing with the other three. Then he repeated the process one more time. By the time he was done, their little black cropped tails wiggled for him. Share a meal and make a friend. He hoped it would work. He hated to kill such beautiful dogs just for the hell of it.

Then Jake stood and gave the dogs commands in Russian. As suspected, they had been trained in that language and they responded to him immediately. New friends and subservient. Nice.

He put his backpack on and made his way toward the outside, but stopped and scooted toward the edge when he saw the large man coming back from the house. Looking around, Jake was trapped.

The man got closer and Jake pulled his gun.

In seconds the dog handler entered the garage. Jake stepped behind the man and said, "Stop right there."

Startled, the big man turned and started for his gun.

"I wouldn't do that," Jake said.

The guy stopped, his hand a few inches from his gun.

"You're the American," the man said through a thick Swedish accent.

"The troll told you about me? I'm flattered. Get on your knees."

The man hesitated and then complied, his eyes shifting toward the dogs in wonder.

"What's the matter?" Jake asked him. "Your dogs don't seem too concerned?"

His thick brow ridges rose.

"They hate you, Sven. You can treat some species of dogs like shit and they'll still do anything for you. But the Russian Terrier will hate and resent you. Gotta be a little nicer to them." Jake came up behind the man and struck him with his gun in the back of his head. He went down but not out. Taking the opportunity, Jake took the man's gun. Then, as the man rolled to his side and tried to get up, Jake kicked the guy in the face, smashing the back of his head against the cement. Now he was out cold.

Jake took off his backpack and pulled out some plastic zip strips, affixed them to the man's hands behind his back, and then also strapped his ankles. Next, he found the duct tape and wrapped it around the man's mouth, around his head. Someone would have to cut it off. Then Jake grabbed the man and pulled him to the other end of the garage. He checked the BMW driver's door. It was unlocked. He pressed the trunk release and it popped open for him. With great difficulty, Jake lifted the man into the trunk and closed him inside. Satisfied, Jake found his backpack and slung it over his shoulder. He looked at the dogs, who seemed interested but not concerned. Telling them to 'sit' in Russian, all four did so immediately. Sweet. Now to get into that house.

CHAPTER 29

A ll of the players had reassembled at the Lillehammer airport. One hour before they would move out, and one and a half until the strike. The Norwegian Police Security Service had the largest contingent, including their SWAT unit, followed by the Norwegian Intelligence Service. The local police were in a secondary, backup position, used mostly to cut off transportation. Sitting back in more of consultant roles were the American Intelligence Network, Toni, and MI6, Jimmy McLean and Velda Crane. Leading them all, to most displeasure, was Interpol's Anna Schult.

Anna stood out on the flight line next to the NIS Bell 407, reviewing a map of the area. Kjersti was in the cockpit talking with the tower and weather, trying to find out when the fog would lift.

Jimmy and Velda came over from a large SUV. "We feel a little left out," Jimmy said to Anna.

Velda nodded agreement.

"I'm sorry," Anna said. She knew that if it was revealed

that there was no flu virus the case would be pulled from her immediately. "Do you have a location on your subject? What's his name?"

"Gary Dixon," Velda said. "Yes. He's out at Petrova's estate."

Jimmy jumped in. "This could be a bloody blood bath with all these weapons. Shouldn't we try something a little less. . .obtrusive?"

Anna had seriously considered that herself. She remembered how everything had gone down two years ago, with her and Jake at the Austrian castle. Jake had lost a good friend that day. Much had gone right, but enough had also gone wrong.

"We can't let this virus get in the wrong hands," Anna said lamely.

Jimmy rubbed the stubble on his strong jaw, looked away, and then back at Anna. "This Jake Adams. I've heard of him. Does he know what he's doing? I mean, why would he bring an active virus to the man who wanted to probably sell it to the highest bidder?"

He had a damn good point, and Anna hoped she wouldn't have to answer that question. At least until she could explain everything.

"I trust Jake with my life," Anna said, "because he's saved it more than once in the past few years. In the past week. Don't judge him until you know the. . ."

"Truth," Jimmy finished.

Anna looked down at Velda and then back at Jimmy. They deserved to know the truth, but she couldn't tell them right now. "Everything will become clear soon."

"Blind faith," Velda said. "Sounds like a good way to get us killed."

"Listen," Anna said. "This Victor Petrova is a bad man. You've read the briefing on him and his organization. We're going to take him down with or without you. You can sit back here in town and drink beer for all I care." That came out much more harsh than she had intended.

Jimmy stepped back, his hands up. "Hey, take it easy Miss Interpol. I play devil's advocate, then salute smartly. We all drink beer when this is over."

"I'm sorry," Anna said. "I've got a lot to consider."

"No problem," Jimmy said. "We'll take the high road. Literally. As planned."

The two MI6 officers left her, but were replaced immediately by Toni Contardo and Colonel Reed.

"What can I do for you?" Anna asked.

"We'd like to change from entering on the road," Toni said, to taking a boat.

Anna shook her head. "Why?"

"Looks like you could use some help there," Toni said. "Hate to leave it only to the local cops."

"I don't know if we have an extra boat," Anna said.

"We've got that covered." Toni put her hand on the colonel's shoulder.

"He shouldn't even be here," Anna said, her gaze harshly fixed on Colonel Reed. "We still don't know for sure if he's working for the Network or Petrova." Or perhaps himself, she thought.

"Colonel Reed has actually been to Petrova's estate," Toni reminded Anna. "And I assure you he is not working for that KGB dwarf."

Anna looked at the colonel, who seemed contrite. "Fine. You better get down to the lake, then."

Toni smiled and she and the colonel walked off to their

car, Anna watching every sway of her hips. Kjersti was wrong. Toni still had it going on.

This was crazy, Anna thought. Why had they put her in charge? Toni had decades more experience than her. She knew the answer, though. If anything went wrong, the Americans, the Brits, and the Norwegians could blame everything on Interpol. Hang her out to dry. But at least she knew something they didn't know—there was no virus. That was one comforting fact.

Kjersti climbed down from the chopper cockpit, throwing her headset onto the seat.

"What's the matter?" Anna asked her.

"We're grounded. Fog isn't expected to lift until later this evening. It would be different if we were heading to Hamar. They've got three mile visibility there."

"That's all right," Anna said. "We'll go by car." She was actually relieved, not trusting her stomach to another flight.

CHAPTER 30

Victor Petrova had just finished a large meal of fish and potatoes and vegetables, topped off with a great apple strudel and ice cream.

Now, sitting in his communications room, he glanced at all of his monitors. But the fog was so thick he could only see a few feet out on the outdoors cameras. So he concentrated on the indoor cameras.

His cell phone rang and he picked up.

"Yes," he said.

Listening carefully, he waited until the caller had finished. He had trained his contact well. A quick briefing. To the point. Just the facts.

Petrova grunted and then hung up. Then he yelled as loud as he could until one of his men came into the room. It was a little person like Petrova. A Ukrainian, though.

"Make sure we're ready," Petrova said. "Looks like we'll have some company soon. Make sure the cars and the boat are ready."

The Ukrainian nodded but waited for more.

"That's all," Petrova said.

The man started to leave.

"Wait. Where's that big Swedish bastard?"

"I don't know," the Ukrainian said. "I'll ask around."

"He was checking on the dogs," Petrova said. "Look there first."

The Ukrainian hurried off, probably to avoid any more instructions.

Damn it! He should have had cameras installed in the garage. Maybe not to watch the damn dogs, but to at least keep an eye on his BMW and MG.

His cell phone rang again and Petrova reluctantly picked up.

"Yes?"

"Hello, my little friend."

My God. What balls. "Jake Adams. Is that you?"

"Afraid so."

"You've got something that's mine," Petrova said. "There's a finders fee."

"Where'd you get all the Alexandrite?" Jake asked him.

Sure. He should have expected Adams would open the damn box. He heard a familiar sound in the background. A dog whine. A smile crossed his face.

"What you do with the big Swede?" Petrova asked.

"He's taking a nap."

Petrova laughed. "I'll bet. Why don't you come into the house and we'll talk."

"Not until you tell all your little friends not to shoot," Jake said. "One of them could actually hit me. Then you'll never find your gems."

"Done. Give me five minutes and you can come in through the front door. Nobody will stop you."

The line went dead. Petrova hunched and then called all his men to tell them to let Jake Adams pass. That man had balls like pumpkins. He smiled with that thought.

◆

Jake had thought about it and realized he could have shot it out with Petrova's men, but that would not accomplish his goal. He would only be killing men he had nothing against—men who were loyal to Petrova, true, but who might not even know the true nature of the man's deeds. Hired guns.

Instead, Jake needed to talk with the man. Maybe he knew this all along. He also knew that Victor Petrova couldn't kill him outright without fear of losing his precious gems. That was his hold card. His queen waiting to pounce on an unsuspecting knight.

Before making the call, he had made a quick call to his own voice mail, leaving a coded message for himself. It was his only insurance policy. Just in case Petrova's men didn't like following orders.

He stuffed his backpack with his gear in a corner of the garage, his only weapon one 9mm handgun with an extra magazine, which hung below his left arm under his jacket. That done, Jake walked out of the garage, his hands out to his sides. Both of the little security guards that had roamed the grounds scurried toward him, their guns pointed in the air. Hopefully they had gotten word from Petrova to let him pass.

The little guards escorted Jake to the front door of the large estate. Before entering the house, they found Jake's gun and extra magazine and took it from him.

Inside, Jake immediately noticed the place had been converted to all things Russian—right out of a St. Petersburg palace—with high ceilings, dark wood floors, and old paintings of Russian aristocracy encased in gilded frames.

When Jake hesitated for a view, one of the men jammed the barrel of his automatic weapon into Jake's back. As they walked slowly through the mansion, more little people poked their heads out of doors and wandered about their business—whatever that was.

Finally, Jake entered a grand room, a library of sorts, with a panel of security screens breaking up the old dark wood style with high tech. Sitting in a leather chair, swiveling from side to side, was Victor Petrova.

He had changed quite a bit since the last time Jake had seen him. Older. A little more weight on his tiny frame.

"You look like shit," Petrova said. "Probably need a drink."

Jake ignored that comment and stretched his arms out, his palms up. "Let me guess. You represent the Lollipop Guild?"

"Ha, fucking ha. Still a comedian. But now a drunk comic. Not very original."

"Can we get on with this," Jake said. "I really need to take a piss."

"Great. Right to the point." Petrova shifted his eyes to his men and then back to Jake.

Jake knew that Petrova had probably calculated every more Jake would make, from Oslo to Svalbard and right to Lillehammer. But Jake still had a few things in his favor. He had the gems.

"I've got something you want," Jake said, "and you

need to keep me alive long enough to find out where I've hidden them. That about do it for you?"

Petrova laughed out a breath through his nostrils. "Yeah, that's about it."

Jake reached into his pocket and found the Alexandrite gem that had fallen from the metal box. When it hit the light it changed color instantly from a purplish-red to a vibrant green under the fluorescent lights overhead.

Nearly gasping, a smile crossed the weathered face of the little man. "Aren't they beautiful?"

They were, Jake had to admit. "More so than diamonds or rubies or emeralds. But why the grand ruse, Victor? Why didn't you just send your men to find the gems your-self? Wait. Let me guess. You either feared the polar bears would eat your men, or they would be enveloped by the glaciers." No smile from Jake. He returned the gem to his pocket and watched Petrova's eyes move along with Jake's hand.

"Now what fun would that have been, Jake?" Petrova shook his big head side to side. "I thought you knew me better than that."

"Right," Jake said. "Why do the easy when the elabo-rate would be so much more fun? You like to fuck with people. You have to do it. Can't breath without finding ways to screw with the minds of others each and every day. Let me know when I'm getting close."

Petrova's head had swayed from shoulder to shoulder as Jake talked. Impatient and impertinent. "You were a pain in the ass in Volgograd. But you cracked then and you'll eventually tell me where to find my Alexandrites."

Shocked, but Jake tried not to show it. He had been held captive in that historic city for two weeks during the Cold

War, beaten and starved and beaten some more. Jake had given them information, anyone would have, but everything he had given them was crap. Not one fraction of actionable intelligence of any kind. He knew it and Victor Petrova knew it. Jake had always guessed that this man had been around somewhere during his captivity, but it had never been confirmed. Until now.

"Sure, I'll give you the location," Jake said. "And then another and another and another. Your men will be running around like true Munchkins searching for a pot of gold." Okay, maybe he shouldn't have mixed his metaphors so drastically.

"I'm a little person," Petrova said, exasperated. "Get over it. Move on. Tell me what I need to know."

This was going about as well as Jake had guessed it would. "You're a fuckin' troll," Jake finally said. "But I'll take you to it. Only you."

One of Petrova's eye's closed. His perplexed look. "Why would you do that?"

"Because then we're going to split it fifty/fifty."

"Why not just take them all for yourself?"

"And have to kill every little person in Europe who happens to bump into me? What would that do to your population?"

Now Petrova finally smiled. "You're right. I would hunt you down like a pig."

They stared at each other for a moment.

"We have a deal?" Jake asked.

The little Russian glanced at his screens and then back to Jake. "Why not. There's enough there for both of us."

That was too easy, Jake thought. But then Victor Petrova was the master of disinformation. He would say just about anything at this point to get him one step closer to the box of Alexandrites.

Suddenly an Elvis song shot from Petrova's cell phone. *Hound Dog.* The Russian picked up and listened carefully. Then he glanced at the window, which showed only fog. He turned his head and mumbled something into the phone, but Jake could only pick up a couple of Russian words. He turned back and slapped his phone shut, then jumped down from his chair and shuffled across the hardwood floor toward the door.

"Let's go," Petrova said. "Elvis is leaving the building."

The two little guards escorted Jake behind their boss, a man grasping each of Jake's hands. Strangely enough, he felt like a dad with his kids at the zoo.

CHAPTER 31

They were all on the move. The local police had cut off any road leading to Victor Petrova's estate, which wasn't hard, since only one road lead out there. Two police boats were in the water; one with two police officers and another with Toni, Colonel Reed, and a police officer at the wheel. All of the others, including the SWAT unit, had driven by vehicle, slowly, through thick, dense fog. There would be no air support, though, and that bothered Anna.

Set up now outside the main gate of Petrova's compound, Anna gave the order for SWAT to crash through the gate. The other vehicles followed closely behind and set up a defensive position near the main house. Officers flowed out of vehicles in all directions to cut off any escape.

Anna and Kjersti stood back at their vehicle monitoring radios. Wind blew across the open grass yard, nearly knocking both from their feet.

Anna knew the plan wasn't perfect. She had wanted to

send police officers around the outside fence, but knew any breech of the fence would surely tip off Petrova. So she had agreed to the direct approach. She watched as SWAT flowed into the house, the huge garage, where dogs barked loudly, and into the surrounding forest.

Within a couple of minutes, reports started coming in from various officers. Not good.

"Petrova has to be here," Kjersti said. She got onto her radio and ordered something in Norwegian. Then she heard back and shook her head.

"What are they saying," Anna asked her.

"The place is entirely empty. Not one person found."

Kjersti's radio squawked, followed by a man speaking English. "We found a backpack in the woods. Also, a canoe hidden in the bushes down by the lake."

"What about Petrova's boat?" Anna asked into the radio. The fog was still so thick they couldn't see the water from their position.

"The dock is empty," the man said.

Great. They left by boat. She got onto her radio and asked for the position of their two boats. "How many could fit on Petrova's boat," Anna asked Kjersti.

"I don't know. It's a twenty-one foot power boat with a two-hundred-twenty-five horse inboard. Perhaps six."

"Six normal-size people?"

"I see where you're going," Kjersti said. "Maybe ten like Petrova."

Finally she got her response from the two police boats. The heavy winds were rocking them all over the place. They were perhaps one hundred yards from the dock. Could barely see even that. Anna ordered them to fan out and search for the missing Petrova boat.

"Where are they heading?" Anna asked Kjersti.

Kjersti hunched her shoulders. "Sweden. But not by boat."

"How far can they get on this lake?"

"Hamar. Hell, almost to the Oslo airport. It's a hundred miles long. But in this fog they could be anywhere."

"If you had to guess," Anna pled.

"There's not much on the southern end of the lake. The highway comes up against it down there. If he had a car waiting, he could pick up the highway and cross into Sweden. But if I were him, I would get off somewhere near Hamar. The Swedish border is closer there. That's assuming he's going to Sweden. I mean, he will find no refuge there."

A man hurried across the grass toward them. He carried a backpack and set it at Anna's feet, opening it for her to see. But she didn't need to see what was in there. She thanked the man and he went away.

Kjersti said the obvious. "That's Jake's backpack."

"So he got here first and is now with Petrova."

"But he wouldn't have brought the box," Kjersti said. "He'd use that for bait. What do you think Jake has planned?"

That was the problem. Anna didn't have a clue. She simply shook her head.

♦

The speed boat cruised along at a remarkable pace, considering the fog and wind. It wasn't maxed out, but enough to bring tears to Jake's eyes as he focused his attention on the men surrounding him. They were all little people like Victor Petrova, who sat on a bench seat next to Jake. There were five other men, one at the wheel, standing on a platform to see over the bow, and the other four spread out on the benches across from Jake and Petrova. Must have been part of Petrova's inner circle, Jake guessed. Then he noticed his backpack at the feet of one man. They had found the one in the garage. He wondered if they had removed his back-up weapon from there.

"I hope your man knows where he's going," Jake yelled into Petrova's ear.

Petrova smiled. "He not only know this lake. He has the best GPS navigation available."

"Where are we going?"

The Russian raised his brows in delight. "I see you noticed your backpack. My men found it and search it completely. They found this." Petrova removed a gem from his pocket and delicately opened his fingers, making sure the wind did not send the Alexandrite flying. "You should have looked more carefully." He laughed and put the gem back in his pocket.

"They are beautiful," Jake said.

"We found the bullet hole in your backpack. You must have been carrying the metal box inside."

Jake wasn't sure of his point, so he said nothing.

Petrova continued. "You asked me where we're going. To get what's mine."

"You don't know where we're going," Jake said, "but we're making damn good progress."

"Right. That, and we're getting away from your friends."

"What do you mean?"

The boat slowed somewhat, as if the pilot was preparing to maneuver around something.

Petrova studied Jake's eyes, obviously trying to read him. "You probably don't know. Your friends just raided my estate. Although I don't know why. Perhaps they think I'm trying to acquire a deadly Soviet-era flu virus to unleash on the world. I have no idea where they get their intel. They're often wrong these days."

Now Jake smiled. "You're the master of deception, Victor. While still playing KGB, you orchestrate this elaborate plan within a plan. You pretend as though a cabal in the Soviet government is trying to turn back the clock, away from the Gorbachav reforms, by an assassination attempt during the Reykjavik Summit. In the process you implicate a bunch of your political enemies, who end up magically disappearing. Then you feed the Americans a bullshit story about a MiG pilot trying to defect and who subsequently crashes in the remote Norwegian islands. You send your hand-picked team to find the crash site to extricate the metal box from the MiG. You probably told your men that it was a deadly biological weapon, since you had stamped the box with biohazard. Let me know when I get something wrong."

Petrova simply stared ahead, not looking at Jake.

He continued. "You didn't have a great fix on the location of the MiG crash site, though. Your men did find it, but they could not relay the location back to you. That had to drive you crazy. Horseshit communications of the late 80s. Let me back up. You also leaked the crash to the Americans, hoping they would send a crew to Svalbard also, which we did. You wanted the Americans to eventually find the site so they could independently verify the plot. You expected your men to get there first and take the bogus biohazard box back to you. But I checked on your whereabouts during that timeframe. You weren't even in Russia. Your diplomatic passport had you in Oslo at the time. You were waiting for your men to show up in Oslo with the box, which you would have taken from them and started fencing. I'm guessing you would have also killed these men to keep them quiet. But you had a problem." Jake stopped to look for a reaction. Nothing. The guy was a rock.

"Yes," Petrova said. "What was my problem?"

"You didn't expect the Americans to shoot it out with your men. You didn't expect all of them to die on Spitsbergen. You didn't calculate the climate. Snow cover was at a low point in history. Immediately following the crash, though, and the area got more and more snow and ice, completely covering the MiG, your dead men, and your precious gems. You redirected satellites at that time to try to find the crash. No luck. You even sent other teams looking for the crash site in nineteen ninety-two and again just before you left the KGB. Nothing. The Soviets abandoned their settlement in Pyramiden on Svalbard, but the Russians recently re-established the mining operation there. Which was fortuitous, considering the more recent summer they've had in Svalbard. The glacial range has melted this year even lower than it had been in the late eighties. When one of the Russian miners found the crash site, you got wind of it and set your plan in motion."

The boat picked up speed again. The fog was not as thick in this area, so Jake could see the shore on both sides of them. Headlights from cars slowly crept along a highway on the right side—the road he had traveled from Hamar.

"Where are we going?" Jake asked again.

"To get my gems," Petrova answered.

"How do you know I didn't leave them at my hotel in Lillehammer?"

Petrova shook his head. "My men already checked. They also checked the car you stole in Sweden."

Great. They had found that. Not completely unexpected, though.

"You going to finish your little yarn?" Petrova asked.

"Just about through. This brings me to me. I kept on asking myself why you would send me to Svalbard to find this box. Of course you first picked Colonel Reed, knowing the two of us had a personal relationship that wouldn't allow me to say no to him. You used the colonel to get me. You already knew that I knew the man who had died on Svalbard, because your men in Volgograd tortured me for two weeks, and one of the questions that kept coming up dealt with my relationship with Captain Steve Olson. That made no sense to me at the time, since Steve had taken a job in Oslo and died in a car crash. I should have known, but didn't, that the car crash story was a cover. So you could have beaten me to death I would have told you nothing else."

"You can't blame a guy for trying," Petrova said.

"Right. But, still. You could have sent your men to Svalbard."

"Trust is a delicate balance to maintain. And I knew that I was under scrutiny from not only the Russian SVR, but the American Network and the Swedish SAPO. Not to mention your girlfriend's Interpol and local police. I can't fart without someone testing the air quality. Besides, life gets quite boring if you can't fuck with people. You came to me one night in Stockholm while I sipped single malt and listened to *Don't Be Cruel*."

Jake thought about that. Petrova had played on Jake's sense of duty. "You knew I'd find the biohazard box and would turn it over to the Network. But then why send the helicopter to shoot us out of the sky."

Petrova shook his head vehemently. "Those weren't my men. They were with Russian SVR."

Christ. He had shot and killed agents with the Russian Foreign Intelligence Service. "Did the SVR think we had the flu virus or the Alexandrite." He already knew the answer to this, but he had to ask anyway.

Petrova laughed. "The SVR couldn't find its own ass with both hands and two mirrors. They thought it was the virus, of course."

"And the men on the train?"

Shrugging, Petrova said, "They were mine. We knew you had the gems by then. It just took us a while to track you down."

Which is also why he knew where he was going, Jake guessed. "You still haven't told me where we're going."

"Yes, I did. To get my Alexandrites. You dumped them somewhere between Falun, Sweden and Hamar, Norway. Now you will bring me to them."

Okay, the guy wasn't an idiot. "That's a large area, Victor."

One of the little men stood up for a better look, and Jake made his move. With one fluid motion, he rushed the man, grasped him by the collar and pants, and threw him overboard. The other men, dumbfounded, suddenly realized what had happened and pointed their guns at Jake.

"No!" Petrova yelled.

The boat slowed and turned to the left.

Jake looked back and saw the man bobbing up and down behind them, his tiny arms waving and his voice barely audible in the wind.

"What was the point of that?" Petrova asked Jake.

Moving back to the bench, Jake took a seat again. "It just looked like fun." Really, he had gotten rid of one MP5 automatic submachine gun. He was sure the guy would have dropped the rifle to the bottom of the lake as soon as he hit the water.

"That was just cruel."

"That means a lot coming from you, Victor."

They picked up the wet little guard, without a rifle, and continued down the lake toward Hamar.

CHAPTER 32

Toni Contardo had heard over the radio that Jake was probably with Victor Petrova and his men in the boat, somewhere in the fog ahead of them. But by then Petrova had gotten a good lead on them. They could have been miles ahead by now. Toni had made sure to tell Anna to redirect some assets along the road between Lillehammer and Hamar. That had angered the Interpol agent. She had already done that.

Now, with the fog lifting somewhat, the police officer driving the boat was able to pick up the pace. Yet they still had not even caught a glimpse of Petrova's boat. Sitting solemnly next to Toni, Colonel Reed shifted his head away from the wind and caught Toni staring at him.

"Jake will be fine," the colonel said, barely above the sound of the motor and the swift breeze.

"Why did you get him involved in the first place?" Toni asked him. She thought she had already asked him this before, but her thoughts were clouded now by the task at hand—finding the little madman.

The colonel lowered his jaw and said, "Petrova suggested it. When he mentioned that our mutual friend Captain Olson had died there, I should have been suspicious. After all, how would he know that?"

That was easy to know. "The KGB had a file on all of our military attaches at each of our embassies—just like we have on them. When Captain Olson and CIA officer John Korkala suddenly no longer worked there, no cover story would have slipped past Victor Petrova. He knew our men had something to do with his own men not coming back from the Arctic."

"Makes sense. Now that you spell it out for me. How we going to find Petrova now?"

They both heard the helicopter approaching from the north at a high rate of speed, and looked up as it buzzed past them fifty feet above the lake.

"That'll help," Toni said.

♦

They were cruising at maximum speed for the Bell 407 at that elevation, over a hundred forty miles per hour. Kjersti looked determined behind the stick. Anna, in the second front seat, turned to the cargo area and saw the two MI6 officers, Jimmy McLean and Velda Crane, strapped into benches, the tall Scotsman calm and cool and the little English woman, white knuckles, holding on for her life.

They had hurried back down the road to Lillehammer, the area still foggy, but Kjersti saying she could take off, clear the low ceiling, and pull back down once they got down the lake a ways. After all, the weather report had

Hamar nearly clear and the fog thinning out the farther they got from Lillehammer. They could have taken more people on the flight, but Kjersti wanted her chopper as light as possible for maximum speed and maneuverability.

Anna had asked for the main highway between Hamar and Lillehammer to be closed, but the local police said that would take a while. It was almost forty miles between the two cities by road—longer by the lake—so it would take some time to clear the cars from that highway. She had also asked the police to set up on the main bridge crossing the lake, but the police had not been able to reach the bridge in time.

Through the headset, Anna said, "Would it be better to vector over the mountains and come at them from the other side?"

Kjersti thought for a moment, no certainty in her expression. "I don't know."

"Victor Petrova could feel cornered, nothing to lose, and decide to kill Jake."

"I don't think so. He wants those gems more than he wants Jake dead."

Anna hoped so, but she still thought she was right. Why not come around and catch them off-guard? "Move to the east," Anna ordered.

Instantly after Anna spoke, Kjersti banked hard left, the helicopter responding to her actions. As they approached the hills around the lake, she pulled back on the stick and they rose over the trees and hills. Once over the top, she banked to the right and continued south. From that position they could only catch periodic glimpses of the lake as they passed river valleys or lower humps in the hills.

The quick maneuvers put a lump in Anna's throat and she thought she might lose her lunch. But she was convinced they had done the right thing.

♦

Jake checked his watch. They had traveled by boat for an hour now. Perhaps thirty miles at their rate. Moments ago, the driver slowed and pulled over to the east bank of the lake. A couple miles back they had passed under the main highway that ran from Hamar to Lillehammer, with Jake guessing they would have had at least a modest police presence on the bridge. But he had only seen a couple cars cruising along the highway as they passed under the bridge, none of them police types.

The boat slowed now and pulled into a small sheltered inlet. Ahead on the shore, Jake saw movement. Victor Petrova had men waiting there. They nudged the shore and two Swedish men, the remaining two that Jake had followed from Falun, including the man he had encountered on the train, held the boat as all but the driver and one of Petrova's men remained on the boat. The man Jake had thrown overboard. Seconds later, the boat was shoved off and it quickly made its way back out to the center of the lake at their original speed.

All of them trudged through the thick woods—no trail at all—until they came to a small dirt road where two identical Volvo sedans sat. They piled in, Jake ending up with the driver who would no longer drink Coke, he and Petrova in the back, and another little man with an MP5 in the front. The one with the blond spiked flat-top.

As they pulled away, Jake said to the driver, "I'm getting kind of thirsty. You wouldn't happen to have a Coke hanging around up there would you?"

The driver scowled at Jake in the rearview mirror. They all ignored Jake. Fine. They can't take a joke. But Jake guessed the Swede hadn't mentioned the incident on the train to anyone.

"You all seem to know where you're going," Jake said. "Glad someone knows. I get all turned around on these back roads in foreign countries."

The front passenger leaned over, digging into Jake's backpack, and came out with his hand-held GPS, showing it to them in the back seat. Good thing Jake had wiped out his waypoints and not written down the location where he had placed the box of gems.

"Yeah, that's mine," Jake admitted.

Jake could see Victor Petrova's smirk from the corner of his eye.

"I think you know precisely where we're going," Petrova said.

"I barely use the thing," Jake said. "A GPS is great for wilderness hikers. When they get lost, those finding their bones years later will know exactly where that person died."

"But I'm guessing you wouldn't hide millions of dollars of Alexandrites without taking an exact GPS reading."

Jake shrugged. "Check it out."

"We have," Petrova said, the snide smile still smack on his face. "You cleared all of your waypoints and locations. But if I had to bet that entire box of Alexandrites, I would guess you placed the location in memory."

Jake laughed and said, "That's a lot of numbers. I can barely remember my banking pin number."

"Your intelligence report says you have a photographic memory."

"Near photographic," Jake corrected. "And I've been drinking a lot lately. I can hardly remember the last time I changed my underwear."

They had been traveling a back road, nothing more than a narrow one-lane that had switched from dirt to pavement. Now they reached the main road to Hamar, and Jake hoped the police had stopped traffic. But they hadn't, because cars flew past heading toward Lillehammer. They picked up speed on the wider road.

Finally, Petrova said, "We have the general area figured out. Thanks to the computer box on the car you stole from the train station in Sweden. As I'm sure you know, many of these new cars have black-box-like computers that not only tell you where your car is now, but also where you have been. They're not perfect, though. We know you went to the hospital in Falun, for instance, before following my men to Lillehammer. It did read a turn somewhere along the way, yet that is not very precise. That's when you dropped off the gems. We'll go there now."

Damn it. Jake knew he should have disabled that system on the car he had acquired. Still, Petrova could know the general area, but finding the gems there would be harder than in the Arctic.

CHAPTER 33

The Bell 407 had swooped down from the mountains, banked to the west and slowed above the lake, waiting for the boat to appear. They had to be in front of the boat, Anna thought, peering through her binoculars to the north.

"Anything?" Kjersti asked her.

Just as she asked the question, a boat appeared in the distance. "There," Anna said. "Moving at a good clip."

Kjersti powered up and pushed the stick forward. The Bell responded, sending them toward the lake surface. She pulled back and leveled off fifty feet from the water, cutting the distance to the boat in a hurry.

Anna called in their position across the radio and waited for response.

Nothing.

She called in again.

Finally, she got a response from the police boat, saying they were perhaps ten minutes back.

Ahead the boat saw them and slowed down. Kjersti

slowed also and eventually hovered to the side of the boat, which had come to a complete stop now.

"Two little people aboard the boat," Anna said, her eyes focused through the binocs.

"You sure?" Kjersti asked.

"That's all I see. Unless there's more hiding under the seats." Anna got on her radio and relayed this info to their police boat.

Jimmy McLean nudged forward, his head between Anna and Kjersti. "Drop me down onto that boat, ladies. That's my target there. Gary Dixon."

"I can't do that," Kjersti said. "We'll wait for the boat."

They didn't have to wait long. Moments later the police boat cruised up alongside Victor Petrova's speedboat. Anna watched as the little men raised their hands and a police officer boarded them. He checked the men for weapons and then searched the rest of the boat. Then the police officer raised his hands in frustration.

"What's going on?" Kjersti asked.

Anna asked over the radio.

This time Toni Contardo answered. "They aren't armed," she said. "Say the boat is Victor Petrova's, but they were just out for a little ride."

"Right!" Anna said. "They must have stopped some- where to drop off Petrova and the others."

"You mean Jake," Toni said.

"Of course. Jake and more of those little people."

"Pull over to that bank," Toni ordered, her arm waving to the nearest lakeshore, with a field where the chopper could land. "I'm coming with you."

Anna knew better than to argue with Toni. "Fine." She clicked off the radio and said to Kjersti, "I hope she has some idea where they are."

McLean leaned back in and said, "Let me at Dixon. I'll make him talk."

The two boats went ashore and then Kjersti set her chopper down in the field a short distance away. Jimmy McLean and Velda Crane got off and went to interrogate the two men from the boat. Meanwhile, Toni Contardo and Colonel Reed ran across to the helo and got aboard.

After putting on a headset, Toni said, "Let's go. How much fuel you have?"

Kjersti checked her fuel gauge. "Depends on where you want to go."

Anna turned to the back and said, "Do you have any idea where they might be going?"

"No," Toni admitted. "But let's get to the Hamar airport and top off the fuel. Maybe the Brit will have some luck with our little friends."

They lifted off the grassy field and flew toward Hamar. Kjersti was familiar with the area and had flown into that airport before.

Once they got to the airport and waited for a fuel truck, Toni went off and made some phone calls. Kjersti went into the operations building to find some bottled water and something to eat for them.

Alone in the helo, Anna got out of the front and went to the back with Colonel Reed.

"You sure you have no idea what Victor Petrova has planned?" she asked the colonel.

The colonel, looking tired and depressed, ran his fingers through his short hair, his eyes avoiding contact with Anna. "I have no clue," he said. "I'm sorry I got the two of you involved."

Anna shrugged. "We're adults. This is my job. Jake is another story, though. He trusted you. But you lied to him."

"Don't you think I know that? But I had to. If that virus got into the wrong hands. . ."

God, she felt like shit. Maybe she should make the guy sweat more, thinking this was still about the virus. And she believed that he believed that was the reason for the whole mission.

The colonel continued, "Jake will kill me. Do you think he'll kill me?"

"Literally?" she said. "Probably not. Might kick your ass, though. Do you have a good dentist?"

He looked concerned and afraid.

"I'm kidding."

Toni and Kjersti both showed up at the same time; both carrying bags of food and water. The colonel and Anna got out while the truck topped off the fuel.

Kjersti had two bags full of chips and other goodies from the machines in the operation building.

"Did you wipe them out?" Anna asked.

Smiling, Kjersti said, "Didn't have any change so I picked the lock."

The fuel truck left and the four of them started back toward the helo. Anna pulled Kjersti back and let the others continue on.

"What's up?" Kjersti asked.

"We need to tell Toni about the gems," Anna said.

Kjersti nodded agreement. "Better now than later."

When they got to the chopper, Toni was on the phone, more listening than talking. Then she hung up.

"Good news or bad news?" Anna asked Toni.

"Jimmy McLean. Said they dropped Victor, Jake, and a few more little people with two Swedes in identical Volvo sedans. But he had no idea where they were going. He didn't even think Victor knew. Not yet anyway. Said that Jake had stashed the metal box somewhere."

"Of course he did," Anna said. "He would have never brought them to Petrova's mansion. He would have wanted some leverage."

"Them?" Toni asked. "You mean the virus."

Anna and Kjersti exchanged glances. Letting out a deep breath, Anna said, "There is no virus."

"What?" Toni looked dumbfounded.

Colonel Reed had been sitting calmly in his seat, and leaned toward the door now. "What do you mean no virus?"

Anna quickly explained what they had really found in the Arctic, how the bullet had broken open the box, which allowed them to take the train at that point, and how Jake had only told Anna and Kjersti just before they had split up in Sweden. When she was done, Colonel Reed looked genuinely relieved. Toni seemed profoundly pissed off.

"Why the hell didn't Jake tell us?" Toni demanded.

"Jake doesn't even know you're involved," Anna explained.

"I didn't mean me personally." Toni had become extremely defensive, as if she had been not only deceived as she had, but not deemed trustworthy. "The two of you knew this in Oslo. You knew this and we still raided Victor Petrova's estate. Who else knows?"

"Other than Petrova and his men," Anna said, "just Jake. As far as we know. We're guessing Petrova had anyone in Russia who knew either killed or shipped off to

Siberia. Regardless, they're probably dead by now."

Toni took a deep breath, calming herself. "All right. It doesn't matter. If Petrova gets the gems he can buy all the weapons he needs."

"That's what Jake thought," Anna said.

"Does anyone have any idea where Jake would stash those gems?" Toni asked.

Kjersti pulled a small map from her pocket and unfolded it. "There are only a couple roads between Falun or Mora, Sweden and Hamar. This is the best route." She pointed to a remote highway.

"That's a long stretch of road," Toni complained.

Anna thought for a moment. "Are you familiar with GPS games?" she asked. Nobody answered so she continued, "In the past year Jake and I have done some geodashing and geocaching."

"What the hell is that?" Toni asked.

Colonel Reed spoke up. "I've heard of geocaching. You get a GPS coordinate and the first person or team to get there wins. . .something. But what's geodashing?"

Anna got onto her cell phone and asked for a pen and paper. Kjersti handed them to her. Anna smiled and scribbled a series of numbers onto the paper. Then she hung up. "Geodashing is usually done by placing GPS receivers somewhere, and then the first to get to various dashpoints or waypoints wins. Jake and I do it once in a while in Austria and Switzerland. The waypoints can be out in the middle of the forest or in a trash dumpster in a city."

"What did you get on the phone?" Kjersti asked Anna.

"I started thinking. Once in a while Jake would leave me a message on my machine with a GPS waypoint and have me meet him there. It usually resulted in. . .sex." She glanced embarrassedly at Toni.

"He left you a message?" Toni asked her.

"Yeah." She smiled. "But it's coded. He probably didn't trust that Victor Petrova wouldn't find the message." She looked at the numbers and converted those quickly to other numbers. "Here we go. Got a location."

"All right," Kjersti yelled. "Let's punch that into my GPS and rock and roll."

The four of them hurried into the chopper and strapped in. As the rotors started to spin faster, Anna punched in the GPS coordinates. Now they had a direction, but would they get there in time?

CHAPTER 34

Jake had plenty of time to consider how he wanted to play this. After all, he knew that Petrova would keep him alive to get his gems back. Jake even guessed how many men Petrova would bring with him for insurance, and he had only been off by a couple men. He didn't think most of the crew would be dwarfs, trolls and other such little people. Regardless, they were probably all pawns to Petrova. Yeah, Jake had thought this through from the moment he found the box in Svalbard. Well, not exactly. At that time he thought the contents were the deadly flu virus. In that case he would have turned the box over to the U.S. Army scientists, tell Petrova he still had it, and meet in a remote location to isolate him.

This location was Jake's turf, even though he had only been there once before. He knew the northern forests. Understood them much more than he understood urban areas. His turf. Petrova couldn't manipulate the situation to his own favor. He'd try, Jake knew.

They had driven toward the Swedish border and turned

down the remote road heading north. Jake sure as hell did-
n't need a GPS to find where he had stopped the car on the
side of the road and buried. . .

"Pull over here," Jake said. They were a quarter mile
from the real location.

The driver pulled to the edge of the road and Jake turned
to see the car behind them pulled in behind them. The forest came right up to the edge of the road, with large trees
surrounded by thick alders and huge boulders dispersed
among them. The ground was spongy moss with pot-holes
of water. A little stream meandered through the lower
areas.

"This is it," Petrova said excitedly, scampering out of
the car.

The driver got out and opened the door for Jake, who
stepped out onto the road. By now the others from the second car were also on the road.

The numbers ran through Jake's mind. Number of men.
His GPS location. Number of seconds it would take them
to react. Numbers.

"All right," Petrova said. "As we discussed on the way,
there will be no funny stuff. No playing around. Oh, it's
here. No, it's here. I thought for sure I put it here. None of
that crap."

"May I at least have my GPS?" Jake asked.

The little man who had Jake's backpack looked to
Petrova for guidance. Petrova nodded, so the spike-haired
little guy found the GPS and handed it to Jake.

Jake turned on his GPS and punched in a series of numbers. "Here we go." Jake started walking, when he heard
the guns click rounds into their chambers. He stopped and
turned slowly, finding them all pointing their guns at him.

He looked at the GPS and said, "I'm only picking up around five satellites, making this accurate to around fifty feet. That's a lot of forest to dig up."

Victor Petrova lowered the guns of two of his closest men. "I'll hold the GPS," he said, and he took it from Jake.

So far so good, Jake thought.

"This way," Petrova said, pointing down the road.

There were two big Swedes, three little people, four counting Petrova, and Jake. Six to one. Time to even the odds somewhat. Twisting to his right, Jake planted his foot in the knee of the closest Swede, heard a snap, and didn't wait for the man to hit the ground screaming in pain. Jake had timed his kick just as they were passing a grove of large trees, which he rushed into now. The first couple of bullets hit the trees near his head as Jake weaved behind a huge spruce.

Petrova yelled at his men not to fire. They still needed Jake alive.

Jake ran as fast as he could through the thick under-brush, jumped the little stream, and turned to the north to run parallel with the road—though he couldn't see anything through the forest. He jumped rocks and fallen trees and kept on running. His only problem was being on the wrong side of the road for what he had planned.

He vectored back toward the road, his pace slowing now to keep down the noise of his progress. He had to believe the other Swede had been sent after him. Petrova's little men would have a hard time negotiating the forest. They would travel down the road. Jake had to beat them to his spot.

As Jake got closer to the road, he could see a pair of the

little men about a hundred yards back. Petrova had probably sent two one way and the other in the opposite direction. He would remain by the cars, just in case Jake swung
back around. But Jake had stopped here for a reason. The
road curved to the right here. So at least Petrova would
not see him cross. His men might, though.

Hesitating on the edge of the forest, catching his breath,
Jake knew he had to make his break now. Mustering
strength, Jake rushed across the road as fast as he could
run. Bullets rattled onto the road at his feet, but he didn't
stop. He hit the other side of the road at full speed and
flew through the underbrush.

The next thing he knew, he was on his face in a soggy
hole. He had hit a deadfall on his shins, the pain shooting
up his legs. Willing himself to his feet, he limped ahead,
pain throbbing at both shins.

He could hear yelling, followed by the sound of cars
moving slowly up the road. He should be close, he
thought, his pace hampered somewhat by his sore legs.
Then he saw the big tree ahead. If he could get there, he
could gain the advantage. He was sure of that.

Getting to the huge tree, Jake found what he was looking for—the plastic trash bag covered with ferns he had
broken and placed on top. Keeping his eyes on the road,
he ripped the bag open and grasped one of the Walter P99
handguns in 9mm he had gotten aboard the Norwegian
Coast Guard ship. He had a full magazine of 16 rounds,
plus one in the chamber, and a second magazine of 16,
which he shoved into his pocket. Thirty-three rounds.
Should be enough. But, considering the number of men
following him, he wished he had also left one of the MP5s
behind.

Jake shoved the plastic bag under some moss and slowly stepped back into the thickest section of alders. He was only about twenty yards from the box of gems now. He would get no closer than that.

When he heard the branch crack, he crouched behind a low spruce. It wouldn't give him protection, but would give him cover.

He waited and watched. Sweat dripped down his forehead into his eyes.

Another slight crunch. Then nothing. Twenty yards?

Jake could finally see a flash of green. It was the military sweater of the coke-bottle Swede. Aiming carefully, he waited for the man to clear some underbrush. The Swede's automatic handgun flowed back and forth as if scanning the forest for Jake.

One more step.

Aim. Squeeze. Jake's gun fired and he saw the bullet strike the man in his right shoulder, dropping him to the forest.

Jake ran through the underbrush toward the Swede. He caught the man as he was trying to pick up his handgun with his left hand, but Jake was too fast, thrusting his foot into the man's face, knocking him back into spongy moss on his back. Jake collected the man's gun, an old Glock 19. Also 9mm.

"You better kill me," the Swede said.

"No, Coke bottle, I think I'll let you live."

"You're fuckin' dead," the man growled.

"You should have been," Jake said. "This damn gun shoots high and to the left."

"Mine's right on."

Really? Jake aimed it at the man, and fired once, shattering the man's right knee. The Swede screamed loudly, his voice echoing through the dark forest. "You're right," Jake said. "It's right on."

Jake left him there screaming. He'd use him for bait. He moved closer to the road and found a hiding spot, lowering himself to the forest floor among high ferns.

He didn't have to wait long. Scurrying. Shuffling. Two sets of feet. Ten yards apart. He lay in the cold, wet forest floor and listened carefully. Mosquitoes started to buzz his head, landing on his neck and ears and his exposed hands. He let them bite and tried his best to concentrate on the steps. The crunching forest.

When they were close, very close, he rose up, a gun in each hand pointed in opposite directions, and fired twice with each gun. One man dropped instantly, the other fired back at him with his submachine gun, peppering the ferns as Jake dropped flat to the ground. Damn it. One gun had fired high and to the left again. He'd need to compensate for that next time. If there'd be a next time.

He rolled to his side and then crawled through the ferns toward the cover of a larger tree. Bullets kept flying. Then they stopped. He had to change his magazine.

Jake raised up and saw only the top of the man's head as he looked down at his rifle, changing the magazine. He aimed low and fired twice. The man dropped with a thud.

Three down. Three to go.

Hopping to his feet, Jake ran deeper into the forest. The first bullet hit Jake in his back left shoulder, knocking him from his feet to the ground. The second and third bullets whizzed by his head and blasted into a big pine trunk.

"I got him," one of Petrova's men yelled. The other Swede. "He's down, boss."

"Shut up!" Victor Petrova yelled. Farther back. Perhaps at the road.

Pain rushed through Jake's body. His shoulder blade had been hit, the pain running all the way down his arm and back toward his chest. He could still breath, so the bullet hadn't hit his lung. One good consolation. He rolled behind the large pine and put his hand on the exit wound. The bullet had bounced off his scapula, the exit the size of Jake's thumb. Blood soaked down his jacket.

He thought quickly. He had to stop the bleeding fast. The pine. Fresh pine pitch flowed from various spots on the rough bark. Jake scooped some up and shoved it into the bullet hole, the exit wound, and then grasped some more for the entrance wound. It worked. Some blood still seeped around the sap, but that slowed in a few seconds. He rubbed the sappy hand on the bark and then shoved his hand into the moist dirt, removing as much of the sticky stuff as he could.

Now he concentrated on the task at hand. Three left, he said to himself again. Then, his head against the tree, he listened carefully for any sound out of the ordinary.

There. A twig snap.

Jake knew he was toast if he stayed there. A sitting duck. He had to move. Now.

Rising to his feet, Jake circled around toward the last man he had shot.

Two shots. He kept running. Two more shots.

He stopped suddenly behind a one-foot pine, his gun aimed toward the shots. When the Swede's gun fired twice more, Jake had him. He shot three times. Heard at least two bullets hitting the man's torso. He was down.

Two left. The little man with the white flat-top, and

Victor Petrova. He guessed the two of them would be together. Out by the road.

But first Jake found the last little man he had shot. The man had taken a bullet through the nose, the back of his head with a hole the size of a baseball. Jake took the man's un-used magazine with thirty rounds of 9mm intact. He shoved the magazine into his back pocket and slipped back into the woods.

Jake moved closer to the road. He could see one of the Volvos ahead. Just a piece of metal through the trees. The two last men, especially Petrova, would not wander far from his only exit.

Closer to the road now, Jake slowed his pace.

"There's just the two of us left," Petrova yelled. He was behind the car. "We can split the gems fifty/fifty."

Jake thought back. Had he shot them all? Did he miss-count? No. Still the spike-haired little fellow. But Jake would have to call him out. Make the little man show himself.

"Why wouldn't I just take all of them for myself," Jake yelled. Then he aimed his gun and scanned the area around the car and to both sides. The little guy could be anywhere.

"You could do that," Petrova said. "But what about a little professional courtesy? After all, they are rightfully mine. I acquired them in the first place. That was hard work."

"Yeah, it's hard being a murderer and a thief," Jake said, trying to throw his voice to one side.

Nothing. Where the hell was that guy?

Then Jake caught a flash of blond hair to his left. Twenty yards. Maybe more. He crouched down behind a little spruce and waited.

"Hey, hey. Working for the old Soviet government wasn't exactly a lucrative venture, Jake. The retirement plan sucks."

One more sequence from Jake and the man would fire. He knew that much.

"Crime does pay," Jake yelled.

There. Just as he saw the blond hair, two shots fired toward Jake. He returned fire with five shots and sunk to the ground. He wasn't sure if he hit anything. Might have. He took the time to reload both guns from the bullets in the MP5 magazine. Now he had 34 rounds to go, plus a handful he shoved into his pocket. He set aside the empty magazine and waited.

"You still with us Jake?" Petrova yelled.

"You can't get rid of me that easily," Jake said.

Bullets buzzed by his head, but instead of returning fire, Jake's focus turned to his left. Something made him turn. As he did, he saw the Swede, coke bottle, dragging his leg, a gun pointed at Jake.

The two of them fired simultaneously. The Swede missed. Jake didn't. He hit the man three times. Twice in the chest and once in the mouth. He dropped instantly.

Okay. Now there were two.

Jake belly crawled toward the man he had just shot, taking a position behind a larger tree. He would be more protected and might have a better angle on the blond man.

Petrova yelled at Jake some more, but now Jake didn't answer. He wanted them to think he was dead. He didn't have to wait too long. Petrova was getting anxious. Now he switched from English to Russian—giving orders.

Seconds later, the little blond man stepped lightly from

behind a tree. Jake aimed and shot three times. This time the guy was down for good. Jake had seen the bullets strike.

Just one left. Victor Petrova.

"Jake, I knew this was going to be fun. You were worth every Krona and Euro."

Slowly making his way through the woods, Jake kept his gun aimed toward the car on the road, his steps as quiet as possible. All he could hear was the tiny brook, song birds, and a couple of ravens flying overhead. Probably anxious to get at those dead bodies, Jake guessed.

Where the hell was that little troll? On the edge of the road now, Jake stopped and waited, his eyes and ears working hard to pick up anything. The pain in his left shoulder made his left arm almost useless.

Concentrating on the car, Jake noticed the rear window down. He aimed his gun there and took another step. Stop.

On the road now, he was vulnerable. In the open.

He saw the barrel clear the top of the window and bullets flew toward him almost immediately.

Diving to his left while he shot three times, he landed hard on his hip and rolled into the ditch. His bullets struck the rear door.

Silence.

He lay in the ditch of water, his gun through the weeds aimed at the car, and saw two little legs under the car. Jake shot twice and the little man's leg shattered, dropping him to the ground on the other side of the car. The old KGB man fired at Jake until his gun was empty.

Jake fired at Petrova until his gun locked the bolt back. Then he put in the last magazine and waited, his heart racing out of control.

He couldn't see the little man anywhere. Where was his body? That's assuming Jake had even hit him. But he had to have hit him a second time.

Using the car as cover, Jake rose up and rounded the front of the car, his gun leading him to his objective. When he got to the front of the car, he finally saw the little Russian in the ditch, his face down in the water.

Jake moved cautiously toward Petrova, thinking he might have one more ruse left for him. But the man's gun was laying at his side, and Jake could see blood everywhere. He kicked the man. Nothing. Felt for a pulse. Again, nothing.

He was dead. Jake rolled the man over, out of the watery ditch. Part of Jake wished the man had lived. He had come to respect his intellect.

Seconds later, Jake thought he heard a helicopter coming from the southwest. He sat down on the ground and wished like hell he had a beer or something stronger. Now the pain in his shoulder brought a chill to him as he sunk lower to the ground. What was that swishing sound?

♦

The helo swooped around a couple of times, Kjersti and crew checking the area for any sign of danger. One car sat down the road, possibly empty. Kjersti set the chopper down and dropped off Toni and Colonel Reed there and then took off toward the second car.

Anna had spotted two men near that second car, and one, she thought, might have been Jake. The jacket looked the same. But both men were down and that bothered and concerned her.

When Kjersti set the Bell down near the second car, Anna was the first out, running toward the car, her gun out and her eyes scanning the area. But she went only one place—toward the one she thought was Jake.

She rounded the car and saw him near the ditch, his body slumped over in the grass. She rushed to Jake now, dropping her gun to the ground as she picked up Jake's head and set it in her lap. His bristly face was covered with blood splatter from where a bullet had struck his shoulder. His clothes were wet and dirty, full of pine pitch. She pried the 9mm handgun from his right hand and started to cry. God, don't take him from me. Not now.

Sobbing, she whispered to him, "Jake. It's Anna. Wake up, lover." She kissed him on the lips, hoping to bring him to life.

Time seemed to linger in a strange tempo of nothingness, the only sound now of birds chirping and trees slowly swaying in a light breeze.

"Wake up, Jake," she said louder. "You've go to wake up. I can't do this alone."

Kjersti came over and checked the man in the ditch. "It's Victor Petrova," she said to Anna. "He's dead."

Jake yawned first and then his eyes opened slowly. "They're all dead," he muttered. "What took you guys so long? I left enough bread crumbs."

Anna kissed him again on the lips and then hugged him tightly.

"Oww," Jake said. "Watch the shoulder."

"I'm sorry."

They both heard someone running up the road and they turned to see Colonel Reed and Toni Contardo.

"What the hell are you two doing here?" Jake said.

But neither of them said a word. They just stopped and stood about ten feet back, both with a look of uncertainty on their faces.

"The Network sent Toni with the scientists," Anna explained.

"I'm sorry, Jake," Colonel Reed finally said.

Jake shook his head. "No problem, colonel. That little troll is dead. He had people running all over for him. We just got caught up in his grand scheme."

Anna tried to help Jake to his feet. When she couldn't do it alone, Kjersti helped her. Together they got Jake up and the three of them struggled toward the helo. Toni and Colonel Reed followed closely behind.

After sitting against the chopper for a minute, drinking a full bottle of water, Jake stood on his own and took in a deep breath, stretching his muscles like a cat getting up from a nap.

"I've gotta get something," Jake said. "And I need to do it alone."

They all let him pass, and he wandered up the road about a hundred yards before scooting into the woods. About two minutes later, he came out carrying a metal box in his left arm like a baby.

He walked up to them smiling. "Now we can go."

Anna said, "What about the bodies? How do we explain them?"

Kjersti said, "I'll take care of that. But first we need to get Jake out of the country and to a doctor."

Now Toni spoke up for the first time. "One of the scientists is a medical doctor. He can patch Jake up on the Network Gulfstream. Where do you want to go?"

Jake shrugged his only good shoulder—the one with the box of gems. "Back to Austria."

"What happens to those?" Colonel Reed asked, his eyes on the metal box.

"Jake taught me an American idiom," Anna said. "Finders keepers?"

"She's right," Toni said. "They were found by Jake. And since he's not affiliated with any government agency, he has the right to keep them."

Jake smiled. "Colonel, do you still work for the Network?"

"Not officially," Colonel Reed said.

"Then you'll get some of this," Jake said. "So will the families of our two officers who died in the Arctic in eighty-six—Steve Olson and John Korkala. Let's go. No offense, Kjersti, but I think I've seen enough of Norway for a while."

Kjersti smiled and got into the chopper. Moments later, they were all inside, airborne, and on their way to Oslo.

EPILOGUE

A week later, nestled in the small chalet in the mountains near Zell am See, Austria, Jake sipped a glass of Italian Chianti and stared at the fire burning in the stone fireplace. It was late evening, darkness complete across the Alps.

He thought about the last week. They had flown on the Network Gulfstream from Oslo to Vienna, the doctor patching up Jake on the plane. Jake had insisted on no stitches, instead asking only for Durmabond liquid sutures. The bullet had bounced off his scapula and collarbone, but had not entered his chest.

From Vienna Jake had taken a couple of days, first traveling to Luxembourg to secure the gems in a large safe deposit box. Then he flew with a couple of the Alexandrites to Zurich to have them examined. As he suspected, each one would be worth thousands of dollars, and he had not even taken the time to find out how many had been contained in the metal box. But he guessed the total would come to at least ten million dollars.

Anna came in from the bathroom, a look of both pleasure and despair on her expressive face. She took a seat next to him on the leather sofa.

"Want me to pour you a glass?" Jake asked her. "It's quite good."

"I can't," she said.

"I told you, I will not start drinking like I did before. I was bored and going through some things. I'm better now. I can handle it. Just a little in moderation. Come on. I don't want to drink alone."

"You're gonna have to. For at least six more months."

Jake stared at her for a moment until he finally understood what she meant. "Are you sure?"

She produced a self-pregnancy stick. "This is the sixth one in the last few days. I wanted to be sure."

"The throwing up wasn't a bug you caught, or your problem with flying in choppers. My God, how the hell did I miss that?"

They stared at each other.

"What will we do?" she asked him.

Without thinking, Jake said, "First, I trade in some of those Russian gems. We'll need to dump our apartment in Vienna and find a place in the mountains. I won't raise a son in the city."

She squeezed down on his leg. "It could be a girl."

Thoughts of young men coming around after his teenage daughter raced through his mind, with Jake grilling each one and threatening to break every bone in their body if they touched his little girl. "No, I think we'll have a boy. But we need to make it legal. How does Monaco sound?"

"I don't care," she said, wrapping her arms around him.

"As long as it's with you."

They kissed long and passionately. Then they sat back in the leather sofa and watched the flames, listening only to the snapping and crackling of fire.

The next few minutes seemed to stand still.

When the first bullet crashed through the front picture window, Jake didn't fully understand what was happening. As he picked up his gun and instinctively rolled to the floor, aiming toward the door, he fired at the first man who crashed through.

In the next thirty seconds, the large room filled with the loud echoing reports of gunfire, the smell of gun powder and cloud of smoke lingering in the air.

Then the noise stopped. Even the ringing in Jake's ears gone.

On his knees now, Jake looked at his gun, the slide locked back and magazine empty. His left eye closed from moisture, which he tried to wipe away with his left sleeve. But the moisture continued to soak into his eye. He didn't feel the pain from the bullet striking his left leg, or the one that had blown through the shoulder that had been shot in Sweden.

Crawling to the sofa, Jake dropped his gun when he saw Anna slumped against the cushions. Her chest had two bullet holes, her stomach a third and her right arm a fourth. Getting to the sofa with her, he checked her pulse as he took her in his arms.

Nothing.

Getting his phone out, Jake called for an ambulance, barely able to tell them his location before setting the cell phone down onto an end table, the phone still on.

He was frozen in time. Couldn't understand that which

was before him. He simply held Anna against him, his own breaths shallow now.

He wouldn't hear the ambulance come. Could not understand what had happened to him. He just drifted off with Anna in his arms, tears streaking his cheeks.

CPSIA information can be obtained at www.ICGtesting.com
Printed in the USA
LVOW011014280911

248246LV00006B/6/P

9 781930 486911